ALEX

ADAM J NICOLAI

LONE ROAD
PUBLISHING LLC

ALSO BY ADAM J NICOLAI

Novels

Alex

Rebecca

Todd

The Redemption Chronicle

Children of a Broken Sky

A Season of Rendings

Of Dark Things Waking (Coming 2018)

If you enjoy Adam's work, sign up to receive free, exclusive fiction straight to your inbox, along with details on upcoming projects, sales promotions, and more. He would love to hear from you!

Just go to AdamJNicolai.com to sign up.

Alex

Adam J Nicolai

Published by Lone Road Publishing, LLC

Cover Design by Kit Foster and Adam J Nicolai

Cover Image © 2011 Adam J Nicolai

For my children, who changed my life.

I love you.

PART I

1

In the hallway, Alex was laughing.

The sound should have grated on Ian. He was late for work, as always—furiously brushing his teeth as the seconds galloped past—and instead of getting dressed, his son was in the hall, playing with toys. The boy had no urgency in the morning, no matter how much Ian begged, threatened, or explained.

Most mornings Ian would be yelling. *Alex, hurry up! Get dressed! We are* late*!* But today was different. Alex had turned five this year, and suddenly, that easy laughter—so simple, so pure—was getting rarer. Sometimes it felt like Ian hardly heard it at all.

He heard Alex scamper into his room, exclaiming something about a big train, and smiled despite himself. His son's joy was infectious. He rinsed his toothbrush, reached for the shirt hanging on the bathroom door—and stopped. Closed his eyes, instead, and relished the simple music of his son's play. *Thirty seconds,* he thought. Thirty seconds wouldn't cost him his job.

But he didn't get thirty seconds. Alex fell quiet. Maybe he'd gotten too absorbed in his toys. Sometimes, when the boy was really into them, Ian could find himself wondering if Alex was even still in the house. He would get up to check on him and find him squatting in his room, crouched over his trains and Star Wars guys like a mystic reading tea leaves, muttering earnest pronouncements.

Ian threw on his shirt and opened the bathroom door, expecting to find exactly that, but when he peered into Alex's room he found only stacks of cold boxes. The light from the window fell across them like riming ice.

It was empty. Of course it was.

His son had been dead for six months.

2

"I'm worried about you."

Ian snorted, and immediately regretted it. It sounded derisive, and that wasn't how he felt. To try and cover it up, he said, "There's nothing to worry about. I'm okay. I promise."

"I don't believe that, Ian." She sounded exhausted. Beaten. That was the effect he had on her now. That was why she wasn't living at home.

"Well, what can I do—" He paused, shifted the phone to his shoulder as he reached for the turn signal. "I mean, what can I do to convince you?" It sounded whiny. "I tell you and you don't believe me."

A sigh. "I already told you what I think you need."

The sigh pissed him off. "And I told you we don't need a shrink. We can get through this. I really think—"

She cut him off. "Are you driving?"

Fuck. "No."

"Dammit, Ian, I told you not to call me when you're driving. This is what I'm talking about. You don't listen to me. Do you even get that? You can't do this by yourself."

"I'm not trying to. Jesus Christ, I called you, didn't I? I don't want to do it by myself."

"Don't swear at me."

Don't fucking leave me. He bit it back. "Sorry. I'm sorry, I just . . .

"I hate not having you at home. I hate it."

A pause, a long one. He wondered if he'd lost her.

"I miss you too. But I don't like talking to you while you're driving. Call me tonight."

"Okay. I love—" he started, but she'd already hung up.

3

The elevator took forever. He could hit the button fourteen times and the thing would still skip the ground floor and go to the basement parking garage. Like it knew Ian was the only one waiting, and he just didn't rate.

The bell finally dinged and he got in. Checked his watch as he felt the ground falling away. 8:05. Late again.

Screw them. I was listening to my son. He pictured Justin glaring at him, looking disappointed. *Don't you get it? You think getting on the phone five minutes late fucking matters to me? I was listening to my son.*

The door opened.

He glued his eyes to the floor, walked down the aisle

between the cubes like a prisoner. He didn't want to see Justin watching him come in late for the second time this week. The mingled anger and exasperation he could stomach—it was the pity that bugged him the most. The only reason he even still had his job was the pity.

He swung around his cube wall and shouldered out of his coat. As he flipped on his PC, Sheila said, "Traffic bad again?"

"Yeah."

She swiveled to face him. She wasn't on a call. She was *never* on a call when he came in.

She was wearing a short, black skirt and a low blouse —what apparently passed for business casual when you're twenty-one. It violated the dress code, but Justin never called her out on it. She could dress like a slut everyday, and it was no problem—but every late morning of Ian's went straight into his file.

Fine. She was hot, and young, and she got away with things. That was fine. That's how it worked. But he was thirteen years her senior, and if he was coming in late, it was none of her fucking business.

He felt her eyes boring into his back, and braced for her pestering. It was about due to start up again.

He tapped in his password and waited for the ancient machine that passed for his computer to grind to life. Then he glanced back at her, and arched his eyebrows. *If you've got something to say, say it.* He wasn't in the mood for any of her shit today.

A couple weeks ago she had actually implied—Jesus, it still made him shake to think of it—that at least now that Alex was dead, Ian should be able to get on the road sooner. No need to bring the kid to daycare, after all, or wrangle him in the mornings.

It was brainless, exactly the kind of ignorant thing a twenty-year-old girl might vomit up without really considering. The old Ian had forgiven stuff like that. The new Ian had wanted to choke her.

You don't talk about my son, he'd said. *Do you under-stand? Not ever.* He had suppressed the *I will fucking kill you,* but just barely.

She must have still remembered it, because she finally pursed her lips and said, "That sucks."

He turned back to his computer. "Yeah."

4

At lunch, Justin pulled him into one of the empty side rooms. Ian was surprised it took that long. Normally he pounced on him right away.

Ian tried to pre-empt him. "I know I was late again this morning. I'm sorry. I just . . ." He reached for an excuse instinctively, but stifled the urge. He was as sick of making excuses as Justin probably was of hearing them.

"Ian, I'm just . . . I'm worried about you, man."

Ian almost snorted. He managed a wan smile that didn't touch his eyes. "That's the same thing Alina said this morning."

"Well, she's a smart woman," Justin answered at once. Justin had an answer for everything. That was why he'd been promoted twice, and was now Ian's boss, even though they'd both started in the same batch of hires nine years ago.

They'd almost been friends, once. Gone out for beers

a few times. Then Justin had realized Ian wasn't really going anywhere, and that had stopped.

"Look, I know what you've been through," Justin pressed on. "I can't even imagine it." He'd said the same thing probably ten times before. "You know we'll make allowances for you."

We. We'll make allowances for you. That was how Ian knew their friendship, if they'd ever really had one, was long over. Justin was a *we* now.

"But it's supposed to be four late starts before a verbal warning. You've had two just this week. You're somewhere around twenty-two for the year. We can't protect you forever."

Ian felt a roaring heat behind his eyes. *I'm sorry I haven't gotten over my son's death fast enough for you. I'm sorry his beaten corpse has created inconvenience for Smartlink. Perhaps you would like me to tell my wife to fuck off and die, as well, since my desire to salvage my marriage is also diminishing my job performance.*

Ian glared at him.

But what he said was, "The year's almost over. I'll shape it up. Just give me time. I know I've blown it for this year, but next year will be fine. You'll see." He swallowed, added: "I really appreciate everything you've done for me. You're right, it is really hard."

"And you're right, you can't imagine it."

Justin had two kids, and his marriage was steady. He was better than Ian in that way, too.

He clapped a hand on Ian's shoulder. "We'll do what we can. I just need to know you're *trying*. You know?"

If I wasn't trying, I wouldn't even be here, you jackass.

He nodded, and Justin finally turned him loose. Their meeting cost him ten minutes of his lunch break.

5

On the way home he stopped at Best Buy, browsed the 3D TVs and the XBox 360 games. The walls shimmered with canned football replays, because all red-blooded American men loved football.

Before Alex was born, Ian had always stopped here on Fridays after work. He wasn't red-blooded enough to enjoy football, but perusing the merchandise had always felt like it granted him some measure of sovereignty. He was married, sure, but he wasn't *tied down*: he could still stop and check out the week's releases without calling his wife.

When Alex came along, he'd ended the little visits. Getting home had felt too urgent. The baby had been a remarkable burden: inscrutable and enormous. He didn't want to make Alina handle it alone. He wanted to be a good husband. He wanted to be a good father.

He'd pined after these lost moments of solitude for years, but now that he had them again, they tasted like ash.

As he got into his car, his phone buzzed with an incoming text.

-*Could use u tnght. Tanklicious cancelld.*-

Derek, probably the only real friend he still had, trying to get him back into online gaming. There was another thing that had once seemed really important.

-*Cant. Thx tho*- He thumbed out the response, hovered over Send as he considered it. It might be nice to see some old online friends again. To spend a little time in a place where he didn't have to be himself.

The phone buzzed again. *-Bring comp over here. I have beer.-*

Ian almost smiled. The idea was appealing.

But he knew he'd just end up crashing Derek's night, probably quitting the game early, and feeling like an ass. So he hit Send and drove home.

When he opened the front door, he heard Alex playing in his room.

6

He froze, listening. He'd heard his son playing in the morning several times now, but he hadn't admitted it to himself yet. He'd never *seen* anything, so he'd told himself it was just his memories, his overactive imagination. Okay, yes, a part of his thoughts had whispered it was more than that—maybe it was actually the first symptoms of schizophrenia. But he'd smothered those worries. It only happened in the morning, after all.

He strained to hear, the door still open behind him, a spray of pale light from the streetlamp frozen on the entry rug.

Nothing. It was gone. He let out a sigh and closed the door. "Jesus," he hissed. He felt like he'd nearly been hit by a bus. His hand trembled as he reached for the light.

"Daddy! You're home!"

Vertigo assailed him; his stomach roiled. *Jesus.* He froze again, unwilling to believe what he'd heard.

That was real. It was clear as a bell.

No. Jesus.

He flipped on the light, peered across the living room toward the short hall that led to the bedrooms. It was all still, all quiet, draped in shadow.

Jesus. He seemed incapable of thinking anything else.

"Daddy! You're home!"

The call was identical to the first: the same one he had heard nearly every day Alina had gotten home with Alex first. But it wasn't the same, it *wasn't*, because the boy was supposed to come bursting around the corner now, grinning ear to ear, ecstatic to see his father. Ian was supposed to be hugging him now, patting his rump, returning his grin and saying, *Hey kiddo!*, fighting to get a word in edgewise as Alex launched into endless repetitive tales about his day, and his friends, and his play, and his learning.

"*Alex*?" he shouted, and bounded around the sharp corner that led to his son's room.

The room was dark, but Ian saw his son as clearly as if he were standing beneath the noon sun: his hair mussed because he'd just taken his hat off, his lips sticky and purple from the sucker Alina always let him have in the car. He was grinning, just like he was supposed to.

"Alex!" Ian shouted again. A geyser of need burst in his chest. He pounced forward, exclaiming, flipped on the light.

But there were only boxes.

7

"Hello?"

"Hey. Derek."

"Ian! You raiding tonight? We still have a spot."

"No. I told you."

A heartbeat. "All right." Another. "What's going on?" In the background, Ian heard a keyboard clacking: *tick-a-tick, tick, tick-tick.*

"I just . . . do you have a minute?"

A second's pause. "Of course." *Tick-tick-tick. Tick.*

"I think something's wrong."

Pause. "What do you mean?"

"I think—I saw Alex tonight."

Pause. "*What*? What do you mean?" The typing stopped.

"I saw him. In his room. It was dark, but I could see him."

"What do you mean?" Derek said again. "Is he there? What happened?"

"No. No, he's not here. I saw him, but . . . he's gone now."

A chair creaked as Derek straightened. "Ian, you're not making any sense. Was he at the house? How can that be? Did the police make a mistake?"

"No. I don't know. I don't think he was really here. I just . . . saw him."

Derek was quiet.

"It was just for a second. I don't . . ." Saying the words, he realized exactly how terrible they were; what they portended. "I just thought I saw him, for a second. Obviously he wasn't really there, but . . . God, it was hard. For a second I really thought he was here."

Derek let out a long breath, said nothing. *What the hell do you say to that?* Ian wondered.

"I'm not going crazy, if that's what you're thinking. I didn't mean to freak you out."

"No." Derek scoffed. "Come on, don't worry about it. You just need to get your mind off it. You've been in that house alone for what? Three months now? Come on, come over, have a beer. You don't have to play."

Don't worry about it.

Don't worry about your dead son, who was found with his face blasted off in a ditch.

It's cool, don't worry about it.

"Not tonight."

8

He sat in the living room, all the lights on, watching TV. Women hawking necklaces—*flip*—a teen mom—*flip*—Linda Blair's head turning all the way around. He put it on Spike and saw some crazy Japanese guy trying to jump from one suspended ball to another. Stupid commentary was being dubbed in.

Alex would've laughed.

He was supposed to call Alina back, and he wanted to, but he was scared he would talk about what he'd seen earlier. Or thought he'd seen. All he knew is he didn't want to sound like a madman on the phone with her, and he wasn't sure he knew how to stop himself.

So he waited, and watched stupid TV, and tried to convince himself that he might be hallucinating, but that didn't necessarily mean he was going crazy. Did it? It had to be normal.

He went to his computer in the basement and Googled *hallucinations grief*.

It did happen sometimes. People reported hearing their lost loved ones, sometimes even whole words.

Catching glimpses of them from the corner of their eyes. There was even an article in Scientific American.

He returned to the couch upstairs, mollified but still uneasy. He hadn't caught a glimpse of Alex from the corner of his eye. He had *seen him*. But maybe the experience was different for everyone.

He didn't realize he had fallen asleep until he heard his son shriek.

9

"*Daddy*!"

Ian bolted upright, every nerve screaming.

"*Daddy*!" It was aggrieved, horrified, on the verge of panic.

"*Alex*?" The cry was coming from his throat, echoing off the walls, before he was even awake. As he became aware of his surroundings, he was already careening around the corner to his son's room.

Alex looked at him. "Donnie went off the *road*," he whined. He was wearing shorts and a t-shirt.

Ian's jaw hung slack, his heart hammering.

"Donnie went off the *road*," Alex repeated.

His toy car—the red one. He named them all. The red one was Donnie.

It was there, at Alex's feet.

His first thought was reflexive. *You woke me up for that? You sounded like you were getting killed.*

"Alex?" he breathed. *Am I dreaming? Is this a dream?*

"Daddy, Donnie went off the *road*," Alex said again, growing impatient.

Well, you better help him. This response, too, was

reflexive. Ian could give it in his sleep. He and Alex had played this game more times than he could count.

His son's eyes gleamed. He knelt and retrieved the toy. "Don't worry, Donnie. I'll help you."

His voice lowered an octave. "Thank you! I was so scared."

He used his normal voice again. "Oh. But that's okay." He looked at Ian. "Right, Dad?" He pronounced it *Dod*. He did that sometimes, to be silly. Now he gave Ian a crafty grin, daring him to challenge his pronunciation.

Ian put a hand to the wall, leaned against it heavily.

"But one other car went off the road! Daddy, there's *two* cars!"

Another part of the game. He was supposed to respond, *Oh no! Two cars!*

"Yeah, two cars!"

But who will help the other one?

Alex disappeared.

10

He checked in to a hotel. He didn't pack a bag.

Every time he was about to fall asleep, he was jerked awake by the memory of his son screaming. The phantom of the sound clattered in his ears as he stared toward the dark ceiling. It reminded him of the first week after Alex had come home from the hospital, when his whole life had become a dream dominated by his son's cries. He had heard them all the time then, too: whether he was awake or asleep; whether he was eating, reading, or talking; whether they were real at any given moment or imagined.

He woke late and checked out, planning to head home, but got on 94 instead. He stopped at Best Buy again, but didn't buy anything, then got a late lunch and spent the afternoon browsing a used book store. The day dragged past, and he wondered what he was waiting for. He had to go home.

But when he saw the front door, he turned and went back to the hotel.

11

He left the TV on, hoping the steady babble would help tamp down the echoes of Alex's cries and let him get some sleep. He had a steely headache, gleaming like a knife. They said that people didn't sleep well in strange beds the first night. Maybe tonight would be better.

He still woke up every couple hours, but at least he slept. Every time he came awake he saw the clock and glanced blearily at the TV. 10:31 pm: some game show. 12:29 am: a music video. 1:47 am: infomercial.

At 3:16, Alex was standing at the foot of the bed, naked and shivering.

"I'll just call for you," he said.

Vines of ice wound up the back of Ian's neck. He sat up, put a hand to his forehead, and tried not to scream.

"I'll just call for you or Mommy," Alex reiterated. The bulge of his preschooler belly glistened with bathwater.

Oh, God. Ian recognized this conversation too.

And what else?

"Kick and scream!" Alex said, louder.

And bite. And kick them in the balls.

"Yeah, and call for you and Mommy!"

Call for anyone who can help you. Anyone. Most people are nice. They'll come running.

But Alex had been smiling in the tub, when Ian had warned him the last time about strangers. Like it was a game to him. He was smiling the same way now.

He didn't understand how badly people could hurt him.

"Yeah, and I'll bite and stick my fingers in their eyes. Right, Dad?"

And he had. The police said that the kidnapper's arms had been bitten in three places. His face had been scratched, one eye a gouged, bloody mess. The gunshot wound that eventually killed him had, they believed, come from the weapon discharging on accident as he wrestled with Ian's son.

Alex had put up a devil's fight. He had almost gotten away. But in the end, Ian's blithe advice hadn't saved him.

"Alex, I'm so sorry," Ian breathed. "God, I am so sorry." *I should've been there.*

I should've been there.

"I'll just call for you," Alex said again.

He was still smiling.

12

Sunday.

On the way home, Ian reached for his phone to call his wife before he remembered how their last call had ended. He waited until he got in the front door. Then he pushed her speed dial number—*1, SEND*—and turned carefully away from the hall leading to his son's room as the tones trilled.

Voicemail.

"Sweetheart, it's me. I'm sorry I didn't call Friday night. I didn't forget, I just have a lot going on. I wanted to talk to you, but I couldn't give you my full attention, and . . . Look. I've been thinking about what you wanted. I want to talk to you about it. Maybe . . . maybe we can do something together? I don't think it would be so bad if you came with me. And I want to tell you—"

"YOU HAVE. TEN. SECONDS TO COMPLETE YOUR MESSAGE. BEGIN AT THE TONE."

BEEP.

"I'm just thinking maybe you can come with me. I just want to tell you some things about why this has been . . ."

He trailed off as the old anger shook its head, climbed to its feet.

Why this had been so hard for him? Alex had been *murdered*. How could she not get that? Why should he have to explain to her why it was so hard that his *son* had been *killed*?

BEEP. Click.

He snapped the phone closed and nearly hurled it against the wall; stopped himself.

Then, before he could think about what he was doing, he cried: "Alex! Are you here?"

13

He did some chores, trying to clear his head. Took out the kitchen garbage; made a dent in the pile of nasty dishes in the sink. His hands finally stopped shaking as he hit the GO button on the dishwasher.

They hadn't been shaking because he was still mad.

Or frustrated, or whatever he was. They'd been shaking because he had called for his dead son, and he was afraid he was losing his mind.

He undressed and turned on the shower. The steaming rivulets on the curtain reminded him of Alex in the bathtub. He turned it back off and put on a bathrobe.

The house was empty, heavy with silence. He thought about dinner, but had no appetite. He reached for the remote, but the noise of the TV would have made the silence worse, not better. He knew this because of all the other nights.

Finally, he went to his computer downstairs. Stale habit forced him to open Facebook, where he stared blankly at a page full of people who had moved on. He had stopped posting after Alex died. What would he say?

Identified Alex's dead body today :(Gonna miss him.

No one had commented on his absence, except for Derek and a couple friends from raiding. Most of his Facebook friend list consisted of old classmates from high school and college. He had been part of the smart group, the ones with sharp minds and a keen eye to the future, the ones who were supposed to change the world. They were living in Singapore and Germany now, had degrees in astrophysics and philosophy. He was working in tech support.

He closed the window and clicked on the folder on his desktop labeled *Alex*.

There were a lot of pictures there, files with names like *BigGrin.jpg*, *FloppyBaby.jpg*, or *ChldrnsMuseum.jpg*, but between these, like thistles in a garden, were Word documents and saved html pages.

MissingChild.doc.

PoliceReport.pdf.
PossblLead.htm.

The worst of these was *news_article.htm*. He opened it and saw Alex smiling, his piercing blue eyes dulled by their translation into cyberspace. The caption read:

BODY IN SHAKOPEE IS MISSING HOPKINS BOY

They'd found him in a ditch just off the road, not far from O'Dowd Lake. He had been shot in the face at point-blank range. At the morgue, Ian had dared to hope it wasn't Alex, at first. The body's face was unrecognizable. But Alex had a mole low on his left side, just above his groin, and it had stood out against the pallid flesh of the corpse like an accusation.

Ian scrolled down to a grainy photo of a white man with wild, grey hair and a clinging scrub of beard. He was wearing a jean jacket. This caption said:

Leroy Eston, Colmes' alleged kidnapper

Mr. Eston had been discovered a few miles away when his rusting van had sidled casually off the road and into a pine tree. When the cops got there they found him with his guts spilling between his hands and onto the brake pedal. He died of blood loss before the ambulance showed up.

The official report theorized that Mr. Eston was taking Alex down to the lakeshore to kill him, intending to bury the body or hide it in the woods, but that the boy had somehow gotten loose. They had fought. Alex was obviously no match for his captor, but he may have had the advantage of surprise. In the struggle, Mr. Eston's weapon had discharged into his own stomach. Finally, Eston had shot Alex in the face, killing him instantly, and apparently returned to his van.

Ian closed the document. He didn't know why he was reading it. It was stupid; a waste of time.

He opened *MissingChild.doc.*

The same picture of Alex, this one slightly less dulled. *Alex Colmes, 5, missing in Hopkins.*

He had been at Rita's house. She was their daycare lady. Ian had gone over there the next day and demanded to know what happened, where Alex was. He had made her show him through the basement and the shed in the backyard. He had refused to leave until she called the police. Alina had apologized for his behavior.

In the next file he saw Alina, Alex, and himself at Lake Superior. Alex had thought it was the ocean.

Ian stared at that one for a long time.

14

In the elevator the next morning, his watch read *8:09*. When the doors opened, the clock on the wall said *8:12*.

Sheila was wearing a brilliant yellow sweater that hugged her breasts and showed off her cleavage. She didn't say anything to him, but she looked at the clock, shook her head, and rolled her eyes. He imagined kicking her chair over.

The callers were idiots, as always. Their computers wouldn't turn off, or they wouldn't turn on. They had moved their taskbars and were too stupid to find them again. Every one of them believed their machine was out to get them.

Just after ten, he got an email from Justin. He braced himself, expecting a summons to his boss's cube for his daily reprimand, but he was surprised. The email said, *Is this something you might be interested in?* It had a link to a job opening for a senior position on another team.

The money was good: at least two dollars an hour more than he was making. More, maybe, if he could shine in the interview. And since it was on another team, he wouldn't have to deal with Sheila or Justin anymore.

He hit Reply and typed out, *Could be. Thanks for the heads up.*

It would be nice to tell Alina he was finally moving up a bit at work. Making some extra money. Those things had nothing to do with why she had left him, but more money always helped make things easier. It would also be a way to show her he was looking forward, moving on . . .

He blinked. That was why Justin had sent him the posting. He wanted to get Ian off his team, turn him into someone else's problem. Maybe he'd even grease the process a bit, just to move him out.

So what? Let him. It's only good for me.

But it still pissed him off.

15

Alina called at lunch. "They have a meeting on Wednesday nights. It's a group grief counseling session. You wouldn't be alone, or even just with me. It would be us, a counselor, and two other couples. What do you think?"

He thought it was bullshit. Nothing any counselor could say would make Alex return, or make Ian stop wishing he would. The very idea that someone would try to convince him to *get over it* made him grit his teeth.

But he missed Alina. God, he missed her. So he said, "Sounds good."

"How does this coming Wednesday look?"

"Well, you know, I have that business trip to Rome, but I can wrap it up early and take my private jet back. I should make it." He'd meant it as a joke, but it came out too sharp. "What about dinner first?"

Silence. "Alina?"

"I don't think that's a good idea. Let's just meet there." *Let's keep it business. You can see me again if you perform the way I want you to at the session.*

"Okay. Do you want to email me the address and stuff?"

"Sure." She fell quiet again. Their conversations were fraught with these pits of silence now. You could stumble into one at any time, without warning, and just fall, and fall—

"Ian, are you serious about this?"

"What? What do you mean?"

"I feel like you're just doing this to make me happy."

No shit. What was he supposed to say? *No, as you know, I am ready to move on. It's like we never even had a kid. Let's pretend that. It'll be easier. See, I've totally come around!* He didn't know how to respond, and he didn't want to stammer—so there was another pit, yawning beneath him just when he thought he was getting his footing.

She said, "It's just not going to work if you don't give it a chance."

"I know. I'll give it a chance. Yes, I'm taking it seriously. I promise." As his lips moved, he remembered how, when he'd first fallen in love with her, he'd promised never to lie. He felt like a jackass.

But lies were the only thing that would make her happy. She didn't want to know what he really thought. She didn't want to know that he still saw Alex, playing with cars—

Shake it off. "Hey. Guess what."

She sighed. "What."

"Justin sent me a posting for a senior position. I guess he thinks I should go for it. It would be at least two bucks more an hour."

"Wow. Really?" She actually sounded pleased. He hadn't heard her sound that way in a long time.

"Yeah."

"Are you gonna apply for it?"

I don't know. Part of me doesn't want to give him what he wants. A year ago, he could've told her that. He could've told her anything.

"Yeah, probably."

"Well, good luck. I hope it goes well for you." Not, *Let me know how it goes,* or, *That would really help us out.*

He felt like he was standing on a cliff's edge, with the wind pushing at his back. "Thanks."

16

He came home late. Alina had already put Alex to bed, but he wanted to say good night.

Alex's door was ajar. Just an inch or so, because if it was open too far, he would use the light to play; but if it was closed, he would scream bloody murder. Ian eased it open, then picked his way over the floor: a minefield of cars and Legos.

His son was lying with his face to the wall. Ian kissed his temple, smiling gently. "Hey, guy."

Alex's eyelids fluttered, but didn't open.

"Daddy's home. He loves you."

Normally he would stop there, creep back out and leave his son to rest, but sometimes he had to say more. Sometimes it felt urgent.

"Daddy will always come home. You never need to worry about that. I'm always gonna come home and keep you safe."

He made this promise because his own dad hadn't; he made it because nothing in the world mattered as much as the little boy in that bed. He made it because he didn't want Alex to worry.

From behind him, Alina cleared her throat. He glanced back at her, smiling, and saw her glare.

"What?" he asked.

"What the hell are you doing?" she said. He had never seen her so irritated.

"What do you mean?"

"Would you just get out of there?"

"I was just saying good night." He turned to give his son another kiss, but the boy's face had been blasted open.

"Alex?" Blood was splattered across his son's temple, over his blankets, up along the wall. A glistening hole gaped where his nose had been. "Oh my God. Alina!"

But when Ian turned back, it was Leroy Eston in the

doorway. His gouged eye burned in the depths of his silhouette.

"Where were you?" he said.

17

It snowed on Wednesday, and when he saw her waiting on the sidewalk for him, the flakes were collecting in her hair. She looked beautiful.

She let him give her a quick peck on the lips. They were warm, and tasted like peppermint. When he pulled away, she gave him a tight smile. "Thanks for coming."

"I'd do anything for you," he said, and meant it. Mostly. Then he remembered that he wasn't supposed to be here for her. Her smile flickered away, but it was too late to take the words back.

The setup was simple: metal folding chairs, arranged in a circle in the school gym. A pretty, black woman greeted them as they came in.

"Ian Colmes?" she said. "And Alina?"

Alina nodded and exchanged big, warm, fake smiles with her. Ian couldn't muster one.

"I'm Shauna. Have a seat anywhere. We're just about to begin."

Ian took off his coat and slung it over the back of a chair as he glanced at the other couples. One was heavy-set, a white man and woman who weren't morbidly obese but could get there with little effort. The other was a thin Asian couple. He didn't recognize either of them.

"Welcome," Shauna said warmly once everyone was settled. "My name is Shauna Douglas, I'm a licensed therapist at the Associate Grief Center in Saint Paul. I've been working with grieving parents for more than fifteen years now." She nodded encouragingly, and grinned a challenge at him. "I live in Pine Springs, so this is a bit of a *haul*"—she chuckled—"but we've been hosting sessions here at the junior high for several years, and I think we've helped a lot of people." Her head bobbed vigorously at no one in particular. Ian felt his neck trying to nod in response, and forced it to be still.

"Let's just start by going around the circle and introducing ourselves. I started"—another overwrought grin—"so you can go next and we'll just go around." She nodded at the Asian couple like an overzealous teacher trying to coax a child into the pool.

"Okay," the woman said without a trace of an accent. "I'm Rachel, Nguyen, and this is my husband Harvey."

Harvey nodded at them; Ian nodded back.

"Should we . . . say who we lost?" Rachel asked.

"If you'd like to," Shauna said. "Whatever you're comfortable with. We'll all be sharing later."

"Okay, well . . ." She glanced at her husband. "It was our daughter, Lana." The words tumbled out, rushed but steady. "She was sixteen and had just gotten her license and was hit by a drunk driver."

A round of condolences followed; then it was the fat man's turn. He took off his hat and his pate shined with sweat. "I'm George Benson, and this here's Mary Ellen. Our son Evan's been missing for three years now. They can't find him. It don't seem like he's coming back." He pinched his lips and looked at his wife, who grabbed his hand. He nodded tightly. "I mean, we don't know, you know? But it don't seem like he's coming back."

"I'm so sorry for your loss," Shauna said, then looked at Ian and Alina.

Ian cleared his throat. "We, ah—" He looked at Alina. "Did you want—?" She shook her head.

"I'm Ian Colmes, and this is my wife Alina. Our son, Alex . . ."

He didn't want to say the words. It wasn't that he didn't want to admit Alex was dead; he could do that. But Alex had been special, divine. He didn't deserve to have his memory desecrated by a fucking round robin of lost children, like just another corpse getting rolled into a pit of rotting bodies.

"Alex was an incredible kid, with these amazing blue eyes. Looking at us you would never have guessed where he got them." He looked at Alina; she gave him a sad, lop-sided smile. "He was really smart, and I know everybody says that about their kids, but it was really true. But most of all he was a great person. He was only five, but he was so outgoing and friendly. For a five-year-old, he was incredibly selfless." He huffed. "Shit, for a thirty-year-old he was incredibly selfless. He never had a problem learning to share, or make friends. He was friends with anyone he met, instantly."

A familiar image burst in his thoughts: Leroy Eston, pulling up alongside Alex as he walked toward home, asking the boy for help finding his way around the neighborhood. *I'm lost. Can you help me?*

That's all it would've taken.

His throat closed. He forced his way past it. "Someone shot him in the face and dumped him in a ditch," he said. "That's it."

Shauna gasped and shook her head. It sounded fake, and it made Ian want to jump out of his chair.

Please don't act like you care. I realize you hear these stories all the time, but for fuck's sake, he was my son. Don't fake it.

But when the group's response ended, Harvey leaned forward and said, "Did they catch the guy who did it?"

He looked earnest. Hungry. "No," Ian said. "But he got shot in the stomach. They think it happened while he and Alex were fighting. Alex fought back." He couldn't keep the pride out of his voice. "The guy died."

Harvey gave a sharp nod and leaned back. "Not the guy who killed Lana," he said. Unlike his wife, he had a slight Cantonese accent. "He was in a giant truck, one of those with the really big tires? He was barely scratched.

"She had a green light. He hit her at eighty miles an hour.

"She was being a good girl, doing everything right. He was barely scratched." Harvey locked on to Ian's eyes. "He lucky to be in jail. You know?"

Ian nodded. He knew.

"Anger is a natural reaction to loss," Shauna said, head bobbing as if they had all made some kind of break-through. "Even when we don't know what happened"—she gave the Bensons a condescending smile—"we get angry."

There was that *we* again. Just like Justin. Ian's back prickled.

"Who have you lost?" he asked.

It caught her off guard. Surprise or annoyance flashed in her eyes. "I lost my mother, when I was fifteen, to cancer."

29

"But I thought this was a group for parents."

The smile came back. "It is."

"Do you have kids?"

She pursed her lips, trying to figure out how to handle him, as Alina hissed his name.

"No, Alina, it's okay. As a matter of fact, I do have two boys. These sessions have made me appreciate them even more.

"But we aren't here to discuss me. We're here because of the terrible loss each of you has suffered. And I think a great way to begin exploring that loss is exactly the way you did, Ian—by remembering the positive things, the wonderful things, about your loved one.

"Alina, Ian said some beautiful things about your son Alex. Would you like to add to that?"

She'd handled him deftly, he had to give her that.

"Sure," Alina said at once. "Ian was right about Alex's personality; he was the friendliest person I have ever known. And he was really well-behaved. Well, most of the time. Sometimes he could be a handful at bedtime." Another lop-sided smile. "He said he was scared of the dark, but I think he just wanted us to leave the door open for him so he could play with his toys in the light. If we shut the door he would howl and scream . . . he sounded like he was . . ."

—*getting murdered*. That had always been their joke.

" . . . like he was miserable. But as soon as you went in, you know, he was fine."

There were tears standing in her eyes. Ian felt something give way when he saw them. They had been fighting so long now, she had been pushing him to *move on* for so long, that he wasn't sure he'd even still believed she hurt. He put his arm around her. He didn't weigh it or think about whether he should do it; he just did it.

But she reached down for some tissues from her purse, and he had to pull it back.

"He was a good boy," she said after wiping her face. "I miss him."

They went around the circle. The Bensons and the Nguyens talked about their kids. Evan Benson sounded like a little hellion, as far as Ian could tell, and Lana had been too old. Ian couldn't comprehend having a child of sixteen. He had barely been able to comprehend Alex starting kindergarten.

"She sounds beautiful," Mary Ellen said when Rachel Nguyen finished talking about her daughter. "You must have loved her so much."

"At least you know," George put in. "The not knowing . . . it ain't easy. I don't want my son to be dead. You know? But I want to *know*."

"Yeah," Ian said. A block of ice had formed in his chest. He looked at George. "At least we know. Everyone says that, but I'd give anything to be in your shoes. To still have hope. You might think you want to hear that your son's dead, but trust me, you don't."

George recoiled. Shauna said, "I think everyone handles that question differently. For you, Ian—"

"No," Ian said. "No one wants to hear that their child is dead, and if you think they do, you're deluding yourself. These guys are hurting. Don't . . . *trick* them. Until they see the body, they still have hope. It's completely different."

18

He didn't get a kiss good night. She would barely look at him. In the parking lot, he said to her back, "Next week?"

"Sure." She got in her car and slammed the door.

19

It was ten thirty when he got home. He flipped the switch in Alex's room, and the light sizzled on, then popped. He caught a single, incandescent view of the room, like he'd just used a flashbulb. It was empty. He didn't know whether he was relieved or disappointed.

He went to the bathroom with the door open. While he was washing his hands, his son screamed, "*Daddy!*"

He jerked as if electrocuted. The soap shot onto the tile.

Alex was standing in his room, vivid and real despite the darkness. Ian shouldn't have been able to see him.

"Donnie went off the *road*," he complained.

"Yeah," Ian said, carefully. The evening's session or his sense of *déjà vu* served to ground him. "I see that." He knelt and tried to look into his son's eyes, but the boy's gaze was unfocused—or focused on something beyond his father. "Alex, is that really you? Are you there?"

Alex grinned. His lips didn't move. "I not *dere*! I Ay-es!"

I'm not "there!" I'm Alex! It was his voice as a toddler. He'd said that when he was two.

The hairs on Ian's arm stood up. "Please, Alex. Listen to me. Why are you here?"

"Donnie went off the *road*," he repeated, pointing at the red car.

"Alex, Jesus . . ." Ian's voice trailed off. "Please. Talk to me."

In a blink, Alex's clothes disappeared; he was again naked and dripping with bathwater, his drying hair curling on his scalp. "I'll just call for you and Mommy!"

"Alex, oh . . ." Ian put a hand to the wall as the hallway swam.

This can't be happening.
You told him to call.
This isn't real.
He must have called a hundred times for you.
You are losing your mind.
He called, and you never came.

"Right, Dad?"

"Alex, honey. I tried. I swear. I tried. I went to Rita's house. I went over every inch of her house. I looked up and down all the streets for you, for any sign of what happened to—"

Shorts and a t-shirt again. "Donnie went off the *road*, Dad!" When he was really tired, these pretend disasters truly alarmed him. He looked like that now.

"I know. I know, honey, but I can't help."

Alex didn't repeat his complaint. He didn't throw a tantrum. His face just fell, disbelieving and hurt, the way it would when he'd ask his father to play with him and Ian said he was too busy. It was a look of absolute dejection, and it wrung Ian's heart.

"Alex . . . God, I would help if I could. But Donnie . . ." He pointed at the red car, impossibly visible in the room's blackness, lying on its side on the carpet. *Off the road.* "Donnie isn't real, Alex. He's not real."

Alex looked up, and he was wearing pajamas—the plaid,

33

flannel two-piece Alina's mom had bought him just before he'd gotten strep throat last year. His cheeks were flushed; fever glittered in his eyes. Ian knew what he was going to say before his mouth opened. He remembered it distinctly.

"I need a hug," Alex moaned.

Ian couldn't resist that request. He would have died to honor it. He lurched forward, arms open, but his son was gone.

20

He went through the charade of bedtime: took a quick shower, brushed his teeth, climbed into bed and lay there for an hour.

Finally he threw off the blankets and stalked, naked, into the hall. Peered into Alex's dark room and found it empty, except for the boxes standing silent vigil.

In the living room, he turned on the TV, then shuffled into the kitchen to make some coffee. He appeared numb, but his thoughts were churning.

Do I believe in ghosts? He had, once, when he was young. When he had still believed in God and UFOs and Santa Claus. Before he had gained a healthy respect for skepticism.

Rationality would indicate he was going mad. Unless . . .

Can other people see him? Does Alina ever see him? If he had truly come back to haunt his dad, wouldn't he haunt her, too?

No. She wasn't the one who had told him to call. She had even been upset with Ian for having the talk about strangers. She had thought it was too early; she didn't want to scare him.

An old, reflexive fury kicked in his chest at the thought. He closed his eyes and waited for it to pass.

That left other people. And no, no one else had ever seen him—but Ian had also only seen him when he was alone. At home, and at the hotel.

His knowledge of schizophrenia was just this side of complete ignorance, limited to horror movies and *A Beautiful Mind*. But he remembered a scene where Russell Crowe had thought he was getting better, and then he found a shack where all his imaginary friends had set up shop. He'd been alone.

Fuck. If he was going crazy, he had to tell someone. But didn't they say that if you *know* you're going crazy, you aren't?

Was that true?

He went to the basement door and put his hand on the knob, ready to go downstairs and do some amateur online research. Then he wheeled back toward the living room.

Fuck it.

He didn't want to know.

21

Jack McCoy delivered his closing arguments. He swayed the jury. The bad guy went to jail.

As the credits streaked past in a tiny corner, the next episode began. Ian flipped the channel; he didn't want to watch another murder.

But the next station was worse. Instead of a fictional tragedy, he was confronted with a real one.

"—missing since April first," the voiceover was saying. A grainy image of Silvia Kalen's face filled his screen. "We are offering a $100,000 reward for any information leading to her whereabouts or status."

She was pretty, smiling, all dimples and dancing brown eyes and dark curls.

"Bitch," Ian murmured.

"Please call 888-55-KALEN if you have any information. That's 888-55-KALEN."

Missing since April first. And since her father was Jarrid Kalen, a man who could afford to do things like buy airtime on cable channels, the local news had latched on to her case at once. The police had thrown a net twice as large as the one for Alex, and the investigation into his son's disappearance had fallen into a black hole. Ian hadn't heard anything else until Alex's body was found the next week.

"Goddammit, Jarrid," Ian said to the empty room. The voiceover ended, and for a moment Silvia's face hung on the screen in awkward silence, smiling sweetly, *888-55-KALEN* quivering just above her eyes and *$100,000* beneath her chin. "There are other kids who need help, you fucker. Get off the fucking airwaves and let the other kids have a chance."

Silvia's face started to fade, but her dramatic departure was abruptly replaced by Vince Shlomi hawking the ShamWow.

"You can't just push everyone out of your way because you're rich," Ian said. "Alex was still alive, you fucker, he was *still alive* when you decided—!

"Or maybe you can. I don't know. Obviously you can. You *did*. You decided fuck the Colmes kid, right? Fuck him, he ain't rich."

Shlomi was soaking up spilled pop with an incredible towel that sold itself.

"Fuck you!" Ian roared. His throat burned as if he'd vomited fire. "Fuck you! You fucking *son of a bitch*!"

He lurched to his feet, cast about for something to break, and grabbed a throw pillow. It glanced dully off the wall when he threw it.

"Why don't you tell *him* to get over it?" he demanded, picturing Alina. "Why aren't you calling fucking *Jarrid Kalen* everyday and telling *him* to get the fuck over it? Why is it okay for him to look for his kid?"

Okay, some part of Ian's mind said. *That's enough. You're acting like a child.*

"I bet his wife is still living at home. I bet he can talk to her without her hanging up on him and slamming her door and looking at him like he's fucking . . . *going crazy*."

He can afford to run ads, and they haven't found his daughter dead in a ravine. If you were him, you'd run the ads too. You wouldn't care about anyone else's kid but your own.

But that didn't matter. All that mattered was that they had been looking for *Alex*, they had been looking for *Ian's son* until that son of a bitch had come along and—

"You'll find her, you shithead. It's gonna kill you like it killed me. I hope they find her in a ditch like they found Alex, with her face . . ."

But he couldn't finish that sentence. When he realized that, the anger drained away. It left him wasted and empty.

When had this happened to him?

Who the hell *was* he?

22

His cell phone buzzed an alarm at six thirty the next morning. He slapped it quiet and fell back against the couch, his head throbbing.

Alex said, "Daddy, I'm dressed."

"Good," Ian murmured, his eyes shut. "Did you brush your teeth and go potty?"

"Yes." He sounded proud.

"Did you flush the toilet?"

"Yes. Can I go play now?"

"For a little bit."

23

The sun streamed through a crack in the curtains. The clock on the wall said *8:17*.

"Shit!" He leapt up, pounded into the bedroom. "Shit, shit, shit!"

He fumbled his shirt buttons closed, pulled on boxers and socks. His pants drawer was empty. "Fuck."

Nothing in the dryer. It was all towels. He dug out a worn pair from the hamper, pulled them on, and grabbed his coat.

As he pulled out he looked in the rearview mirror and saw Alex in the house's front window, waving goodbye in a red turtleneck and jeans. It was the same thing he'd done on the day he disappeared.

Ian's hands started shaking so badly he could barely

keep a grip on the wheel. He kept driving. He wanted to get the house out of view.

When he rounded the corner, he pulled over. His heart hammered like it was gasping for air. *Palpitations.* He'd never had them before, never read the definition, but he'd heard the word. It described perfectly what was happening in his chest.

Jesus, he thought like a whimper. He closed his eyes, tried to breathe deeply, tried to calm down. *Jesus Christ.*

Finally, he was able to pull out his phone and call his boss. He barely had the strength in his hands to press the keys.

"Ian?"

"Justin, I'm sorry, I overslept—last night I had my first counseling session with Alina and it didn't go well. I'm on my way."

He sighed. "Okay."

"I'm sorry."

"Ian, this really can't keep happening."

"I know. I'm on my way."

"We'll talk about it when you get here."

Ian glanced into the rearview mirror. He couldn't see the house. "Okay."

24

He had expected some kind of reckoning: a final warning, if not a final dismissal. Justin gave him neither, just the same tired bullshit. On a different morning, Ian would've actually felt his opinion of the man drop. Today, he didn't care.

"Ian, you look terrible." Billi Swanson, kneeling at

Sheila's desk to help her with some problem. "Are you okay?"

Ian nodded.

"He looks like that every morning," Sheila scoffed, and glanced at the clock. "Ten after nine. New record for you, Colmes."

It didn't even get a rise out of him. *Something is wrong with me. I need to get checked out.* He thought about the counseling sessions. Wondered if they would help him.

"So, what do you think?" Sheila asked Billi. "He obviously screwed something up pretty bad, but I'm not sure it's hardware. Should I try to walk him through the system restore first?"

"Yeah," Billi said. She was an ample woman, out of shape: levering herself back to her feet was a production. She blew out a breath. "If that doesn't work, shoot it up to tier two."

"Kay."

Ian listened to his computer grind through its morning ritual. The screen flickered once and presented him with an image of himself, Alina, Derek, and Alex last Halloween. *Brown eyes, brown eyes, brown eyes, blue.* He had the weird little thought every time the screen appeared.

"Hey," Billi said, resting a hand on his desk. "Everything okay?"

He glanced at her. "Yeah. Sorry."

She scoffed, waving his apology away. "I don't care when you come in. That's Justin's problem."

"I know." He shrugged and lowered his voice. "It's just hard not to feel like shit about it with . . ." He nodded toward Sheila, who was working her best, high-pitched, *I-really-care* voice with her caller.

"Screw her," Billi whispered back. "She ain't gonna be perfect forever."

Ian managed an amused snort.

"Really though. How are you holding up?"

He debated how much to say. Billi was cool; probably the only person at Smartlink he even trusted. "Not well," he admitted. "Couldn't get to sleep last night. Passed out on the couch. I set my cell alarm but it must not have gone off."

"I'm telling you, look at FMLA."

He rubbed his head. "Yeah."

"Seriously. If Kal can take six weeks for depression—and I'm pretty sure that was all bullshit—you can sure as hell take some time to get level. You have a lot going on."

He looked at her. "For what, though? I don't need medical leave. I'm not sick."

"That didn't stop Kal. Talk to a doctor, tell them what's going on. You know, the stuff you *don't* tell me."

He double-clicked the little phone icon and positioned his headset. "Really nothing to tell." *My son died. I saw him buried, and now I see him in the window.*

"You're grieving." Billi tapped her temple. "It's *mental*."

25

He had a microwave meal for supper, one of those salisbury steak deals. He ate it in the living room, watching a *Law & Order* rerun.

He'd tried sitcoms, reality, the news, *The Daily Show*. Only *Law & Order* and maybe the occasional infomercial really let him escape. The show was weirdly comforting. They didn't always catch the bad guy, but they usually did. The cops on *Law & Order* would never let themselves get diverted from something important (a kidnapping) by a sudden high-profile case (a rich girl's kidnapping). They had too much integrity.

Of course, they didn't handle kidnappings, usually. That was the other *Law & Order* show, SVU. Ian couldn't watch that one.

He threw the plastic tray in the garbage in the kitchen. He was fighting hard not to let the house go to shit. One day, a few weeks after Alina had left, he'd come home from work and recognized the growing pile of dirty dishes and old pop cans in the living room as the sign of a man sinking back into bachelorhood. He'd gone on a rampage of cleaning that night. His life was falling apart, but he didn't have to let the seams show.

Alex was sitting on the couch when he got back to the living room. "Daddy, will you play hide and seek with me?" The couch was too high for him, so he was kicking his legs over the side.

Ian stopped short, felt a familiar pang like his chest was getting wrung dry. *That's how I'll know I've lost it,* he suddenly realized. *When I stop getting surprised. When I expect to see him. That's how I'll know.*

He approached the couch carefully, picked up the remote and muted Detective Green's wry dialogue. Alex looked up—he'd been watching the TV when he spoke first—and smiled. "Daddy, can we play hide and seek?"

Ian knelt in front of his son. He wanted to take his hands, like he'd used to when they had to have a *serious talk*. But it seemed like every time he touched him, Alex disappeared.

"Alex, listen, okay?"

The smile faltered; the boy's brilliant eyes started to wander.

Look at me. It's what he would have said if Alex had been alive.

Alex looked at him.

"You have to tell me why you're here."

His son fidgeted. "But, I just want to play hide and seek."

"Alex . . ." He felt a whisper of anger in his gut. "There's no more time for playing. Okay? God, I wish there were." How many times had Alex asked Ian to play with him, and Ian hadn't had time?

It was a stupid, pointless recrimination. He couldn't take back his refusals now. And they had been *valid*: he couldn't play with his son every moment of every day. They played sometimes, and other times Alex had to play by himself. He had to learn how to do that. And Ian needed time for himself, sometimes, just to think—and time with Alina, even just a few minutes to talk, and touch . . .

Alex's eyes were heavy with rejection. "Do I have to do *jobs*?" he asked. In the boy's mind there had only been two types of activity: playing, and jobs.

Ian made a hoarse sound, something between a chuckle and a sob. He reached for his son's hands, and became alone.

26

Somehow he made it to work on time the next morning. He spent the time between calls Googling the Family Medical Leave Act. At lunch he tried to call Alina, but hung up when he got voicemail.

On the way home he indulged in another Friday Best Buy stop. He flipped through the video games, then the movies, then the computer games. He looked at the cell phones and the digital cameras, fended off at least half a dozen attempts to *help him out today*.

After dinner, Alex was on the couch again. "Daddy, can we play hide and seek?"

Ian looked at his son's brilliant azure eyes and broke. "Sure, pal."

27

Alex's face lit up; he leapt from the couch like he had weasels in his pants. "Me first, me first!" he shouted.

"All right," Ian conceded. He didn't want to smile, but he couldn't stop himself. "I'll count to twenty."

"And close your eyes," Alex urged.

"And close my eyes." Ian obeyed the rule. As he counted he heard Alex tearing off, a herd of elephants condensed into two tiny feet. The boy was always loud when he set out, which gave Ian a good idea of which direction he went, but he was surprisingly good at hiding once he found his spot.

" . . . eighteen, nineteen, twenty. Ready or not, here I come!" Now Ian would look at Alina, and they'd share a secret smile. She would creep toward the bedrooms while he went into the dining room and then the kitchen, checking to make sure the basement door was still closed. Alex wasn't allowed down there alone.

Except when he opened his eyes, the living room was empty.

He's gone. Just like in the mornings, when Ian would look in his room after hearing him play.

Ian's unfounded anticipation shattered. His guts were twisting. *I can't do this. I can't keep doing this.*

Alex, why are you doing this to me?

From the kitchen, he heard the distinct creak of the basement door.

That simple sound froze everything, made his ears prick like a cat's and his arms turn cold with sweat. He tried to tell himself it was nothing, that he was imagining it or the house was just settling.

It couldn't have been Alex. The boy had never changed or moved anything. He appeared, spoke, and disappeared. He couldn't actually affect—

Yes, he can. The curtains, the other morning, when he looked out after you.

Ian drew a deep breath and sneaked into the kitchen. The basement door was ajar. The lights in the stairwell were still off.

You're not supposed to go downstairs, Alex! You know that!

He padded to the door and eased it the rest of the way open, fumbled for the light switch like a man slapping at ants, and saw his little work table and computer waiting in the sterile light at the bottom of the stairs. The thread-bare carpet, the fading white walls, regarded him as silently as a painting.

"Alex?" he called, but there was no response.

He's gone. Close the door and go back. But instead he crept down the stairs, each wooden step like ice beneath his bare feet as his brain whispered warnings.

The door to the utility room, that secret lair where the furnace and the water heater labored on black, naked concrete, hung open. The space beyond gaped with darkness and must.

"Alex?" Ian said again. His legs carried him to the door, and he waved blindly for the pull chain. Alina always made him turn this light on for her. She was scared of bugs.

Click.

The room was like a cave, walls bulging with the weight of the house's foundation, stained with moisture and neglect. At its far end was a rickety wooden door to an old cellar pantry he and Alina had never touched.

It was open a crack.

Okay. Enough. Go upstairs. This isn't even real. You're probably imagining it.

But he had told Alex to *call for me*. He had told Alex they'd play hide and seek. So he pulled the door open.

Alex was naked, his arms splayed out, bruised at the elbows. He lay belly-down on a bare, dingy mattress, jerking as if—

Ian fumbled for a scream, but his voice was gone. His son's eyes were clenched shut, his face streaked with tears. Ian crawled forward, choking on horror, and reached for his hand.

When the boy disappeared, Ian vomited until he had nothing left.

28

"Derek?"

"Who is this?"

"Derek, do you mind if I come over there tonight?"

"*Ian*?"

"Yeah, please. You still have that guest bed, right? Or the couch?"

"What? Yeah. Yeah, of course. What's going on? Are you okay?"

"I just can't stay here tonight. I can't . . . I can't fucking be in this house. I can't . . ." He swallowed a gag. He would scrub out his eyes if it would make him stop seeing—

"Of course, sure. Yeah. Do you need me to pick you up?"

"No." He fought for control of his voice, of his thoughts. "I'm already on my way."

29

"Ian. Jeez, you look terrible. Are you sick?"

He ushered him in, closed the door. A swirl of cold air ruffled the papers on the nearby kitchen table.

"No. I mean . . . No. I don't think so."

"Sit down, okay? You don't look good." Derek took his coat, and Ian sat down in the living room, the images from the basement lashing him like whips.

Had that happened to Alex? Is that how he had spent the last days of his life: getting raped by Leroy Eston?

Where the fuck were you, Ian? Where the fuck were you?

He shuddered, felt his stomach quake again. He glanced around as if suddenly becoming aware of his surroundings. He was alone. Alex would come if he stayed alone.

"Derek?" Ian took to his feet. "Where are you?"

"Kitchen," Derek called. "Getting you a beer, you fucking need one."

Ian got up and went to the kitchen. Derek was closing the fridge door. "Ian, God, would you sit down? Seriously. You're freaking me out here."

I don't want to be alone, Ian almost said. *When I'm alone I see things.* "Okay. Sorry."

Derek gave him a Coors Light as they sat down. Ian turned it in his hands, feeling the cold aluminum, staring at it like he'd unearthed an alien artifact.

"Light?" he finally observed. "You must not be *too* worried about me."

Derek let out a relieved sigh, like his friend had been in a trance and he had just been starting to wonder if he needed to call 911. "Yeah. Well. Jake doesn't like the hard stuff."

"Things going well with him?" Ian asked, not because it had been on his mind, but because he needed time.

"Yeah, I think so. He doesn't love the raiding schedule. You know how that goes. But he's smart and funny and has a great ass." Derek waggled his eyebrows.

Ian looked at his friend, but he wasn't really seeing him. He was seeing the cellar pantry. "That's good."

Derek's grin faded. "Ian, come on. Are you gonna tell me what's going on? Did something happen with Alina? Did she . . . ?" He stopped. They both knew what he was going to ask.

"No. No, we're still happily married." Ian shook his head. He was profoundly grateful to have company, but maybe it had been stupid to come over here. He couldn't tell Derek what had happened. He couldn't tell anyone, unless he wanted to end up getting committed.

"What then?"

"I just . . . I couldn't stay in that house tonight. You know? Not tonight."

Derek watched him. "Getting pretty quiet over there, I bet."

Ian nodded at his beer.

"Well, you know you can come over anytime. And you have a key, right?"

Ian had forgotten about that. Derek had proudly shared keys with a few of his closest friends when he'd bought the house last year.

"I mean, you know. Call first. But yeah. Whenever."

"Thanks."

They were quiet for awhile.

"Were you raiding tonight?" Ian asked.

"I was going to. I cancelled when you called. You freaked me out."

"Go ahead, if they still have your spot. I'll watch."

"You sure? Do you want to play?"

Ian shook his head. "Not tonight."

30

He came awake suddenly, coughing back a snore, drool sticky on his cheek. A scream of light was stabbing into his eyes.

"Ah, shit. Sorry about that." Derek repositioned the curtains, blocked the sun. "I didn't mean to wake you up."

"S'okay," Ian croaked, and cleared his throat. "What

time is it?" He pushed himself to a sitting position. Apparently he had passed out on a bean bag. Last night he had lounged in it, briefly, watching Derek's game.

"Little after eleven."

"Holy shit," Ian stated. He groaned to his feet. "Fucking hell. I am getting too old to sleep on beanbags."

Derek chuckled. "You didn't look very comfortable, but you were sleeping like the dead. I was gonna bring you to the guest bed, but I figured I wouldn't fuck with it. You were out cold."

"Fuck," Ian answered. He stretched his stiff arms, tried to roll the hard knot out of his neck. It ignored him.

They got breakfast at the Osseo Cafe. Derek paid, despite Ian's insistence to the contrary. Then Ian tagged along while Derek ran some errands: Target, Cub, the post office. They shot the shit, made fun of people, and generally behaved like they were still in high school. Ian couldn't remember the last time he had relaxed so much.

"So what's the plan?" Derek asked as they drove home. The sky was bruising already. Daylight Saving would be over soon, and the days would start ending at like five o'clock.

It was nice not to be driving; to just be the guy in shotgun, fiddling with the iPod. Ian clicked his tongue. "I don't want to go home yet. If that's cool."

"That should be fine. Jake's out of town this weekend anyway."

"Sweet." Ian cracked a smile, still looking at the iPod menu. "Just make sure you keep your fag paws in your bedroom."

Derek cackled. "Whateva, cracka. Like I'd want to tap that anyway."

31

"You know what's weird?" Ian said. They were in the living room, watching a rerun of Star Trek: TNG, eating delivered pizza. Derek arched a brow.

"I see kidnapped kids everywhere now. Billboards, milk cartons. Alina talked me into counseling, and there's a couple there whose kid disappeared. And those ads for Jarrid Kalen's daughter that are always on. *Everywhere.*

"It's just like when Alina got pregnant. Both of us started noticing all the pregnant women. It seemed like there were a million of them, all of a sudden. Or when Alex was born, and we both started seeing kids every place." Ian smiled. "Ours was the best, of course."

"Yeah he was," Derek agreed.

"Those blue eyes," Ian said. "Those blue eyes just kill me." He'd said it a hundred times before. He indulged anyway.

"They were . . . captivating, is the only word," Derek said, and smiled. "He was gonna slay the ladies, that's for sure."

Without transition, Ian said, "I've been sleeping like shit."

Derek picked up on the comment, turned the TV down a bit. "No surprise there, I suppose."

"Well, yeah. But I mean, even when I do get to sleep, I have these dreams. They're just . . . so *real*. I feel like I'm not sleeping at all."

He waited. Derek said, "What kind of dreams?"

"They're about Alex."

Derek's face softened. "You remembering him?"

"Well . . . yes. I mean, he's always doing something he

did when he was alive. Playing with his cars, or . . ." His stomach clenched. "Or playing Hide and Seek."

"That sounds nice, but from your face . . . they're not?"

"I'm not just *remembering* him. In the dreams, I'm walking around the house. You know? The empty house. It's just me, just . . . just like it is now. And he's *there*. I know he's dead, but I'll just come across him all of a sudden, just sitting on the couch."

Derek let out a low breath. "Wow."

"Yeah. And these dreams are so vivid, a few times I've . . ." Ian stole a glance at his friend, his stomach still twisting. "Gotten confused. I'll wake up and it seems like it really happened.

"You remember when I called you last week."

"Yeah."

"That was the first time it happened."

"Wow," Derek repeated. He sounded like he didn't know what else to say. *I can't even imagine,* Ian heard Justin saying. It was probably true.

He suddenly felt like an asshole, cheapening his son's memory by telling ghost stories. The fact that he was talking to an old high school friend only made it worse. *Grow up,* he told himself.

But now that he'd started talking, he couldn't stop.

"It's always like he's trying to guilt me," Ian said. He couldn't look at Derek; he looked at the wall instead, saw Picard holding forth on some grave matter of Starfleet protocol from the corner of his eye. "We had this talk before he . . . before he got kidnapped. And I told him to scream for help, and to bite and fight back. And he throws that back in my face. He says, 'I'll just call for you and . . .'"

Ian's throat closed off. While he fought for control, Derek waited.

Finally, Ian whispered, "Can you imagine how many times he must have called for me?"

"Ian." Derek leaned forward, tensed his elbows against his knees. "No. You did everything you could."

"Did I? I could've been in Shakopee."

"You had no way of knowing that's where he was. You were counting on the police for—"

"Yeah, and *he* was counting on *me*. I should've been there, and he wants me to know."

Derek clapped his mouth shut. Ian could feel his eyes but still wouldn't meet them.

"What else have you dreamt about him?"

Ian wasn't ready to answer. Giving voice to the thoughts left him certain they were right. Alex had every reason to torment his father: the man who had promised to keep him safe, to come home every night, to die to protect him. Big words that had meant nothing.

There was no answer for Alex's accusations.

"Come on," Derek pressed. "What else? Are they all about that? I thought you said you dreamt about him playing."

Ian flicked a glance at him, then away. "Yeah. Playing with his cars. I've had that one twice. He wants me to play with him."

Derek gestured, as if to say, *Well, there you go.*

"What?"

"Is it a good dream?"

"Well . . ." Ian remembered the furious need in his chest, the crippling pain when Alex disappeared. "No.

Because it's like he's back, even though I know he's dead. And when I try to touch him, he disappears. Every time."

Again, Derek exhaled. "Wow. It sounds . . . horrible."

"Yeah." Ian nodded. "It is." He had hoped talking about it would help get it off his chest, put it in perspective. Instead, it was just making him feel more trapped.

"But still," Derek said. "It sounds *better*, at least.

"Look, I wasn't his dad. But I knew Alex. He was an incredible kid. Gentle, and a ton of empathy for a five-year-old. I can believe you're beating yourself up. I would too. But have you considered that your brain is just using the idea of Alex to do it?

"I only say that because I don't think you should let that fuck up your memories of him. I just don't see Alex coming back to you in your dreams and . . . accusing you like that. I can see you doing it to yourself, but don't pin that on him."

"He'd have every right."

"Maybe he would, maybe he wouldn't. But I don't think Alex would do that."

Alex had also said, *Daddy, you're home!* and, *I need a hug.* Part of Ian yearned to accept what Derek was saying.

But if he did, it meant the visions weren't real. It meant that he was seeing things. Was that better or worse?

"I know they're just dreams. I know that. And I'm not religious or anything, I haven't been for years, but . . ." Ian looked at the floor. "Do you think there's any chance . . . I mean, they're so *real*. What if he's trying to talk to me somehow?" He looked up, to catch Derek's reaction.

Carefully neutral, weighing. Finally, he answered,

"'There are more things in heaven and earth, Horatio, than are dreamt of in your philosophy.'"

Ian felt a sad smile on his lips. "And what does that mean?"

Derek shrugged. "It means, who fucking knows?"

Ian scoffed. "Great."

"Well, seriously. There's nothing I'll be able to say to convince you one way or another. You're the one having the dreams. But if it really is Alex, I think you should focus on the good things. I think it's far more likely that he'd come back to say goodbye. You know? I just don't see him coming back to make you feel bad.

"Look, if there's a heaven, Alex is in it. You know that."

Ian hadn't believed in heaven for years, but the question was hypothetical. He imagined a place of eternal peace, reserved for those who had suffered, and found himself nodding.

"And that kid would not hold a grudge, from heaven, against his daddy. He just . . . he wouldn't.

"He was too good for that."

32

Sunday night. Home again. He hesitated at the door, autumn leaves whispering in the breeze behind him.

He felt like he had as a kid, after coming home from a couple nights at a friend's house. When the limitless possibilities of the weekend had all been realized or wasted, leaving a taste of disappointment in his mouth.

He opened the door and went into the empty house. The familiar glare of the streetlight splayed past him into the dark entry. He listened and heard nothing.

Like an old movie reel grinding to life, his brain supplied an image of Alex getting raped in the dark. He turned on the light to dispel it.

On the dining room table, his forgotten cell phone blinked at him. *Low power*, it said, and *Voicemail*.

"Hi Ian, it's your mom. Just wondering about Thanksgiving this year. I know it's a month out, but I just want to start making plans. I hope you can make it. Alina is welcome, too. Should I call her?"

Ian winced. *Mom, God.*

"I won't call her unless you want me to, just in case. But anyway, I think it's gonna be at three. Let me know if you're gonna bring anything. You don't have to, but you can if you want. Give me a call. I haven't talked to you in a long time. I love you, honey."

"END OF MESSAGE."

He erased it.

"SECOND. NEW MESSAGE. LEFT? YESTERDAY, AT NINE. ELEVEN. PM. FROM ALIHNUH KOL-MES."

The phone was still sitting on the table, on speaker mode. Ian paused on his way to the kitchen, turned toward it.

Click. "END OF MESSAGE."

33

He woke around four in the morning and stumbled into the bathroom to pee. Alex was on the toilet already, his pants and underwear in a crushed jumble on the floor.

"Sorry I scared you, Daddy." He sounded resigned, but reticent. "I only didn't think you could hear me. So that's why I yelled so loud."

That's okay, pal. When he was three and four, Alex had needed help cleaning up after using the toilet. He hadn't mastered that skill until he turned five. *It's hard to hear you from downstairs. Next time I'll stay up here.*

"Okay. Will you wipe my butt now?" Alex hopped down to the floor, and was gone.

Ian flipped the light on, still bleary and unsteady.

"That's okay, Alex," Ian said to the empty room. "No more hide and seek, okay?"

34

On Monday he filled out the online application for the job Justin had sent him. It wanted him to attach a résumé. He crafted one between calls.

Billi caught him working on it. "You bailing on us?"

"Trying," Ian said.

She lowered her voice. "Where you applying?"

"Just the senior job on Kate's team."

"*Oh.* I thought you were applying *elsewhere*." She gestured at the wall.

"Nah. I need a reference though, can I put you down?"

"Sure. You'll like it. It beats being on the phones. You only have to talk to the real jackasses." A grin.

"What a treat." He matched her tone. "Mainly I just want to get away from . . ."

She caught his nod toward Sheila, answered with a nod of her own. "Just don't mention that as your main reason in the interview."

"Nope, I know."

"You'd be good at it. Kate's less of a stickler on the whole time thing. I'll put in the good word."

He was coming in late nearly every morning, had trouble lately keeping his temper with his coworkers and sometimes with callers, but Billi would put in the good word.

"Why?" The word took him by surprise; it hung in the air like he'd just coughed up a fur ball.

Billi looked at him. "Why . . . will I put in the good word?"

He felt like an idiot, wished he'd kept his mouth shut. "Never mind."

She scoffed. "Ian, come on. You can't mean that. You're fantastic."

It had been so long since he'd heard praise, he wondered at first if she was mocking him. His skepticism must've shown, because she said, "You get the right answers, the first time. You hardly ever ask me for help. You don't need it. Everybody's comfortable coming to you, you don't put anyone down, you're easy to under-stand and approachable."

"I'm late every goddamn morning and I feel like I'm sniping at everybody all the time."

Billi shrugged. "You snipe at Sheila, maybe, but she deserves it. Jorge was telling me the other day he didn't know what he'd do if you weren't here for him to bug."

He must've still looked confused, because she went on. "Look. You are going through things none of us can even comprehend. But you're still one of the best people working here. So you're coming in late. So what? You never used to. You'll get there again.

"You just can't rush something like this."

At lunch he drove to Burger King and ate in the parking lot with the engine off. On the way back he called his mom and confirmed that he'd be coming to Thanksgiving.

"Okay. Do you want me to call Alina?"

Ian sighed. "No. If she wants to come I'll call her."

"Are you sure? I don't mind—"

"Mom, I don't want you to call my estranged wife and invite her to Thanksgiving. Please. I'm seeing her every Wednesday and I'll talk to her about it then."

"She's still married to you, and she's still part of the family. You two are good for each other. I know what happened was terrible, Ian, but don't let it ruin your marriage."

"Thank you. That's a great idea. I'll keep it in mind."

A stung silence. *Goddammit.*

"Mom, I'm not trying to be mean. But really, you don't think I've thought of that? She's my wife, I love her. Yes. I think she still loves me, okay. But we can't just pretend like nothing's happened. That's not . . . I'm not gonna do that."

"All right. I'm not trying to nag."

"I know."

In the rearview mirror, Ian saw Alex in his booster. He was looking out the window and kicking the back of Ian's seat.

"I just want you to be happy."

Thump. Thump. Like a squirrel jumping across his back. He twisted around. Alex smiled and waved at him.

"You know?" Mom said.

He faced forward again, slammed on the brakes as he nearly ran a red light.

"Ian?"

"Yup, okay. Bye, Mom." He fumbled at the End Call button.

"Dad, what's that *noise*?" Alex screamed.

Ian flinched. His phone tumbled between the seats.

"Alex, please don't—"

"Dad, what's that *noise*?" he yelled again, louder.

"I don't—what noise? What are you—"

"Dad, what's that *NOISE*?" Alex shrieked, and Ian whipped around in his seat.

"Alex, goddammit, not right now! Not right *now*!"

The car behind him laid into its horn. The light was green.

He lurched an arm toward the back seat, flailing toward Alex, but couldn't quite reach him. Another honk screeched.

He started across the intersection as Alex screamed again. He turned on the radio, blasted some classic Metallica until he couldn't hear him anymore.

At the office, he left Alex in the car and ran inside.

36

Four times that afternoon he put himself into *After Call Work* to stop the calls for a minute, and went out to make sure his car was empty. When he went to the bathroom, he expected to find Alex on the toilet. When he came back to his desk, he expected to find him playing in the chair.

He got home as the sun set. To delay going into the

house, he detoured and got the mail. The box was nearly overflowing.

He grabbed it all, stuffed it under his arm, and went inside. Flipped the light on right away. Went into the dining room and tossed the mail on the table, where it splayed out like a bug splatting on a windshield.

The mortgage bill. The Visa bill. The other Visa bill. DELINQUENT, the last envelope admonished, in case he'd forgotten.

He snapped up the mortgage bill and ripped it open. He hadn't been able to make a full payment last month, and the balance had carried over. Alina had said she'd keep contributing to the house payments, but he didn't want to bug her with it.

That's all I fucking need, is to call her asking for money. He tossed the bill back on the table, with no idea how he was going to pay it. It knocked aside another envelope, and suddenly, Alex's face smiled at him from a mailer.

MISSING SINCE MARCH, the caption said. *LAST SEEN IN HOPKINS.*

Another boy's face was next to his son's: Edward Jameson, missing since September. And next to that, the obligatory Silvia Kalen, missing since April. There were three more on the other side.

He remembered, all at once, how bleak it had felt to see his son's face on that piece of paper for the first time.

The boy was dead now, but Ian still had to endure his picture—

He grabbed the mailer and punched out the number on it. A live voice answered.

"Hi, I just received your mailer. It shows a picture of

Alex Colmes. I'm his father. He died six months ago. Please take his picture off."

The voice said he'd look into it.

"Please do. Please. I can't keep seeing his face every time I come home and get the mail. There's been some kind of mistake."

Of course. The voice assured him if there was a mistake, they would fix it.

Ian hung up.

37

He went to the counseling session Wednesday night. He didn't see Alina outside, but when he got to the gym she was there, sitting in the same place as last week, her coat on her lap.

The group talked mostly about their feelings for their kids that night: how much they loved them, how much they missed them, how much their lives had been changed by them. He spoke when Shauna dragged something out of him, but kept his tongue the rest of the time. He didn't want to piss Alina off again, but more than that . . .

Love was not a strong enough word to describe how he felt about his son. *Miss* didn't begin to describe the hole the boy's murder had left in his life. He couldn't talk about those ideas like they were just words. They were too much more than that.

I didn't even know there was a feeling like this, Ian had told Alina one night as he held the sleeping baby. Alex's heartbeat had been warm and trembling against Ian's chest. *I don't just love him. I've* fallen *for him. I'm infatuated.*

I mean, you know . . . it's platonic, obviously. But it's more like when I fell in love with you, than anything. His effort to explain himself was pathetically inarticulate, but Alina had smiled at him anyway.

She'd understood.

He thought about trying to explain that feeling to this group, and rejected the idea. Sometimes that moment felt so close, he could still imagine the warmth of Alex's weight on his chest. But those times were getting further and further between, and tonight, while he still loved his son, he was angry with him, too. Angry, and scared.

Whether intentionally or unintentionally, the boy he loved so much was driving him mad.

After the session, Alina turned away to put her coat on. He thought she was going to leave without speaking, but she touched his arm as they stepped into the parking lot.

"You were quiet tonight."

Being quiet is wrong. Saying what I think is wrong. What the fuck do you want me to do? But her eyes weren't accusing. Maybe she hadn't meant it that way.

"I think . . . sometimes, it helps just to listen."

She nodded. Her face was gentle. "I can understand that."

"You can?"

"Yeah."

"Listen, I'm sorry about last week. I didn't mean to go off on Shauna."

"You should give her a chance, Ian. She's not as bad as you think."

"Yeah. I'll try. I'm just . . . I don't know, ever since . . . they found him, I'm just so angry all the time.

"All the time."

Her face was unreadable. "I know."

He had forced her out. She said it when she left: *I can't breathe in this fucking house anymore.* Of course she knew.

"I don't mean to be. I'm trying . . . I just don't know what to do."

She touched his face. "Thank you for trying. It means a lot."

He remembered her being at home, smiling at him when he came in, making furious, quiet love to him in the dark so they wouldn't wake their son. *I need you,* he wanted to say. *I still love you, and I need you back.*

Then he thought: *If you're at home, Alex won't be.* It cheapened the urgency of his desire, turned her into a tool he was trying to use. The words died on his tongue.

Because there was nothing else to say, he said, "Next week?"

She smiled and nodded before hurrying to her car. It was getting cold.

38

Alex was in the backseat again. "Good," he said, as if Ian had just asked him a question.

Ian turned the engine on to let the car warm up, watching the boy in the rearview. *Alex, you have to stop talking to me like this. You have to stop.*

But saying that wouldn't do anything. He'd tried reasoning with Alex already. It didn't work.

"Good, Daddy," Alex repeated.

"What's good?" Ian asked.

"It was *good.*"

"What was?" But suddenly he knew. "Your day at Rita's?"

"Yeah. But it was not . . . not quite . . . it wasn't quite fun."

"It wasn't quite fun?" His heart hammered. *This is it,* he realized. *He's trying to tell me something. She was involved. She had to be.*

"No," Alex drawled. He was looking out the window. "There were too many kids."

"Too many kids at Rita's?" His heart sank. He remembered this conversation now. It wasn't anything new.

"Yeah, Julie was there. And Big Alex was there. And Delilah was there."

Delilah? Is that a new girl?

"Yeah, but she's only three. I'm older than her . . . than her is, Daddy."

Than she is.

"Yeah, than *she* is."

Well, that's good, maybe you can help her out. You were three once, you know.

"But now I'm a *big* boy!"

You sure are! Does she know her alphabet?

"Yeah, but . . . not *quite.*"

You can teach her, I bet.

"Yeah, I can teach her! And also we can do some *puzzles!*" Alex bounced up and down in his booster, excited.

That sounds good. I'd be so proud of you if you taught someone their letters, kiddo.

"Yeah. I'll do that tomorrow. Right, Dod?" Alex grinned, hoping to bait Ian into their old game.

Ian closed his eyes. *This has to stop. It has to.* If it was in his head, maybe there were some drugs he could take. He remembered taking something a few years ago for over-active dreams, when he was having trouble sleeping at night. Maybe he had some of those left at home.

When he opened his eyes, he flipped the rearview mirror up so he couldn't see Alex. He'd rather face the glare of other cars' headlights.

39

He searched his cabinet for the pills when he got home, but couldn't find anything. Maybe he'd thrown them out. *Probably shouldn't take them anyway, they're probably not for this.* But he didn't care about that. He just wanted to stop seeing his dead son.

There was probably something else he could get, that would treat—*What? Overactive dreams? These aren't dreams. If you're looking at medication, you need something for schizophrenia.*

Was there even a treatment for schizophrenia? He thought there was. Pills, weren't there? He seemed to remember that a lot of patients had to be forced to take them. They were fine while they were on them, but they would never take them on their own.

Was that right?

He wanted to Google it, but he couldn't bring himself to open the basement door. He hadn't been down there since last weekend, when they'd played hide and seek.

I won't go into the basement. I don't like to shower. I check Alex's room every night before I go to bed. This is getting bad, Ian.

But it didn't change anything. He left the basement door and turned on *Law & Order*.

Is every night going to be like this, from here on out? He dreaded coming home. He was always looking over his shoulder.

How long could he live like that?

40

As he lay in bed, he figured it broke down like this.

There were two possibilities. Or four, depending on how he looked at it.

Maybe he was going crazy. That could be something temporary, brought on by the grief, or it could be something more serious that would've developed anyway, that just happened to coincide with Alex's death. If it was temporary, it would go away. Right? So he could just get through it. If it was permanent . . .

That was bad. That was the worst possibility. He set it aside.

The other possibility was that he was actually seeing a ghost. He was a grown man, and he didn't believe in ghosts, but there was no way he could pretend this wasn't a possibility. If Alex were haunting him, then there could be one of two reasons: either he was trying to make Ian miserable for letting him be killed—

He choked. He knew that was it.

Derek had thought otherwise, and at the time his argument had been persuasive, but Ian was no longer sure he agreed. An angry spirit wouldn't have the compunctions his son had had in life.

Would I be the same person, if I were abandoned by my family, raped, and killed?

So Alex was appearing to remind Ian what he had lost and how he had failed. Of the promises he'd broken.

Pills wouldn't help with that. *So, what then?* Again, his mind grasped at movies, because it was all he knew. *A psychic? An exorcist? A . . . séance, or something?*

The whole idea was so ridiculous, he laughed. In the dark, alone in his room. The noise echoed off his bare walls like the cry of a loon.

41

Alex had been a talkative boy. Ian used to joke that they spent the first two years of his life teaching him how to talk, and the next three teaching him to shut up.

"Good morning, Daddy! I peed already," he announced, standing in the hallway the next morning. He was in his pajamas. Ian went past him and into the bathroom. As he relieved himself and brushed his teeth, Alex kept up a constant barrage from the other side of the bathroom door.

"Daddy, can I have Pop Tarts today?"

"Daddy when I was sleeping I had a good dream about elephants. But only not about zebras too. The zebras are just sleeping."

"Daddy I know what's two plus two. It's four! Did you see the picture I made? I think you should bring it to work and hang it up."

Ian ignored him. This was his resolution upon waking: ignore it, and see if it would go away. If Alex had truly come back to torment him, perhaps Ian could make him tire of it. If Alex wasn't real, ignoring him was the smartest option anyway.

"Daddy I need to brush my teeth! Don't forget! Or I will get the cavities!"

"Where is Donnie? *Donnie!*"

"BAAAA-OOOO! BAAAA-OOOO! BAAAA-OOOO!"

"*Okay!*" Ian snapped. He tore the bathroom door open. Alex was balanced on one of the dining room chairs, holding his hands above his head and spinning as he yelled. "Alex! Get down! You're gonna—"

He slapped his mouth shut. He wouldn't finish that sentence. His thoughts did it for him.

—hurt yourself.

"Sorry, Dod!" Alex was always quick to apologize. "I will never ever do it again."

Sure you won't. But he didn't say it. He fixed his eyes on the kitchen, skirted past the dining room table, and resolutely ignored his son.

"Daddy are you making Pop Tarts?"

"Daddy can I have Pop Tarts today?"

"Daddy are you making Pop Tarts?"

They'd been teaching him how to wait for other people to acknowledge him before speaking, how to only make requests once. The urge to correct him—*Alex, stop and wait until I answer. Be quiet now*—resurged in his chest as though it had never left.

He refused it.

"Daddy? Can I have Pop Tarts today?"

Ian went back to the bedroom, hunted for clean clothes while his coffee brewed.

"Daddy, why can't I have Pop Tarts?"

Because you aren't really there.

"Daddy? Daddy, *why*?"

No.

"Daddy, please? Daddy *please!*"

No!

Alex heaved an exaggerated sigh and hurled himself to the hallway floor.

Go stand in the corner if you're going to act like that.

"No!"

Right now, Alex. Right—

Ian clenched his eyes closed, ground his teeth. This wasn't easy.

"I won't!"

Six months ago Ian would've taken the boy by the shoulders and steered him to the corner; carried him bodily if needed. Now he stalked to the stereo in the living room, flipped it to FM and turned it up. Dessa's voice blared from the speakers, observing that the years passed by now in twos and threes.

Beneath the music, Alex screamed.

42

At the first red light, Alex said, "Daddy, I don't like that black hat."

He was talking about Ian's ski mask, the one he took out when it was time to shovel the snow from the driveway. *That's fine,* Ian had told him. *You're not the one who has to go shoveling.*

"The eyes are scary on that black hat. Will you leave it inside, please?"

No, Alex. I need it for shoveling.

Alex fell silent. As the cross traffic slowed, Ian flipped the mirror down and saw the backseat was empty.

It's easier to answer him, he thought. *He goes away if I play out the conversations. Maybe I should just do that.*

And then, immediately: *Just resign myself to him being there, just talk to him alone in my head like I used to talk to him out loud. Whenever he wants to, forever.*

The light turned green, and Ian pushed on the gas, cursing.

43

He hadn't finished his résumé on Monday, so he worked doggedly on it between calls. Billi gave him some pointers.

At lunch he stayed in the cafeteria. He didn't want to see Alex in the car. He got back to his desk ten minutes before his break ended, and looked up bus schedules. He could get to work that way without being alone. If it took an extra hour each way, he didn't care. It wasn't like he had a family waiting for him.

That afternoon he finished up the application and sent it in along with the makeshift résumé. Both of them were crap. But the deadline was tomorrow, and he didn't want to miss it.

Sheila flounced past him on the way back from one of her bathroom trips. He got chewed out every time he was as much as a minute late, but she could take fifteen trips to the bathroom over the course of a day. He alt-tabbed as she went by, but he wasn't quick enough. She took a step backward, peering over his shoulder.

"'Supernatural.com,'" she announced. "Go back to that, I want to see."

"Look it up yourself," he answered.

"I don't like to surf on company time," she said, without a hint of sarcasm.

"Then I guess you're screwed."

"God, what is wrong with you? Why are you such a prick? I just want to see." She leaned across him, reaching for his keyboard. He caught a heady whiff of perfume, got a close-up view of the tanned swell of her breasts inside a black bra, and felt an embarrassing stirring in his crotch.

She flipped the window back and stood up. "'Home Exorcisms.'" She clicked her tongue. "Sounds . . . dangerous. Colmes, you wild man."

"Jesus Christ," he answered as he closed the browser. "You are not in high school anymore, Sheila. Do you get that? Would you leave me the fuck alone?"

She made an affronted sound. "You talk about me being in high school? You're the guy who's forty-five minutes late every morning."

"And you're on your fifteenth bathroom break of the day. You know, normally I don't bother the people I work with. I'm pretty live-and-let-live. You ought to try it. It's a great way to get along."

Jorge stood up, glaring over the cube wall. "I'm on a call, guys."

"Sorry," Ian answered, but Sheila just went back to her desk. He glanced back at her, fuming, and she gave him a smile that said, *I win.*

No. You know what? Fuck that. No. He tore his headset off and threw it on the desk.

"Going on a bathroom break?" she asked as he stalked past.

His hand twitched out. He nearly flipped her off. Instead he balled it into a fist and held it at his side.

You have no fucking idea what I'm going through. Do you? You just have to push and push and push. Do you know that I'm hallucinating, bitch? Do you? I'm fucking unstable. Keep pushing and find out.

But it was an empty, stupid threat. He wasn't one of those guys who was going to bring a gun to work and kill everyone. He wasn't going to throw his life—such as it was—away over Sheila Fucking Swanson.

You don't have the guts, he imagined her saying.

He rapped sharply on Justin's cube wall. "I need to talk to—"

Justin waved at him, pointed at the headset he was wearing. "Mm hm. Well, that's possible. I can look into it."

Ian took a deep breath. He wanted to scream, to break something.

"Tomorrow's Friday, and we're already down three people. Would next week work? Otherwise Kate may be available too." Pause. "Yeah. Okay, just take a look at the calendar. My schedule's up to date." Pause. "All right, sounds good!" Pause. "Okay. Thanks. Bye.

"Ian! What's going on?" He took off the headset, gestured at one of the chairs in his cube.

"I'd like to move desks. Across the wall." Ian didn't sit down.

"Okay. What's going on?" Justin repeated.

"I'm just . . . Sheila is driving me nuts. It's like she lives to bug me." Jesus, he sounded whiny. "You know, she's twenty years old and doesn't really get what I'm going through, and she . . .

"She actually told me that I should be getting here on time in the mornings since I don't have to worry about Alex anymore." He scoffed. "Can you fucking believe that? It's so . . . fucking . . . *callous*."

Justin recoiled from the vulgarity, like he'd just watched Ian whip his dick out. "Okay. Okay. Are you sure you're not just taking a little too much offense to that?"

A hand of ice grasped Ian's stomach. "Excuse me?" His hand was trembling.

"No, I just mean . . . Maybe she's just trying to give you some advice?"

Or maybe you love looking down her shirt so much that you'll take her fucking side on anything. "I didn't ask for her advice." He pronounced each syllable carefully, neutrally. "She needs to mind her own goddamn business."

"Ian, *please*. Mind your language, we have people on the phone."

Ian blinked.

"Tell you what. Let's go into a side room to discuss—"

"No. You know what? Forget it."

44

"Daddy, I don't like that black hat."

Yeah, you said that this morning. He hit his signal, eased into the next lane.

"Daddy, I don't like that black hat."

Alex, please.

"Daddy, I don't like—"

Alex, goddammit!

45

He made a frozen pizza for dinner, and burned his thumb pulling it out of the oven. He recoiled, roaring, and dropped the thing on the floor.

"*Fuck*!"

He almost kicked the oven rack with his bare foot, but stopped himself when he realized how stupid it would be; instead, he tried to slam the oven door closed with the rack still halfway out.

Bam! Bam! BAM!

The door closed.

"Daddy, are you okay?" His son was in the doorway to the dining room, eyes wide with worry, and Ian suddenly felt acutely ashamed.

"Yeah. I'm okay." He slopped up the pizza with a towel, wincing at the pain in his thumb, before turning to the sink to run his burn under cold water. "Sorry. I didn't mean to yell."

Alex didn't hear; he'd already gone.

Fuck it. Ian grabbed a box of cereal from the cupboard and the half gallon carton of milk from the fridge. He remembered when they'd had to buy two full gallons at a time to keep up with Alex's voracious appetite for milk. *Cinnamon Toast Crunch it is.*

He carried the meal into the living room, where Alex was sitting on the couch.

"Daddy, can we watch Word Girl?"

Ian resolutely flipped the TV to *Law & Order* and poured himself a bowl of cereal.

"Daddy, can we watch Word Girl please?"

No. Not tonight.

"Why *not*?"

Ian chewed through a mouthful of crunchy cinnamon cereal. Disgusted, Alex ran into his room to play.

46

He came back into the living room at eight o'clock, in footie pajamas and holding a beaten copy of *More More More, Said the Baby*. "I picked my book, Daddy," he announced.

Ian and Alina hadn't been perfect. They'd fucked up plenty. Hell, every day had felt like an exercise in discovering new ways to screw up as parents. But this one thing, they had managed: every night, rain or shine, they'd taken turns reading a book to their son.

Williams' simple story of children loved deeply by their guardians had left Ian shaken the first time he'd read it. He'd felt his love for his son like a river in his soul, infinite and fathomless. At the sight of the book, he felt a whisper of that sensation again. As Alex stood watching him, bright eyes shining eagerly, the whisper grew to a shout.

"Alex . . ." Ian said. He turned off the TV.

He'd never been good at ignoring his son. It wasn't something he could do now. If he'd gone mad, so be it. If Alex was real, if he had come back to torment his father for failing him . . .

Then Ian was still his father, and he would still be there for his son.

He slid off the couch to the floor.

"Alex, you know we can't read that book. Don't you?"

"It's *More More More, Said the Baby*," Alex explained.

"I know it is. I love that book. You know why?"

"Why?" Alex said.

"Because it reminds me of you, and of how much I love you. And how I would do anything for you."

"Yeah. But let's read it, Daddy." He took a step toward the couch.

"We can't do that. I think you know that."

Alex drew up short. Ian was deviating from the script.

"We can't do that. No matter how much I want to. Do you know why?"

"It's *More More More, Said the Baby*."

"Because you're gone, Alex. You died. Do you remember what that means?"

He changed. The book disappeared and he was in a grey dress shirt and black slacks, impressively sharp and somber for a four-year-old. *Ready for Alina's mom's funeral.*

"It means we'll never see her again?"

"It means we can never see each other again. Right. You were killed—" The word cracked on his tongue. He waited while the familiar grief squeezed his chest, watching his beautiful son watch him.

"A man—an *evil* man, a terrible man—killed you. And Daddy wanted to help, he would've done anything . . . ." He wrestled with himself. "Oh, God, Alex, *anything* to save you, but he couldn't. He couldn't. And now . . ."

"We can never see Grandma again?"

Alex didn't understand. It was just like when he'd been alive, when he'd seemed to get what Ian was saying and then asked if Grandma was going to be at the church for the funeral too. His innocent effort to comprehend left Ian reeling.

"Right, Alex. Right. Except it's you. Not Grandma. You are the one who died this time."

Alex's brows furrowed.

"You can see her, I bet. You can find her there. But you just can't stay here. It's not a place for you . . ." *Oh, God, Alex.* "Not a place for you anymore."

The clothes disappeared. He was wet and cold. "I'll just call for you and mommy!"

"No, Alex. It's too late for that now."

"I'll just call for you and mommy!"

"Alex, no. I'm sorry. It's too late."

He was on the ground in a red turtleneck and jeans, his face bruised, his hands and feet lashed together with duct tape. "*Daddy!*"

It was nothing like the cries he gave when his toys were lost, *nothing*. It was feral, anguished; the cry of a lost child, desperate for his father to hear him.

Ian doubled over as if he'd been punched in the stomach.

"*Daddy!*" Alex was sobbing.

"Alex," Ian managed. "I can hear you. I'm here. This is over." *Oh, Jesus. Oh, God.* "Do you understand? This is over. He can't hurt you any more. You are safe now."

"Daddy . . ." Whimpering, snorting like an animal.

"Alex, oh God, honey. Please. It's over. Okay? He killed you, but that means you're free. Please just think of that. Please think—"

"Daddy, where are you?"

"Alex." There was nothing he could do. He was as powerless now as he had been then. What had he been doing while his son screamed for him? Had he been in

bed sleeping? Making love to his wife? Watching *Law &
Order*? "Alex . . . is there a light?"

Alex's head snapped up, as if he'd heard a sudden noise.

"There's a light. Right? Somewhere, by you, you see a
light? And you have to go into it. Okay, Alex? Do you hear
me? Go into that light. Grandma is there—"

Alex rolled to the wall, put his back against it, staggered to a stand despite his taped hands and feet.

"—and the bad man isn't, the bad man's not there.
The light is safe from him. Okay?"

He was staring at the far wall, eyes wide.

"Alex, God, please listen. Find the light. Okay? Find
the light."

"*No!*" he shrieked. He started hopping toward the hallway. It was pathetic, gangly. "No! No! Leave me alone!

"*Daddy!*"

He limped out of sight around the corner. His door
slammed.

47

Ian fell like an untied balloon, sent whizzing around the
room until it collapses to the floor, empty. He had
nothing left. He couldn't move. A boulder had pinned
him to the earth.

He wondered if Alex had found a light. He wondered
if there was such a thing. He wondered if he would go to
hell for telling his tormented son to look for something
he himself did not believe in.

And he wished there was a heaven. He wished that
harder than he had ever wished anything in his life.

48

He woke a little after two in the morning, his face raw from chafing against the carpet, his head throbbing like he had torn it in half. Groaning, he climbed to all fours and then to a stand.

He stumbled to the bathroom, thinking to pee, and ended up collapsing to his knees and spewing his modest dinner into the toilet.

When he finished, he held his breath and listened.

The furnace kicking on. The house settling. An autumn wind tugging at the windows.

Nothing else.

The toilet flushed like thunder in the silence. His upper lip was crusted with dried snot; he scrubbed it off and rinsed his mouth several times. In the mirror he saw a haggard, red-eyed madman.

His son's door was still closed as he stepped out of the bathroom. He left it that way, and went to bed.

49

The alarm went off at seven, sawing at his ears like a cheese grater. He hit the snooze button and repeated the process nine minutes later. Then again. Then again.

At 7:40 he staggered into the living room and called in sick. He was lucky enough to get Justin's voicemail. That was good. He didn't want to talk to him.

He thought about going back to bed, but knew it wouldn't do any good. He stayed on the couch instead, staring blankly at the TV as the curtains over the windows slowly started glowing with daylight.

Justin would be pissed when he got the voicemail. *Wonder if I'll still have a job on Monday.* Ian remembered Billi telling him to look into FMLA. Maybe if he qualified for that, Justin wouldn't be able to fire him. He idly considered Googling it, but that would mean going downstairs.

His listless gaze strayed away from the jumble of images on the TV to the hallway, half expecting to find Alex there, but it was empty. For both of their sakes, he hoped the boy was gone.

Some channel was playing an all-day marathon of *The Simpsons* Halloween shows, and he realized dully that Halloween was Sunday already. *Gotta get some candy.* He remembered Alex's first Halloween, and how amazed he and Alina had been that the kid seemed to know exactly what to do. His mastery of the phrase "Trick or Treat" had come faster than "I'm hungry" or "I love you." After two houses had given him candy, he was running to the next one.

He shook off the memory, stood up, and went to make breakfast.

50

At Target, he picked up four bags of candy (two Sour Patch Kids, one Snickers, and one Almond Joy), various supplies for the house, and a few more frozen pizzas. He wasn't much of a cook, but on a lark he also stopped at the grocery store and bought a raw steak and a baking potato.

His back seat remained empty for the entire trip.

He stopped off at home, made a quick lunch, and put

the groceries away. He couldn't see the door to Alex's room most of the time, but when he stepped out of the bathroom and into the hall, he drew up short, staring at it.

That door had been open for months, ever since Alina moved out. To see it closed now felt wrong. He didn't like closed doors. He always left the doors to the bedroom and bathroom open—the only doors in the house that he normally left closed were the ones in the basement. A part of him wanted to open this one again, even if just a crack.

He remembered playing hide and seek, opening the cellar pantry. He left the door closed.

Just to be out of the house, he left again that afternoon. It was a cold, clear October day. He drove around aimlessly, his mind wandering. It was hard not to think about Alex, but he also thought about work. He thought about Sheila leaning over his lap, and the curve of her breasts. She'd done that on purpose, he was pretty sure, but not because she had any interest in him. She'd wanted to prove that she could do what she wanted, and he wouldn't have the backbone to stop her. It was a stupid power game, but he'd lost.

Alina had never done anything like that when they were dating, in college. He wondered if it was something all women recognized as an option: using their sexuality to get their way. It seemed like a dangerous way to live. He knew there were men who wouldn't tolerate it, who would think of it as cock-teasing.

That was one of the things that had so attracted him to Alina. They had never played games. They'd always been straight with each other.

He saw the library ahead on the right, and decided to stop. In the parking lot, he pulled out his phone and texted her. -*Thinking of you. I love you.*- He didn't know if he was supposed to do that. He had never been estranged before. She wasn't living at home, but they weren't divorced. He knew they had some things to work through. And yes, a lot of it was his own shit. But he was sure they could do it.

The truth was, he would go to counseling if that's what he needed to do to get things under control. Shauna annoyed the bejesus out of him, but he could see why Alina wanted him to go. He used to know how to handle his temper. He could do it again. He could be the man his wife fell in love with.

In the library, Ian used one of the public computers to Google FMLA. He'd be eligible for up to twelve weeks of unpaid leave if he had a "serious health condition" that made him unable to do his job. That sounded like cancer, or something. Not grieving.

He was pretty sure the company would argue that his situation fell under the corporate policy on bereavement leave. Under that policy, when his son had died, he had received three days off. According to Smartlink, that was enough. Get your ass back to the office.

Jesus, it pissed him off. He'd seen the soulless machine at work before. But the contrast between Alex—his vitality, his joy, his boundless enthusiasm for life—and the grey, iron gaze of Ian's employer was just staggering. Weren't the Smartlink executives human beings? Did any of them have children, did they understand that losing your only child was like having your heart torn from your chest? How could someone become so caught up in profits and the need to oil the machine that they no longer cared when the brightest points of light in the world were snuffed out?

Kal can take six weeks for depression, he remembered Billi saying, *and I'm pretty sure that was all bullshit.*

He printed out the page and took it home with him.

51

The house was empty and quiet when he got back.

He set the books he'd checked out on the dining room table and went to the bathroom. Coming out, he saw that Alex's door was still closed. He kept expecting to find it open.

Is he still in there? he wondered. *Is he sitting there right now, waiting for me to come find him?*

But if he was, he was being quiet. That in itself was strange enough that it seemed to rule out the possibility. *Or maybe there really was a light, and he really found it.*

Maybe I actually helped him.

A warm glow blossomed in his chest. It felt *right*, somehow, that notion. Maybe that was even the reason Alex had come back. It was horrible, what he had gone through. Maybe he just hadn't been able to escape it, and he had just needed to hear from his Daddy that it was over. That he was safe now, and it was okay to go on.

Ian shook his head, let out a breath of disbelief. It sounded like something from a stupid primetime drama, one of those supernatural ones that took itself far too seriously.

All the same, the warm glow didn't go away.

52

The steak wasn't gourmet, but it wasn't a total fuck-up, either. The hardest part was seasoning the thing. He wasn't sure what was best, so he just used a little seasoning salt and pepper. For good measure, he sprinkled on some italian seasoning. He considered the paprika, but that didn't seem appropriate.

As he brought the dishes back into the kitchen, his phone buzzed with a text message from Alina.

-I love you too. See you Wed.-

He wondered what she had done today. Worked, probably. What were her plans for the weekend? Was she finding her life easier without him?

He carried the phone back into the living room. The message said, *I love you too.* Because of that, he was able to let the other questions go.

53

"Hey, it's me."

"Hey, what's going on?"

"Nothin'. Called in sick today."

"*Nice.*"

Ian chuckled. "Raid on for tonight?"

"Yeah, planning on it." The creak of furniture as Derek twisted to see the clock. "Like an hour, I think? We're starting invites at seven."

"Got room for a tank?"

"You coming?"

"Yeah, I think so."

"Then we will *make* room."

Ian smiled. "Don't . . . kick anyone out or anything."

"Nah, I mean I know we have cancellations. We'll make the tank part work out."

"Sweet." He wondered whether to say anything else. "How . . . is everything?"

Ian let out a long breath. "Okay. I mean, not great. I don't know if I'll ever be able to say again that things are good. I know that sounds . . . what? Fatalistic? But I can't say it." Silence. "It just seems dishonest."

"That's fair."

"I had another one of those dreams last night."

"About Alex?"

"Yeah."

Derek waited.

"It's like I was seeing him after he was kidnapped. His arms and legs were taped together. He was . . . calling for me. Calling for help. I couldn't get to him. Of course."

"Jesus."

"Yeah. But I told him it was over. That . . . you know, because he was gone, the ugly part was over. The guy who took him can't hurt him anymore. I told him he was safe now, and he just had to let go. To go on."

A pause. "What happened?"

"Well, I haven't—" Ian stopped himself. He was about to say, *I haven't seen him all day.* "I mean, there was no light for him to go into or anything. But he left. I think . . . I don't know, it sounds stupid, but I think he might be okay."

"Doesn't sound stupid to me."

"Yeah. I hope you're right."

"'More things in heaven and earth,'" Derek said. "I

don't know what's out there, but I know a good thing when I hear it. So should you."

"Yeah." Ian tasted the idea that Alex was okay in some kind of afterlife. That he'd been through hell, but it was over; and that he had forgiven his father.

It was good. He smiled a little bit. "All right. See you at seven."

54

The raid was fun, and distracting. His skills at tanking had atrophied in the seven months or more since he had last played, but his online friends were too happy to see him to really give him any grief about it. It felt comforting to get the private whispers welcoming him back, to receive the blithe assurances from people he'd never met in real life that they'd missed him. To participate in something so trivial, with people who took it so seriously.

He played at his computer in the basement, and when his monitor went dark between loading screens, its depths reflected the closed utility room door behind him. It only caught him by surprise once. Every time after that, he just closed his eyes for a few seconds until the game's display came back.

They finished up around eleven. Ian thanked the raid for bringing him, sent Derek a separate message to thank *him*, and logged off. He went upstairs without looking at the door.

He considered grabbing a snack and watching some infomercials to ease the tension in his neck (it cramped a bit sometimes while he played), but opted against it. He didn't want to spend tonight the same way he had spent so many other nights. Tonight had been different. Tonight he hadn't been alone, or tormented. Tonight he could imagine playing online again, excelling at work again, having Alina home again. He went to bed right away, instead, daring to imagine that he could recover.

He was in that twilight place between sleeping and awareness, where the edges of mundane thought just start to bleed into dreaming, when Alex screamed.

55

Ian's body seized. His eyes shot open and he stared upwards, into the dark and the silence, heart hammering. The red gaze of his alarm clock glimmered on the wall. The blurry shape of the ceiling fan crouched above him. He waited for the second scream, the one that would confirm it hadn't been a nightmare. His nightmares had woken him more than once since Alex had been taken. Maybe—

"DAD-*DEEEEEEEEE*!"

He squeezed his eyes shut, fighting his own sudden urge to scream. Grabbed his pillow and clamped it against his ears.

"DAD-*DEEEEEEEEE*!" The pillow didn't help. "IT'S TOO *DARK*! DAD-DEEEE! *OPEN THE DOOR*!"

Ian jumped out of bed, ran into the hall, grabbed the knob on his son's door.

"DADDY! IT'S TOO DARK!"

His hand clenched the knob, but he didn't turn it. He wanted to throw the door open and scream, or throw the door open and comfort his son. He wanted to run outside, right now, and get away.

He'd thought he was done. He'd thought he'd really made a difference.

"DAD-*DEEEEEEEEE*—"

"Alex!" he barked through the door. The screaming stopped. He didn't know what to say next. He had just needed that screaming to stop.

Through the door he heard sobbing. It wasn't the same as the noises Alex had made the night before. It was heart-rending, yes. But it was bearable.

"Alex," he said again, less sharply. "Why are you crying?"

"Be—be—be—" The boy stammered over his words, choking on tears. "Because you—you—you closed the *door!*"

We warned you, Alex. You knew if you kept playing instead of going to sleep like you were supposed to, that we would close the door. But he said, "Alex, do you remember what we talked about last night?"

Silence.

"This isn't a place for you, anymore. Do you remember?"

Quiet sobbing.

"You need to go on to the next place. Remember? You're too sad here, and you need to go on. You'll be happier—"

"Dad—Dad—" Huge, gulping breaths. "Daddy?"

"Yes?"

Alex's voice trembled as he fought to keep it under control. "May you open the door, please?"

Ian winced, felt tears burning down his cheeks. This had been hard for him when it had been real—he and Alina had constantly reminded each other that Alex had to learn that bedtime meant bedtime. They weren't flaying the flesh from his bones as his cries would seem to indicate; they were merely closing his door so he didn't have light to play by. They were in the right, they were the parents, and teaching him to go to sleep at night was their job, however difficult he might make it—

But that logic was obsolete. Alex was still in the dark, still screaming for his father, but the nightmares that must plague that darkness now . . . !

He turned the knob, nearly pushed the door open—and remembered caving to his son in life.

All right, Alex. Listen to me. We'll leave the door open a crack. Okay? But you have to go to sleep. No more playing. It is really late, you need your sleep, and Mommy and Daddy have to work in the morning. Do you understand?

And five minutes later the boy had been out of bed again, racing Donnie in the tiny strip of light from the cracked doorway.

The stakes were higher now. But the methods were the same.

"Alex, I can't do that."

From the other side of the door came a guttural moan that slowly crescendoed to a wail.

"You need to find another way. Look, like I told you. Look for a light, or another way to . . . to go on. There has to be something."

"DAD-*DEEEEEE!*"

Ian lurched into the living room and turned on the TV.

56

He steadfastly ignored his son's screams. He thought about going downstairs, to see if it was quieter, but couldn't bear the thought of those cries echoing through the floor so close to the room where he had seen Alex getting raped.

After an hour, he threw on his coat and left through the front door. Standing on the porch, his breath pluming in the frozen air, he waited and heard nothing. But it was too cold to stay outside, and when he went back in the cries resumed.

He curled into a ball on the couch and turned up the TV until the music and the voices from the speakers crackled with distortion, and still he heard Alex shrieking in the snatches of silence between commercials. At two thirty he put his coat back on, got in his car, and drove.

Alex didn't follow him. Ian turned on the radio and listened to whatever was on, his mind racing, his soul raw.

He can't keep doing this. He can't.

I have to figure out a way to tell him. He has to understand. There has to be something to convince him.

He thought again about séances and exorcists, Ouija boards and psychics.

The lights of oncoming cars on 169 mesmerized him. They looked like a river of souls, flowing to heaven. They were running past him, the other way. He was in a different river—the one filled with red lights, the one going to hell.

The scream of a horn jerked him awake as he started

drifting across the lane marker and into another car. He wrenched the wheel back and managed not to crash.

He got back home just as dawn broke. The house was quiet. He collapsed on the couch, and slept.

57

He woke at ten, and again at noon. Each time he struggled to get up as a brick of exhaustion behind his eyes dragged him down. Each time he surrendered to it, and fell into the grey.

When he woke the next time, the light from the curtains was starting to die. His bladder drove him from the couch, and once he was up, the jagged kink in his neck made him recoil from the thought of going back to it.

He couldn't stand to stay in the house so he drove away, wincing at the pain in his neck every time he had to check his mirror. Alex left him alone, and somehow he ended up at the mall where he and Alina used to come to walk.

His stomach grumbled as he parked, but he didn't get anything to eat. Instead he just wandered the broad halls, shuffled past the other shoppers, surrounded by people but completely alone. He passed a store that sold Ouija boards and stared at one in the window, wondering if its arcane face would let Alex speak in plain language instead of always aping things he had said in life. The hand-written price tag said $17.50. He bought it.

When the mall closed he threw the board in his trunk and thought about calling Derek, or Alina, or his mom. Then he went home, ate a banana, and tried to go to bed, hoping to get his sleep schedule back to something resembling normal before work on Monday.

Alex started screaming around eleven.

58

Ian stood in the empty hallway of his empty house, outside a closed door, and spoke.

"Alex, I know what you're trying to do."

"Dad-*dy*!"

"I know you want me to open the door so you can keep talking to me in the car, and in the living room, and try to get me to read books with you. Right?"

Screeching. A tantrum to tear down the heavens.

"But you're still not listening to me." God, his head hurt. Exhaustion bulged at the backs of his eyes. His ability to keep his voice level astounded him. Thinking back, though, it always had. Short of an occasional snap or sharp outburst, he had never had trouble keeping his temper with his son. Even reasoning had always seemed to work best, and Alex was the one person on earth that Ian had always been able to stay level with. He didn't want to hurt him. He didn't want him to feel unloved or disliked. But he still had to teach Alex how to behave, and that meant administering the rules firmly but dispassionately.

It had worked, eventually, with the bedtime tantrums. In the months before he had been kidnapped, Alex had slept with the door closed every night. Maybe it would work again.

"I love you, Alex. You know that. I need you to trust me."

"OPEN THE *DOOR!*"

"I'm not going to do that."

"*OPEN THE DOOR!*"

"Alex, the answer is no. You need to find your own way. I can't help you with that." The depth of his fatigue actually made it easier to keep his calm, to stay detached.

"*DAD-DEEEE!*"

"Go to sleep, Alex."

"*DAD-DEEE! NO, DAD-DEEEEE!*"

"It's time for bed now."

59

Ian went into the living room, tried the same failed strategies there as he had the night before. Eventually his detachment frayed, and he winced at every new shriek like it was a cattle prod. They drove him into the kitchen, where he stared at the basement door for several minutes, flinching, before going through.

He and Alina had sought refuge in the basement before—when Alex was an infant, learning to sleep through the night. Sometimes he'd been hungry, sure, but sometimes he had just been defiant, and in an effort to get him to start recognizing the difference, they would let him cry for up to twenty minutes at a time.

They'd always go into the basement for that, where his cries would be somewhat muffled. The trips below were Ian's idea, because his wife seemed to be going mad from sleep deprivation, and he wanted to shield her from the yawning, bottomless demands of motherhood as much as he could.

You stay here, he'd tell her. *In twenty minutes I'll go up. I'll take care of him. Just try to get some sleep.*

Her haggard eyes would accost him—*You can't care for him. He needs to be breastfed. It's my job.*—and he would stare back, or even say out loud, *One bottle of formula every couple days is not going to kill him. We can't let him run us into the ground. We both still need to sleep, and you especially.*

She had gotten so mad at him, sometimes! The literature had convinced her that every time she let Alex cry or let him drink formula, she was shortening his lifespan or destroying his brain cells. But later, when Alex had started sleeping through, she had thanked Ian. For being there when she was too exhausted to think. For standing up for her.

The stairs lurched beneath him, and he tripped. He shot a hand out to grab the railing, but momentum twisted him around and knocked his feet from the steps. He ended up stretched like a man on a rack, his feet brushing the cheap carpet, his arm bent weirdly to hang on.

"Goddammit," he whispered. The floor was thinner than it used to be, or Alex's voice was stronger. His shrieks were barely muffled at all.

60

Walgreen's sold earplugs. He bought a pack and drove home. Just as it had been Saturday night, the air outside the house was still. As he locked the door behind him, Alex's shrieks started up again as if they had never stopped.

Ian closed his bedroom door and put in two of the

plugs. They expanded in his ears like a rush of water over his head, bulging against his flesh and filling his head with echoing stillness.

He crawled into bed and buried his head under the blankets, clenching his eyes shut. He could still hear his son.

After an hour he gave up, ripped out the plugs, and went again to his son's door to entreat him to stop. It didn't work, but a little later the sun rose, and Alex's screams wound down to sobs, then to moans, then to silence.

61

Sunday night he handed out candy, but when the trick-or-treaters stopped, Alex began.

Ian stayed up all night, reeling, and finally found one place in the house where he could barely hear Alex: the shower. He used it at four in the morning, dressed, then left for work. He parked at the far end of the lot, set his cell phone alarm for 7:55, and slept for two and a half hours.

The callers he got all had nasty viruses or registry issues; no one needed a simple driver update or an advertised program install. Their questions scraped against his brain like sandpaper.

Once, he nodded off with a caller on hold. He jerked awake in such a panic that he nearly toppled out of his chair.

At lunch, he sneaked out to his car for a nap. He awoke even groggier, his head throbbing. The advantage to this was that his headache would not permit him to doze between calls.

He drove home in a stupor, and fell asleep on the couch until Alex's screaming woke him for the night.

62

"Mr. Ian Colmes!" Derek sounded like an announcer on a game show.

"Hey."

"What's goin' on?"

"I . . . I'm sorry to ask, I know it's weird, is there any chance I could stay over there tonight again?"

A heartbeat. "*Tonight*?"

Ian bit back the urge to apologize again. "Yeah." The road was swimming as he drove home; he blinked at it, trying to make it hold still.

"God . . . you do know it's Tuesday?"

"Yeah."

"Ah, man. Tonight . . . Jake's staying here tonight, we've had it set up for like a week now."

Absurdly, tears boiled into Ian's eyes. "Oh."

"I'm sorry, Ian, I wish I could. Those dreams coming back?"

Ian blinked again. "I . . . yeah, I guess so. They're waking me up, every night, waking me."

A concerned sigh. "Oh, man."

"I can't . . . I haven't slept in days, he just . . . keeps *screaming*." From a distant cavern in his mind, Ian wondered if this had been saying too much. It didn't matter. His brain felt like a leaking orange juice carton on the fridge shelf. The words had just seeped out.

"Ian . . . God, you sound terrible."

"I'm so tired."

"Man . . . listen. I'm really sorry about tonight. Just . . . try to get some sleep, okay? Maybe take some, like . . . . sleep medicine? Or something? It might help. I never dream when I'm on that stuff."

"Yeah." Ian thought about a hotel room again, but he couldn't afford it. He could call his mom, but she would freak. "Yeah, that's a good idea. Okay."

"And . . ." Derek hesitated. "Look, I hate to say this, I know you hate the idea, but it might help to talk about it. You know, or see someone who can help you. There's got to be something."

"Yeah." He was headed home, where Alex would be screaming.

63

"Ian."

The world beneath him quivered and he jerked awake, casting left and right, trying to figure out where he was.

Justin waited for Ian to get his bearings. Behind him, Sheila was looking back from her desk, her lips pursed like she'd found a maggot on the carpet.

"Shit," Ian said, hoarsely. "Sorry, I'm sorry."

"Can you come into a side room for a minute?"

"Yeah. Yeah." He started to set his phone to *After Call Work* so he wouldn't get calls, but it was already set. *Shit,* he almost said again.

Justin led him to a side room and closed the door. As they sat down, Ian started.

"Justin, I'm sorry. I didn't mean to. I've just . . . I've

been sleeping so bad. I can't get any sleep at home. I keep having these nightmares." He felt like a worm, groveling to this man.

"Ian, you can't sleep on the job."

"No, no, I know I can't—"

"We have to write you up for this. It's gonna go in your file."

"Yeah. Of course." What could he say? "Okay." He had expected to be fired.

Justin's pen scratched across the paper, all in neat little caps.

WED, 11/3/10. IAN COLMES WAS SLEEPING AT HIS DESK ON ACW. I HAVE ADVISED IAN THAT HE IS ON WRITTEN NOTICE AND ANOTHER

Justin paused, at a rare loss for words.

INCIDENT MAY RESULT IN TERMINATION.

He signed his name in impeccable cursive, and handed Ian the pen. Ian's sprawling scribble went on the line labelled *Employee Signature*.

"Take the afternoon off," Justin said as he stood. "Go home and get some sleep. Take it easy."

Ian wondered if he would get paid for the rest of the day. He was out of vacation time for the year. But he didn't ask. The image of his couch—or, oh God, his *bed*—glimmered like an oasis.

Justin paused at the door. "Maybe give SER a call. I've heard they're really good."

Smartlink Employee Resources. Ian had seen the fliers. They could get him some free mental health care. Probably a couple hours. That should be enough, right? Fix everything.

"Okay. Yeah." Ian nodded. "Thanks."

64

It was cold outside, the first really cold day of the season. He trudged through the parking lot under a grey sky, head bowed against the wind, as brown and yellow leaves chased each other over his shoes.

He had to stop for gas. The wind gusted as he climbed out of the car, making him shiver. He remembered being young, and running around in autumn without a coat on. He had relished the cold, then, but the fire of youth had burned out sometime since, and now the wind sliced right through him.

There was an old coat in the trunk—left there since last March, when he'd torn it off one day in a sweat. That had been before Alex was taken. *How long before?* he wondered, but couldn't remember. Long enough that something like the first warm day of spring had still been notable.

He popped the trunk to grab his coat, and saw the Ouija board.

REACH OUT TO GHOSTS, the package read. *CONTACT LOST LOVED ONES!*

Hokey bullshit. A scam made for suckers. He threw his coat on and slammed the trunk. But as he watched the dollar display on the pump rocket upwards, he kept thinking about it.

CONTACT LOST LOVED ONES!

Maybe it will let him talk. Maybe he'll be able to just tell me what he wants.

It's bullshit. Jesus, I thought you outgrew this shit when you were twelve.

I did. But obviously I got something wrong.

It's fucking stupid. Don't be an idiot. If you want to do something about this, do like Derek said. Get some fucking Tylenol PM. Call a shrink. Call SER.

He slapped the gas dispenser on to the pump and climbed back into the car.

He was so *tired*.

65

The Ouija board's box slid on to the kitchen table with a whispered *thunk*, and he turned away from it at once. He hung up his coat and grabbed a pop from the fridge, something with caffeine, and stood staring out the kitchen window into his little backyard as his thoughts chased each other in circles.

He was ashamed of the thing sitting on the table. He wanted to bury it in the closet like a rented porn video, but of course that was ridiculous. There was no one to see it but him.

Then again, maybe that was enough reason to do it.

In the backyard there was a swing hanging by a pair of rusty chains from a broad tree branch. It had been part of the house when they had bought it, and when he'd gotten old enough, Alex had loved it. Now it was twisting with the autumn breeze, banging against the trunk, its chains jingling like a poorly-made wind chime.

The thing was, the board was the only way forward that he could keep a secret. The other options—*all* the other options: talking to a psychic, trying to perform a séance, shit, even taking an FMLA leave—involved telling someone what was happening. He wasn't ready for that. He didn't know that he ever would be.

Finally, he made up his mind and marched away from the window, toward Alex's room.

Outside, the wind blew and the dead leaves danced.

66

Wait outside the door and listen, some part of him said. *Make sure he's not in there.* But he steamrolled this warning, grabbed the knob and threw the door open. It was *his* house, he'd go wherever the hell he wanted.

Boxes, stacked two and three high. Faded white walls, flecked with bits of tape and old nail-holes.

It had to be done in here. He was sure of that much.

He flipped the switch, but the light was dead. That was okay. It was dim, and the overcast day didn't help, but he could still see.

The boxes were heavier than he'd expected, but he moved them out of the middle of the room. He and Alina hadn't labeled them. He still remembered the day they had packed it all up. Alina had started in the middle of a Saturday afternoon, after mentioning that it had to be done several times over the preceding months. She had come in here and worked silently, periodically walking out with a full garbage bag or a plastic dish.

She hadn't said anything, but she hadn't needed to. Waves of condemnation had rolled off of her. *I can't believe you're making me do this by myself.* Hurt, anger, frustration: all the hallmarks of their new relationship.

Finally, he'd caved. He really didn't want her to have to do it alone. It was a horrible job. He didn't wish it on anyone, least of all her or himself. Why he had to respect her wishes (to do it *now*), but she couldn't respect his wishes (to wait), he didn't know. It didn't matter. She was doing it, and he either had to be there for her, or abandon her.

He stood and stretched his back. The boxes lined the walls now, crouched in the dimness like blocks of stone. Uncarved statues, waiting to watch the show.

He settled on the floor in the middle of the room and slid the board from the box. There were no instructions: just the board, and a simple planchette. Who needed instructions? Everyone had seen The Exorcist.

All the Ouija stories Ian had heard growing up involved inadvertently contacting something evil and bringing it into the user's house. Even when he had believed in the possibility of an afterlife, he wouldn't touch a board for exactly that reason. Now, concern for that outcome barely flickered across his mind.

He'd already spoken with his son; he knew Alex could move things. He still didn't believe in demons, or any of the rest of it. But he knew something was happening with his son. He just wanted to talk to *him*.

"I'm sorry, Daddy."

Ian jerked his head up. Alex stood by the door in jean overalls. He was shorter, plumper, his cheeks stuffed with chub. After speaking, he popped his thumb in his mouth and sucked at it furiously.

"For what?" Ian rasped.

"For . . . for . . . the owl-it." His eyes were big and heavy. He pointed at the nearest electrical outlet.

It came back. Alex had been playing with the outlets. Somehow, he had found a fork. Ian had caught him.

It was the first time Ian had really let loose yelling at him. It had also been Alex's first spanking. Ian could count the others on one hand.

I'm glad you're here to say you're sorry. It could've hurt you really bad, you know that? Really, really bad, so bad you wouldn't be able to talk or call for help or anything. The outlet is not a toy, Alex. You need to leave it alone.

"It's not a toy," Alex agreed miserably. But he wasn't looking at the outlet now. He was looking at the Ouija board.

Ian felt his mouth run dry. His breath whistled in his lungs as if he'd tumbled into a freefall.

"It's not a toy," Alex said again.

"You mean this?" Ian asked carefully. He tapped the board with one finger. "You don't think I should use this?"

"It's not a toy."

Ian sat, slack-jawed, working it through. "Well . . . Alex, I don't know what else to do. You want to tell me something, I think, but I don't know what that is. I can't understand you. I'm trying, but I just can't understand, and every night you've been *screaming*, and I just can't keep doing that. Do you understand that? I *can't*."

Shorts and a t-shirt. "Donnie went off the *road*."

"I don't know what that means, Alex!"

The boy winced.

"Just . . . look, you are a smart boy. The smartest boy I know. And you know how to read, and write. You can show me." Ian pointed at the board. "I'll ask you, and you can tell me. Plainly. Okay? And if you don't know the words, or how to spell them, just . . ." He floundered, his palm up in front of him, grasping for ideas. "You know, just . . ." He tapped his head. "Read me. Can you do that? And I'll help you."

Three years old again, eyes heavy with remorse. "It's not a toy," he whispered, and was gone.

Ian ground his jaw, opened and clenched his fists, fought the urge to scream. Then he grabbed the planchette and slapped it onto the board, somewhere in the middle, where there were no markings.

"Alex, this is your dad," he said in his best, no-nonsense Dad voice. "Are you here to try to tell me something?"

He waited, eyes glued to the planchette, fighting the ridiculous urge to move it to *Yes* himself. That's not how it was supposed to work.

"Alex, I know you can hear me. Answer me, now. Are you here to try to tell me something?"

Nothing. Of course, nothing. This was idiocy. He waited, counted to thirty, and another question occurred to him.

"Are you just here to hurt me? To make me sad?"

He stared at the board again, cold dread curling in his chest, certain that this time his son would respond.

"Are you just mad that Daddy let this happen to you?"

Nothing. He'd read something on the internet once about the power of true names, so he threw that out.

"Alexander Isaiah Colmes, you need to answer me. I won't even be upset. I just need to *know*."

The wind gusted outside, rattling the window and

throwing the chimes on the front porch into a frenzy of mad jangles. The planchette didn't move.

"*Goddammit!*" He hurled it; it ricocheted to the carpet in a splash of busted drywall.

"*Fuck!*" He lurched to his feet, leveled a kick at the board, missed, snatched it up, whipped it like a frisbee. It struck a giant gouge in the wall and tottered there for a second before slipping loose to the floor. Ian stalked across the floor, grabbed it again, and slammed it into a box over and over, screaming.

"What am I supposed to *do*? What the *fuck am I supposed to do*?"

Chunks of cardboard exploded like confetti. Then he lost his grip on the board and it flew backwards to glance off the ceiling. Popcorn ceiling bits rained down.

His head roared with pain as he panted; something in his elbow had popped and now throbbed dully.

"God damn it," he whined. "Just *tell* me."

No answer. He stalked out of the room and slammed the door behind him.

67

He got to the junior high before Alina, for once. He waited in the parking lot, staring at the front doors through a haze of exhaustion, wishing the ibuprofen he'd taken would do something for his headache, or his sprained elbow, or his dead son.

At ten to eight he went inside and took his seat. He was the first one there, except for Shauna, of course.

"Hi Ian," she said brightly.

He nodded, wished he had brought a book.

"You're here early tonight!"

"Yeah," he said.

"Find a new route?"

He blinked. "What?"

"Did you find a faster route here?"

"I—no. No, I just left the house early."

"Oh, okay." She smiled.

He spread his hands, annoyed. "Is that okay? Should I leave?" *What the fuck do you want from me?*

"Oh, no, no, of course not. The Nguyens usually get here a bit early too, they should be coming in any minute." She continued smiling at him, and he bristled. Finally, she said, "Well, I'd better finish setting up."

The others filtered in in pairs. He and Alina were the only ones that ever arrived separately.

"Sorry," Alina called as she came in to the gym. She was the last one there.

"No, no," Shauna answered. "It's all right, you're right on time."

His wife bustled to her seat; as she took her coat off, she gave him a little smile. On some level, he understood how important that was. But it was buried beneath so many suffocating layers of fatigue and despair that he couldn't grasp it. Her brief display of affection played out like a movie scene behind a thick wall of plastic wrap.

He was still trying to figure out what it meant when Shauna said, "Tonight I'd like to talk about guilt."

Ian peered at her.

"All of us feel it sometimes, and especially in these kinds of circumstances, when we've lost a dear child, it's easy to feel responsible. We wonder if there was something else we could have done, something we could have

ADAM J NICOLAI

said. Harvey, you're nodding. Is there something you'd like to share?"

Harvey shrugged, but started talking. "Lana. She was working late as a waitress. I didn't like how late she was working, you know? A couple times I even thought . . ." He looked at his wife. "I even thought, 'I don't want her out driving at that time of night.' But I didn't say anything. I should've. But I didn't."

"Do you think it would have made a difference if you had?" Shauna asked.

"I don't know. Maybe? If she listened to me, and changed her hours, maybe she wouldn't have been at that red light at two in the morning. And that asshole . . ." In the silence, Ian's eyes slipped effortlessly closed. When Harvey spoke again, they flicked back open. "That asshole could've crashed into a fucking tree."

Shauna worked him over, trying to get him to talk about how much or how little that regret ate at him. When she was done, she turned her attention to the Bensons, but Alina said, "We know something about that, too."

Shauna nodded, and Alina went on.

"It was Alex's first day walking home alone. Neither one of us was there with him. We'd shown him the way before, walked it together as a family before, but it was his first time—you know, walking it by himself. It was really hard for us."

"She means it was really hard for me," Ian said. He was hardly aware he had spoken.

"Ian?" Shauna said. "What do you mean by that?"

Alina was looking at him, but he didn't look back. "I mean that we're really just here for me. I'm the one that

108

can't just put this behind me and move on with my life like I'm supposed to. I'm the one that's always wondering how far he was from the house when he got grabbed, or why we had to make him walk it *that day, that fucking day* of all days, when that crazy . . . *fucker* was driving around. I'm the one. We're here for me."

That buried part of him was surprised at what he'd said; was sending up alarms. He ignored it and jerked his thumb toward Alina. "She was good to go the day after we heard he was dead."

The Bensons recoiled from his words; the Nguyens' faces remained carefully neutral.

Alina whispered something, but Shauna spoke over her. "I doubt that, Ian. I think it would be best if we each speak only for ourselves."

He nodded—*Fine, sure, yeah*—and lifted his hands in surrender, but then he said, "Okay, speaking for myself, *I* wouldn't have let him walk home alone yet. *I* didn't think he was ready. *I* was scared shitless."

From the corner of his eye, he saw Alina's face flicker between something like a smirk and a grimace. "He would've been going to Kindergarten in September, Ian," she hissed. "He had to learn how to walk home by himself, we *talked* about that, we *both* decided—"

"I would've picked him up every day at school for the rest of my life if it would've kept him safe," Ian snarled. "Every. Fucking. Day."

"All right," Shauna said. "Let's all just take a quick break."

"And you think I wouldn't?" Alina lashed back. "You think I . . . what, that I *planned* this? You think I *wanted* this to happen?"

"You knew I wasn't comfortable with it!" Ian snapped. A long, tearing pain started behind his left eye and wormed slowly toward the nape of his neck. His eyelid spasmed uncontrollably. "You did it anyway! You didn't care what I—"

"If you thought it was so God damned important—"

"—thought, because *you* knew better, you always—"

"—why the hell didn't you just take matters into your own hands—"

"Ian, Alina, please—"

"—know better than me, how the fuck can I know anything, I didn't even have a dad—"

"—and *save* him, since you knew what would happen!"

"—so why fucking listen to Ian? Why fucking listen to anything I say? Just a dumb piece of shit—"

"*Please*, both of you, this isn't helping!"

Alina leapt to her feet, her face burning. Her coat slid to the floor and he suddenly realized why she had been sitting with it on her lap at these meetings. She was trying to hide her midsection.

Oh God. His mouth slapped shut. His eyes searched her livid face like he could find the words there and take them back.

Her mouth worked in silence; her whole body seemed to quiver with wounded rage. But finally she snatched up her purse and her coat and stalked out, in silence.

"Alina!" He bounded out of his chair, caught up to her in the hallway and grabbed her arm. "I'm sorry, I'm not—"

"*Get off me!*" she screamed. He stumbled backward, and she banged through the door and into the night.

68

He called her four times in the car on the way home. Each time, when the voicemail picked up, he disconnected and tried again.

At the house he stalked from the living room into the dining room and back again, a tiger pacing its cage. God, why couldn't he shut up? She didn't deserve anything he'd said to her. Why couldn't he just *shut up*?

He tried again to call her. This time, he left a message.

"Alina, I'm so sorry. I didn't mean anything I said. I know I really screwed up. I just . . . I'm . . . I haven't slept well in days, I can't sleep, and I just wasn't thinking. I wasn't thinking at all. Please call me. Please. I love you."

He hit *END*. Her face, at the session, haunted him. She looked like he had stabbed her in the stomach.

At the start of the night, she had *smiled* at him.

"God!" he screamed. "God damn it, God fucking *damn it*!" His voice broke, still raw from his tantrum earlier in the day, and he sat down hard on the couch, staring at the floor.

She couldn't be pregnant. It was nearly impossible, unless she'd been with someone else. He couldn't imagine she would do that. She'd handled Alex's death better than he had, but surely not enough to have an affair? If she were with someone else, why would she still bother with the sessions, or their occasional calls?

With Alex, she had started showing late in the third month. Three months ago they hadn't even been in the same house anymore. She had moved out, gone to live with her father—

Right after their last night together. It had been good,

their first sex in months, but it hadn't been enough. A couple weeks later the same old shit had started up, and she'd gone.

One night? There was no way. They had tried for months to get Alex. And she was on birth control, too—unless she had stopped that after Alex went missing.

His stomach flipped at the thought of a second child. It flipped back at the thought of Alina having the baby without him.

You're ahead of yourself. You don't even know she's pregnant. And it doesn't matter. You have to fix this. You have to figure out how to calm down—

He clenched his fist against the couch. How could he calm down, how could he move on, with Alex screaming every night?

He had to tell her. That was all. Tell her what was going on, that he was hallucinating, that he was going to get help. She might understand. They had been married for ten years, and they had been *good* years. They had. She might forgive him, might wait for him, if she knew—

The home phone rang.

He grabbed at his cell out of habit, and the home phone trilled again. He scrambled to his feet and into the kitchen, caught it on its third ring.

"Hello?"

The line was quiet.

"Alina?"

Her voice was a like a pane of cracked glass. "I'm done, Ian."

"Alina, I'm so sorry. Please, listen—"

"No. I'm done listening. I'm done trying to fix you. You have to fix yourself."

"I know. I know, you're right—"

"*No*, Ian. Are you listening to me at all? I'm *done*."

The room tilted. He stumbled to the closest chair and sat.

"I wish . . ." She paused, pulling together the shards of her broken voice. "*God*. I wish you were still strong. You used to be so strong, the whole time we were together. And this is hard, I know it is, but life moves *on*, Ian. *My* life moves on, and you . . . you won't move. You won't come along. You . . . you're making me go alone."

"No," he whimpered.

Her voice writhed, high-pitched, nearly breaking. "I don't *want* to be alone."

"I don't want you to—"

"But you *do*! You do. Or you would come with."

"Alina . . ."

"Do you have any idea . . . how *embarrassed* I was tonight." It wasn't a question.

"Yes. I'm sorry."

"I felt . . . like an *idiot*." She spat the word like a curse.

His tongue cleaved to the roof of his mouth and stayed there.

"You say . . . you miss me. And you say . . . you love me. But you think I killed our son."

"No!"

"And there's nothing I can do to change that, and I can't live with that. I can't live with a person who would believe that of me."

"Okay. Okay." The room was swimming. His head throbbed. "Okay."

"Goodbye, Ian," she said, but before the words were done he blurted:

"How long have you been pregnant?"

He waited for her to scoff, to hang up on him, to deny it. Then she said, "Three months."

He had expected this answer, but it still made the floor tremble beneath his chair.

"Is it mine?"

An exasperated, disbelieving sigh. "Yes, Ian. It's yours." Then a muttered, "Jesus."

"You should have told me." It wasn't the right thing to say, not with things as precarious as they were, but—

"And what would you have done, Ian?" she said, acidly. "*God*. You probably would've thought I did it to you on purpose, just to force you to deal with it."

"It changes everything, Alina."

"No, it *doesn't*. Don't you get that? That's exactly the problem, it *doesn't*. That's why I didn't tell you. You are not the man I married, Ian. You're not the guy I wanted to have children with anymore. I miss that man, I miss him really bad." Her voice cracked. "God, I *dream* about him, I miss him so bad. But he's gone and he's not coming back."

"How can you say it doesn't change anything? A second child? That . . ."

"Every day, you would look at this kid and think, 'They wouldn't be here if Alex still was.' Tell me you wouldn't."

His heart labored in his chest, but he couldn't answer her.

"You know," she said, "when I first found out, I thought, 'This will be good. This'll give us something to grab hold of, something to look forward to. He'll be . . .'" The words whined upwards in pitch, tumbled off a cliff. She finished hoarsely: "'He'll be so happy.'"

The room spun slowly around him as he listened.

"I took the test at work. I was actually in a good mood all day. Terrified, but happy. I couldn't wait to tell you. And the second I walked in the door, you started in on me about the dishes, or some shit, and I realized . . ."

He remembered it. He had delivered another stupid round of accusations at her, and she had fallen silent for the night.

The next day, she'd left.

"You're grieving, Ian, and you're doing it by hurting everyone around—" Her voice choked off.

"I'm sorry," he said into the silence. "I'm really hurting, Alina."

"Well, *so am I!*" she snapped. "*So am I!* You're not the only one who loved him, Ian! You're not the only one who feels guilty! But I thought this was something we could get through together, and you . . . you won't even *hold me at night* anymore!"

"I will, if you give me another chance, I will—"

"Oh, fuck that," she spat. "That's all I've done, is give you chance after chance. I can't keep getting hurt by you, Ian. Don't you get that? I am already hurting *enough*."

"Okay. Okay. You're right. I know I've been an absolute bastard."

Silence.

"Look, I was wrong tonight, everything I said was wrong. If I had been more awake, I wouldn't have said any of it, but I haven't slept at all this week, I keep having these nightmares—"

"You wouldn't have *said* it?" she seethed. "You would've just sat there pretending everything was okay, the whole time thinking, 'What a shitty mother'?"

"No! Let me finish!"

She snorted. He could see her shaking her head.

"Look, I . . ." He was losing her. He had fucked this up so badly there was no way to save it. "I was really trying, I *was*. I sent you that text this weekend because it was true. I still love you, I *swear to God*, and I want to be the person you need. I want to be strong. I'm just not perfect. I'm trying, but I'm not perfect. But I think I'm getting better. I just haven't been able to sleep and it's . . . it's turning me into a lunatic. I'm going to get help. But . . . I was really looking forward to tonight. I was really hoping we were gonna get through this."

A long pause.

"Goodbye, Ian," she whispered, and hung up.

69

He sat with the phone pressed to his ear, staring at the wall as it clicked and fell silent, trying to understand what had happened. Sick disbelief, heavy as an oil spill, floated on the surface of his empty thoughts. Eventually the phone began blaring a warning—*BLAT BLAT BLAT BLAT BLAT*—and he still stared. But the noise aggravated the pain in his head, already searing. To make it stop, he let the phone slip out of his hands and clatter to the floor.

70

The cold table pressed against his face as he woke. Jagged pains crackled in his neck and back; his elbow groaned as he straightened his arm.

The phone had stopped its noise. The clock on the microwave read *1:03 AM*.

He stumbled to his feet, lurched toward his bedroom like the walking dead. Alina's face hovered in the darkness: hurt, incriminating. It made him feel like vomiting.

After he collapsed in the bed, the thick soup of his thoughts swirled.

He and Alina had fallen in love over the phone. They'd talked every night in college. Since the first night he called her, they had talked every night until the day she left. They'd fallen in love over the phone, and she had left him over the phone.

She was right—he didn't hold her anymore. He used to, especially when she had nightmares. He would pull her close, caress her face, whisper lovingly in her ear until she calmed. He had that power over her, but he stopped using it after Alex died. When she woke him with her night terrors now, he just stared at the ceiling.

He was going to be late for work tomorrow. He hadn't even set his alarm. There was no point in it now. Who was he trying to support?

There was a gun in the closet—a .22. He'd bought it after Alex had gone missing. He'd never told Alina. She would've flipped. It was stupid, anyway. There was no one to shoot.

Talking to Alina on the phone. Her voice so inviting, so feminine, so *smart*. Her laugh. God, he loved that laugh. She thought he was funny. He could make her laugh. He could bring her to orgasm. It was hard to say which was better. They were both divine, both heaven in his ears.

Alex wasn't screaming tonight. Why wasn't he

screaming? Had he come back to break them up? Was that Ian's punishment for losing his son, and now the haunting was done?

He'd be fired tomorrow when he came in late. Did that matter? He could just stay home. Take the .22 and blow his brains out. He would never hear Alex screaming again, then.

His bed swallowed him and he drifted away.

Two hours later, Alex screamed.

Ian sat up, sucked in a giant breath like he was drowning. Blind panic, madness, gibbered at the edges of his consciousness.

"*Noooooooo!*" the boy shrieked. "*Nooooooo!*" He sounded crazed, feral, but Ian could match him, Ian was mad with exhaustion, and white rage boiled out of his stomach, seized his throat, made him shriek back, "*Alex!* Shut the fuck up! Shut up! *Shut up!*"

"*Nooooooo! Help!*"

Ian flailed against his blankets, kicked them away, hissing, spitting. "*Shut up!*" He tripped as he jumped from the bed, smacked his face against the carpet, burst back to his feet on a geyser of fury that rocketed him across the hallway and into Alex's door like a cannon.

"*GODDAMMIT!*" he roared, hurling it open. "*YOU FUCKING—!*"

Leroy Eston crouched in the empty space above the carpet, eyes casting about like a lion on the hunt, his nose twitching, a light dusting of snow on his jean jacket.

Seven feet away Alex was hiding behind a tree, deathly quiet, mouth open, breath pluming.

"Alex!" Eston called. "Come on out, now! We'll bring you home!"

Ian's scream died on his tongue. He froze in the door-way, empty and cold.

"Come on, Alex!" Eston shouted, still tossing his head back and forth, searching. "It's okay! I promise! If you don't like our games, we'll bring you home. Let's go!" He stumbled forward, down the hill toward Alex's tree, and the boy tensed, squeezed his eyes shut, his lips moving silently, waiting—

"*Kelly!*" Eston called over his shoulder. "I lost him, get down to the shore, I think he got—"

But the grass was slick, and he slipped; fell back onto his ass and slid past Alex's tree. His eyes widened as he saw the boy, and he started to shout something else—but Alex leapt on him like a jackal, raging, his hand raking like a claw towards the kidnapper's eye.

"*Alex!*" Ian roared and dove forward to help, scram-bling for Eston's gun. His hand plunged through the kidnapper's arm, and it and Alex and the tree and the gun disappeared, leaving Ian alone in the darkness, scrabbling against the carpet and screaming.

PART II

71

He stumbled out, eventually, like a man staggering out of a collapsed coal mine. He left the door open.

Because he didn't know where else to go, he retreated back to his bed and curled beneath the tangled skein of blankets, shivering and broken. He clenched his eyes shut, but behind his eyelids he saw only Alex praying, Eston sniffing at the air—

So he opened them again, and stared down the hall into the black pit of his son's room.

He had fumbled at the light switch as he left, but the bulb was still dead. He wished he could flood the room with light, *saturate* it—burn it, if he had to, to purge that darkness from his sight. But he couldn't, so he closed his eyes again, and the cycle repeated—Eston then blackness, screaming then silence—until finally his heart slowed and some glimmer of his rational mind began again to whisper.

He couldn't stand to stare at Alex's empty room anymore, but he didn't want to lose the comfort of his blankets. So he sat up, clutched them tight around his shoulders and made his way into the living room: a ragged priest, his stole trailing behind him.

72

The TV pulsed with silent light.

His brain worked over what he had seen, pushing at it from every angle, flinching from it, picking it apart. But he was too tired. There was nothing to be gleaned from it but more pain.

He longed to share it with Alina, to attack it together, to make sense of it. Nothing had been too much for them when they had been together. But this yearning only amplified the problem, made it twist inside his heart like a shiv.

Finally, blessedly, he started nodding off—sometimes for as long as a whole infomercial. He wanted to lie down, to sink into the couch and disappear, but he couldn't. It was almost time to get ready for work.

The very notion made him want to sob. He had lost his son. He had lost his wife. He wanted to *sleep*. It was the only thing left for him. He imagined stretching out, leaving the world behind. It would be worth the loss of his job.

But some remnant of his work ethic drove him to his feet, to the dining room, where he stared at his cell phone and tried to remember how it worked.

"Smartlink Tech Support Specialists, this is Justin."

Ian blinked and looked at the clock. Justin was in early.

He had expected voicemail—had been *counting* on voicemail.

"Justin?"

"Yes. Who's calling?"

"It's Ian."

"Oh, Ian." He sounded glib, almost expectant. "What can I do for you?"

Ian briefly considered giving it up, saying, *Nothing,* and forcing himself into the shower, but his exhaustion was so deep that this was never really more than a fanciful delusion. "I won't be in today."

A long, deep sigh. "Ian, you know you're on probation."

"I know that."

"If you don't come in to work today . . ." He sighed again. "Look, I'm sorry, I know you're going through a lot. But if you don't come in to work today, we have to let you go." Pause. "Company policy."

"Justin, I am so tired. I haven't slept in days. I've been having terrible nightmares that have kept me awake constantly. I'm looking into FMLA, I just don't have the paperwork done yet—"

"Have you talked to HR about that?"

"No. Not yet, no, I—"

"Ian, look. You have gotten more mileage out of our attendance policy than anyone. We've bent every rule in the book. I sent you home yesterday with pay. But you're on written warning. We can't bend the rules any more. If you want to keep your job, you need to come in and do it."

Ian gritted his teeth. "I am physically incapable of doing that today, Justin."

"Well, then . . ." He saw Justin from behind his chair, his smart headset positioned perfectly, lifting his palms to say, *It's out of my hands.* "You're done. It's your decision."

"Don't fire me."

Justin scoffed, finally at his wit's end. "Why not, Ian?"

"Because if you do," Ian snarled, "I'll call your wife and tell her you're fucking Sheila Swanson."

He hung up and went to bed.

73

He slept dreamlessly—or at least, his dreams echoed so deeply below his waking mind that when he got up to pee in the early afternoon, he remembered none of them. He stumbled back to bed in an eager haze, anxious to return to nothingness.

Sleep held him until a sudden honking horn on the street outside pried his eyelids apart, and he found himself staring at the wall of his bedroom in the fading daylight, wondering fiercely who Kelly was.

Eston had called for her last night. While he was hunting Alex.

Ian's brain hunted through memories of daycare, of Rita's friends and relatives, for a Kelly. Nothing. It combed through work, and his and Alina's friends. Through college. Through *news stories*. No Kelly—or at least, none that made sense.

Kelly, I lost him, get down to the shore.

Ian sat up, alert and awake for the first time in days.

Who the fuck was Kelly?

74

"Hi Daddy," Alex said in the dining room. "Were you taking a nap?"

"Yeah, bud." Ian answered aloud without thinking. He wasn't surprised to see Alex out of his room. He had expected it to happen, once he opened the boy's door again.

"But is your headache . . . does your head . . . is your headache all better now?"

Ian stopped at the table. Alex had a blue plastic bowl in front of him, filled with cut hot dog slices. A streak of ketchup marred his cheek like a line of war paint.

Alex claimed it was his favorite, but that didn't mean he'd eat it all. Instead, he'd swing his legs and sing and chatter incessantly while the food cooled and the ketchup congealed. It drove Ian and Alina nuts.

It used to, Ian thought. *Not anymore, because Alina doesn't live here anymore.*

And neither does Alex, he remembered.

"Daddy? Does your head feel better now because of your nap?"

Ian blinked. "Yeah. Yeah, actually it does."

"Mommy told me to be quiet. Did you think I was quiet?" His cheeks had bright spots of red; he must have been playing outside before dinner. He was watching his dad intently, waiting for confirmation that he'd done well.

"Alex, do you remember last night?"

The boy screwed up his eyebrows in an exaggerated grimace of concentration. "Mommy didn't make hot dogs last night. But she only made icky stuff."

"Leroy Eston was in your room last night." The name tasted like bile. "Do you remember—?"

"Daddy, did you think I was quiet." It wasn't a question; just an insistent reminder of the question Ian hadn't answered.

"You have to listen to me, Alex. This is important. Le—" He started to say the man's name again, but it conjured images of Eston's stringy hair and jean jacket that made Ian want to gag. "The bad man, the one that hurt you—he said something about someone named Kelly. Did you see someone named Kelly? Did she hurt you?"

"*Mommy* made the hot dog," Alex corrected him. "Because you were *sleeping*."

"Alex," Ian started, but bit his tongue. He'd been down this road. It never led anywhere.

He said it anyway.

"Honey, I really need you to think about this. Okay? You're here for a reason, and I'm trying as hard as I can. Was there a lady named Kelly, who hurt you?"

The hot dog was gone. Alex was bundled into his winter coat, a hood low over his eyes, sitting in a booster car seat perched absurdly on the dining room chair.

"Daddy, I don't like that black hat."

He felt an instant of sharp frustration, but then Ian's heart quickened. "My ski mask? The one I used when I was shoveling?"

"The eyes are scary on that black hat. Will you leave it inside, please?"

His mind groped for explanations, desperate. "Did Kelly have a ski mask? Is that what you mean?"

The bowl returned; the car seat disappeared. Alex was smiling. "I'm glad you're feeling better, Daddy."

75

He went downstairs and went through every file he had from the time of the investigation, looking for a woman named Kelly or any sign that Eston hadn't acted alone. He Googled *Kelly Eston*, *Leroy Eston Kelly*, *Kelly Shakopee Minnesota*, even *Kelly Eston black hat* and *Kelly* by itself. He scoured Facebook, MySpace, LinkedIn, WhitePages.com.

If he'd found nothing, it would have been easier.

There were dozens of possibilities, hundreds of permutations of the name and location. He pored over all of them for some sign of a person who could kidnap and murder a little boy, but of course that was far too broad a criterion. None of them were related by blood, as far as he could tell, to Eston. None of them appeared to have a public criminal record. He couldn't place any of them in Shakopee on the day Alex was found, not with the tools he was familiar with. Some of them were even men, a possibility he hadn't considered before he sat down.

Every hit eroded his resolution, made him doubt what he had heard the night before.

I'm so desperate to believe his spirit is here, and here for a reason, that now my mind is making things up, he realized. *It's my subconscious, or something. I was already seeing things, but I was trying to get away from it, and now it's given me something to look for. Something to believe I can affect, so I'll stop trying to get away.*

He imagined cornering one of the women, demanding to know where she had been the first week of

April. Maybe he'd see Leroy Eston again while he was there, insisting that she was the one, that she had helped kill Alex, and then Ian could sneak in through her window the next night with his gun—

His stomach lurched. *Oh God.* The thought was sobering as a bucket of water to the face. He closed the search windows, shut down the computer. As the monitor fell dark he saw his own face reflected, with the utility room door standing behind it.

76

Despite sleeping all day, he was yawning as he came up the stairs. He grabbed a banana and a yogurt from the fridge, and ate them both at the table as he fought to stay awake awhile longer.

Okay, so he wouldn't go to anyone's house. That would be crazy. But did that mean he had to forget what he had heard altogether? What if it really meant something? What if Alex had shown it to him for a reason?

Alex didn't show it to you. You are seeing things, and your brain made that up.

Fine, maybe. But even then. *Even then.*

He'd still heard the name. What if it meant something? He fought past his own raging skepticism and stubbornly explored the idea.

There was nothing in the stuff Ian had saved about Eston possibly having an accomplice, but that didn't mean the police hadn't had their own suspicions. Maybe he had seen the name somewhere, during the investigation, and his subconscious was trying to remind him of it. An off-hand comment during a news report, or a scrawled sticky note in a police file. Maybe he could call Detective Olson, the chief detective on Alex's case, and ask him—

What?

Ask him what?

I'm not going to tell him that I saw the ghost of Leroy Eston in my son's old room. And if I don't tell him that then I have nothing to say.

"Fuck," he muttered. He put his elbow on the table and rested his head in his hand. He stayed that way for several minutes as endless scenarios played through his head, all of them ending in madness.

Finally, he sighed and stood up. The clock on the microwave read *11:34*. It was getting late, and Alex hadn't started screaming. Ian regarded this fact with a sharp sigh of relief. He hadn't wanted to go back to seeing his son everywhere he went, but if it meant being able to sleep at night again, he would accept the tradeoff.

That meant, of course, that he had to decide what to do tomorrow.

The sudden memory of that morning's conversation with Justin made his stomach turn. Part of him wanted to crawl into his room and hide. The job market was horrible right now. There was no guarantee he'd find anything else quickly enough to keep the house without Alina's support. He couldn't afford to lose his job, yet surely that was exactly what had happened this morning?

A moment ago he'd been pondering his growing madness; now, he considered the very real possibility that he'd end up on the street. The two ideas had a dreadful synergy.

He had to hold on to his job.

There was no reason to believe that Justin was actually having an affair with Sheila. And he'd hung up too quickly to determine whether his threat alone had had any effect.

But it might have. Justin was many things, but at his heart, Ian was sure he was a wuss.

Ian hadn't meant to threaten him. It had just come out. Now it was there, and he was either going to own it or run from it.

Fuck it, he decided. If Justin was really going to fire him, Ian would find out about it as soon as he got to work. It would hardly be the most embarrassing situation he'd ever encountered at a workplace.

Go in, go to my desk, work like nothing happened. His stomach roiled. He ignored it and went to bed.

77

The alarm went off at six thirty. He snoozed it until seven, then got up, took a shower, and got dressed. He didn't see Alex. He got to work about ten to.

The roiling in his gut from the night before had become full-fledged somersaults. When the elevator passed him and went down to the basement like it always seemed to do, he was grateful for the delay.

The sensation of the floor falling away was amplified; as the doors slid open on his floor, he felt a clammy wave of nausea wash over him. He forced his feet to carry him down the row toward his cube, his eyes glued to the floor.

Don't look at Justin's cube. Just walk past. Don't look. Don't look up.

He looked up.

Justin was in his cubicle, one of the supervisor ones with the clear walls. His eyes met Ian's for just an instant. Then he looked back to his computer screen, the color draining from his face.

Ian averted his eyes as if he'd just caught the other man picking his nose.

"Wow, Colmes," Sheila said. As usual, she wasn't on a call. She was dressed modestly, for a change: a loose skirt that hung to mid-calf, and no cleavage. "Not just on time, but five minutes early." She was smiling, like it was a joke, and for the first time he wondered if maybe she wasn't the bitch he always treated her as. Maybe she was just teasing, trying to be friendly and fit in.

If so, she wasn't very good at taking hints.

"Morning," he answered. He pushed the power button, tapped in his username and password, and watched the screen go dark. He didn't realize he had been holding his breath, waiting to see if his access had been revoked, until his desktop popped up. Four faces from last Halloween, pocked with little icons.

Brown eyes, brown eyes, brown eyes, blue.

He blew out a long, slow breath and logged into his phone.

78

Lunchtime.

"Hello, you've reached Shauna Douglas. I'm not available at the moment, but please leave your information and I'll return your call. If you have your session number, that would help me as well. Thanks."

BEEP.

"Hi, Shauna, this is Ian Colmes from your Wednesday night counseling session at the junior high in Champlin? I'm sorry, I don't have the session number. But I'm sure . . ."

I'm sure you'll remember me, I'm the guy who got into a huge fight with his wife and accused her of murdering her son through negligence.

" . . . ahm, you probably remember me. I just wanted to check with someone, and if you wouldn't be the right person, maybe you could let me know . . . but I am looking into FMLA at work. I have been having these extreme bouts of . . . I don't know, depression I guess, and it can get really bad. It's making me miss work and now I'm in trouble because of my attendance, basically."

He rubbed his temple. He hadn't intended to go into this much detail.

"I just . . . so basically I just need, um, someone to sign this form about my situation so I can get approved and hopefully not lose my job over this. I'm hoping you can help me with that, if not, maybe you can point me in the right direction? I'd appreciate any help you can give me."

He left his cell phone number and hung up, feeling like an awkward jackass.

79

He glanced at Justin's cube as he left for the day, but it was empty. The man hadn't so much as e-mailed him. Ian wasn't sure what that meant, but whatever it was, he was willing to accept it.

A small crowd was milling quietly at the elevator. It was Friday, and no one could wait to get out of this place.

Ian joined them, wondering what he would do with his weekend.

He deeply regretted the things he'd said to Alina; he yearned to ease the pain he'd given her, but didn't know how. If she wanted to end their marriage, he wouldn't stop her, but he didn't want her believing that he'd meant anything he'd said on Wednesday. He hadn't. He had agreed to let Alex walk home. It didn't matter whose idea it was. Obviously, it had been a mistake, but it was as much his as it was hers.

If she wouldn't listen to him on the phone, maybe he could write her a letter. Try to explain. But that prospect was quickly swept into an eddying current of clashing questions.

How much should he tell her? Should he mention Alex, or Eston? Should he gloss over the reasons he couldn't sleep? He could take the dream angle, as he had with Derek. But he *hated* the idea of lying to her. He wanted to share the truth with someone. And he trusted her. God, it would be good to hear her talking about this problem, working with him to figure out the best way to handle it. Maybe she even saw Alex too. Maybe she—

Justin said, "Ian."

Ian whipped around. His boss was standing behind him.

"Do you have a minute?"

"I actually have some running around to do, I can't really—"

"Just a minute," Justin insisted, and gestured to the nearest side room.

Shit. Here it was. Ian clenched his teeth, trying to

keep his hands from trembling. *Just let him talk. Don't open your mouth. Don't say anything stupid.*

"Sure."

It was the same room as Wednesday, where Ian had had to sign his name. Justin closed the door behind them and sat down, staring at the table.

Ian wanted to say, *What is this about?* or *Look, I'm sorry about what I said, I was just so exhausted I wasn't thinking clearly.* But he forced himself to stay quiet, to wait the man out.

"I didn't go to HR," Justin finally said. He was still staring at the table. "And I won't. Okay? But seriously . . . even if I don't, eventually Barb's going to ask me some questions. Eventually she's going to do it, even if I don't."

Barb was Justin's boss, the director of phone operations in the Minnesota office. When Ian opened his mouth, he meant to say, *I understand.*

What he said instead was, "Well, you'd better make sure she doesn't."

Justin flinched as if he'd been whipped. Ian's heart pounded.

"How . . . ?" Justin started, then shook his head. He grabbed his temples with both hands and leaned against his elbows. Ian remembered doing something very similar the night before. "It's only been a few times. I had already told her it couldn't keep happening, before you even said anything. It's . . . history, over and done with."

Ian kept silent. The back of his mind was crowing in disbelief.

"Don't tell my wife. I can't control what Barb does. But please, I'm asking you man-to-man. Don't tell my wife."

"I'm working on FMLA," Ian said. "When that's done,

Barb won't be able to do anything. You keep her off me until then. Or Daney will be finding some very interesting pictures in her e-mail."

Justin nodded, pale as death, his head bobbing like a jack-in-the-box. Ian left him like that, and walked away feeling like he had just won the World Series of Poker.

He cackled most of the way home.

80

Best Buy had a huge display for the new XBox 360 thing that let you play without using a controller. Ian walked past it and browsed the movies instead. Finally, as usual, he bought nothing.

As he was walking back to the car, Derek called.

"Hey," he said. "How are you holding up?"

"I'm all right." He hesitated. "Sleeping better. Sorry for freaking you out on . . ." What night had he called Derek? Tuesday? Monday? Most of the week had been a blur. "Earlier."

"That's okay, I'm just sorry I couldn't tell you to come over."

"Don't worry about it. I can take care of myself."

"Yeah, well, I felt like an asshole. You sure you're doing better?"

"Yeah. It comes and goes, you know? This last week was really ugly. Hopefully the weekend will be better."

"Have you . . . signed up for, like . . . sessions, or anything?"

"Like a psychiatrist?"

"A counselor, or something."

Ian debated. "Yeah, I guess so. I made a call."

ADAM J NICOLAI

He could feel Derek's relief emanating from the phone. "Good," he said. "Good, I really think that'll help."

Ian got to the car, swung inside. "Maybe. I think it's just shit I need to work through."

"What?"

"Just shit I need to work through."

"Well, that's what they do. Help people work through shit."

Ian chuckled. "I suppose they do."

He started the car. The conversation tapered off. It was weird.

"You need a tank tonight?"

"I don't know," Derek said appraisingly. "You want to come along again?"

"Yeah," Ian mused. "Yeah, I think so. If you got room."

"All right. Shoot me a tell around seven."

81

When he came in the front door, Leroy Eston was kneeling over Alex in the darkness of the living room.

Alex had his clothes on. That was the first thing Ian noticed. He wasn't being raped. But Eston was leaning into his face, his stringy hair brushing the boy's cheek, catching on his gag. The killer's voice grated in the silence.

A flare burst from Ian's heart, igniting his limbs with rage. He bounded forward, a roar at his lips, and forced himself to stop.

No. Listen. Listen.

Eston had given him one clue already.

"—understand?"

Alex nodded, his cheek scraping against the floor.

"Even if you get through the door somehow, there's nothing around here for miles and miles and miles. No phone. No police. No help. You can scream and scream and no one will hear you, no one will come. Do you understand *that*?"

Another nod. Alex's face was streaked with grime and tears above his red turtleneck.

"And let's pretend that you get away somehow. You make it back home. Do you know what will happen then?"

A whimper.

"That's the worst thing. The worst thing you can do. You're really fucked, then. I will come to your house, and I will kill your mom and dad. Because I know where you live. You know that, right?"

Alex shook his head, clenched his eyes shut.

"I will come in while they're sleeping, and I'll kill both of them." His voice was weirdly soft, a knife draped in velvet. "They won't even know I'm there. And then I'll come in your room, and play my games with you in your own room. You don't know about my games yet, but you will. And you won't want to play them in your room, Alex."

The boy was sobbing around his gag.

"Leave him the fuck alone." The command hissed between Ian's teeth, steam from a teapot. Eston glanced suddenly towards the wall, as if he'd heard a noise from that direction.

Alex disappeared.

Every muscle in Ian's body coiled like a spring. He clamped his lips shut, waiting as Eston glanced at the other wall, then the near wall again, trying to figure out where Ian's voice had come from. Then he looked down, where Alex had been a moment before, and was gone.

82

Ian gasped, grabbed the knob of the still-open front door to keep his balance. He reached for the light switch and flicked it on. The living room was empty.

"Fuck," he wheezed. "You fucking . . ."

He closed the door and stumbled forward, his hands shaking. He sank to his knees where Alex had been, his eyes scouring the carpet.

Inside his coat pocket, his cell phone buzzed. He fumbled it out, gazed at it like it was an alien artifact.

Shauna Douglas was calling. He stared at her number until the phone stopped making noise, then he looked back at the floor. Alex was still gone.

"Alex!" he shouted, and climbed back to his feet. He went into the dining room, then into Alex's room. "Alex! I need to talk to you! Are you here?" They were both empty.

He looked in his own bedroom, looked in the bathroom. Then he stalked through the kitchen and opened the door to the basement.

"Alex! Come on, can you hear me? I need—"

"Hi, Daddy," Alex said. He was at the bottom of the stairs. He looked nervous, like he'd done something wrong. "I was playing on your computer, but I didn't mean to."

Ian started down the stairs, but backtracked to flip on the light. "That's okay," he said, breathless. "Hey, that's all right. Don't worry." He hurried down the stairs. "Are you okay?"

"Yeah, but I was only playing Super Why." Relief at his dad's reaction radiated from Alex's face. He smiled. "You want to see?"

He was here: whole, unharmed, still innocent. The horrors that had transpired a minute ago with Leroy Eston didn't exist for this boy.

Ian wanted to weep.

"No," he said. "No, not right now. Maybe later, okay? Can you show me later?"

Alex was disappointed, but he nodded. "Sure, Dod."

The word stabbed Ian in the heart, and he grimaced. But he smiled, too.

"I'm 'Dad,'" he said.

"Okay, Dod," Alex answered, his impish grin shining.

"That's 'Dad' to you," Ian insisted.

"Okay, Dod!"

"All right. Alex?"

"Yeah, Dod!"

"I love you," he whispered fiercely.

"I love you too," Alex said back, as if it were the simplest thing in the world.

83

The frozen pizza needed to bake at 450, so he set the oven to pre-heat and started hunting for the pizza cutter. It was always dirty, because he was having frozen pizza for dinner far more often than was probably healthy. He had considered buying a second one, but had rejected the idea at once. If he was too lazy to clean one

ADAM J NICOLAI

goddamn pizza cutter, he'd be too lazy to clean two. Where did it stop? He'd end up with a sink full of filthy pizza cutters. The image made him recoil. It reeked of craziness.

While he dug through the dirty plates and bowls in the sink, he thought about Leroy Eston.

Seeing Alex again was hard, but he was beginning to think he could come to terms with it, maybe even resolve it, somehow. Seeing Alex's killer was something else entirely.

Part of his mind was simply babbling uncontrollably, gibbering with rage and grief. It wanted to destroy Eston, to finish gouging out the man's eyes, at the same time that it wanted to curl up in the corner and wail. But after weeks of direct confrontation with the horrors of his son's final days, he was getting used to those feelings. He could set them aside and let the other part of his mind work.

That part was wondering, *Why am I seeing Eston now?*

The typical responses took their places. Speaking for the prosecution was the hotshot upstart, Alex Is Haunting You. And tasked with the defense was the aging, but ever stalwart, You're Fucking Crazy.

Alex wants to show you more, Alex Is Haunting You argued. *There's something about Eston that he wants you to know. Maybe some kind of clue about Kelly that you haven't seen yet.*

You're Fucking Crazy mounted a strong defense. *You had it figured out downstairs the other night. You're making the hallucinations more elaborate and more horrible as a way to make sure you don't escape them. Your own brain won't let you put this behind you.*

If that's true, a little therapy will take care of it, or you can work the issues out in time. But if Alex is trying to tell you something, don't you need to hear it?

Ian shook his head. He didn't care about the underlying motivations. He wanted to know what the new appearances *meant*.

They mean your illness has advanced, You're Fucking Crazy asserted. *Eston is a powerful symbol for you. If you continue to treat him like he's real you'll eventually do something stupid and possibly dangerous trying to hurt him.*

Alex Is Haunting You scoffed. *It means there's something you missed, something critical. Even if my colleague is correct, even if it's all in your head, that doesn't mean you have nothing to learn from it. It could still be your own mind trying to work through some kind of unprocessed clue. Either way, you need to pay attention.*

But Crazy wasn't having it. *If that were true, therapy could help you figure out those clues just as well. Better, even. And without the risk of dissolving completely into some fantasy realm where your son is still alive and you have the power to kill his attacker. If you—*

Haunting cut him off. *Without risk? You promised Alex that you would always be there for him. Think of what he's done, the barriers he's broken, to reach out to you. If he's somehow found a way to call to his Daddy even after he died, wouldn't the greater risk be to ignore that call?*

Ian remembered Alex saying, *I'll just call for you.* What if he hadn't meant it as a recrimination? What if he was trying to explain why he was appearing?

Jesus, what if he had meant he was calling *now*?

It was Crazy's turn to scoff. *Everything he says can be interpreted that way. Of course it can, it's your own brain creating his dialogue. That's why it's never anything new.*

Your mind is just replaying scenes from when he was alive. It lacks the courage to create something new. And it even punishes you for failing to play along. These are warning signs, Ian.

Spoken like a true fatalist, Haunting rejoined. *But what if it's the other way around: what if Alex is simply restricted to showing you pieces of his life? "More things in heaven and earth." You don't understand the rules here. That doesn't mean you can afford to ignore what's actually happening.*

The oven buzzed, signaling that it was done pre-heating, and Ian gave a start. He still hadn't found the pizza cutter. He'd been staring into the sink for the last ten minutes.

84

"Brutus!" a voice crackled from the computer speaker. "Good to see you again, man! How have you been holding up?" It was EpicGodwin, a mage who raided with Derek often but hadn't been around last week when Ian played.

Ian pushed the left Ctrl button on his keyboard, activating his mic. "Oh, you know. Not easy. Time helps. But it's still not easy."

"Yeah, I can't even imagine. I'm so sorry about what happened. At least they caught the guy."

A lot of people said this. Not just the *I can't imagine* part, but the *at least they caught the guy* part. Like it fucking mattered that the guy had died. *Alex* had died. That was the only part that mattered.

Ian stared at the fantasy characters milling about the bank of Brutus's digital home city, and fought against saying anything abrasive. "Yeah," he finally answered. "I would've preferred to get my son back alive. But yeah."

Silence greeted this response. In the chat window on-screen, someone said simply:

: (

Ian tried again to remember why he had decided to raid tonight. Some kind of act of defiance against Eston? He was reminded of a David Cross bit, something about people forging on with their irrelevant plans in the wake of 9/11, trying to make sure that the "terrorists didn't win." Cross had made them out to be delusional morons.

Which is pretty much what I am.

He started to type out a whisper to Derek—*Sorry, this just isn't going to work for me tonight. Sorry to leave you in a lurch.*—when Epic spoke again.

"Well, I'm glad you're here. We missed you. And doing something just for fun will help, I bet."

How badly could anyone he only associated with in a digital fantasy world really have missed him? He bristled. For a second.

Then he realized he didn't care.

"Yeah," he said into his mic. "Thanks. That's what I'm here for." He hit Escape, cancelling the message to Derek, and settled stubbornly in to tank.

85

A red light pulsed on the side of his cell phone when he emerged from the basement three hours later, and he remembered suddenly that Shauna had called.

"Hi, Ian, this is Shauna Douglas returning your call. I'm sorry to hear you're not sleeping well. I'll sign your form if you like, but my guess is that you would need a doctor's signature. You may want to check with your HR on that. If that is what you need, I can certainly recommend some very good psychiatrists in this area. If you're coming to the meeting Wednesday night, we can talk about it then. Hopefully I'll see you then." A heartbeat, then she added: "You would still be more than welcome."

He made a noise partway between a snort and a chuckle, and closed his phone.

Hopefully I'll see you then.

He hadn't even considered going back to the weekly sessions. He'd been going for Alina, really, and there was no way she'd be there again this week. Not after what he'd said to her, or her response later that night.

He felt a sudden lurch, as if he had just dropped ten feet. He sat down hard on the couch.

Was it really over? Was it . . . was that even possible?

The woman who had laughed at his sarcasm, who would sink into his arms when he embraced her from behind—the woman he could talk to for hours, into the night, even after ten years of marriage.

People said you had to work on a relationship to hold it together, and he and Alina had learned that was true. But their relationship was founded on communication— it had started on the *phone*, for Christ's sake—and they had always been able to work everything out. They'd been able to talk through anything.

He should be able to call her, and talk through this. But he couldn't. He ended up yelling, every time, and she was sick of it. How many times had they gone down that road? How many times had he made her think they would work it out, like they always used to, only to change the rules on her midstream and start blaming her, screaming at her, clamming up on her? Of course she was done with him.

You used to be so strong.

People grew apart, sometimes. That hadn't happened to them. He had forced them apart, because he was so goddamn *weak* that he couldn't move on. He had forced her out, just to find air to breathe—but she still hadn't left him, not really. She had called. They had talked. She tried for months to get him help. Why? Because she still loved him? Because she knew she was pregnant? Maybe both?

It didn't matter now. He had fucked it up.

He didn't want to hurt her. He missed her—ah, God, he missed her. When he could quiet his thoughts enough to picture it, he could imagine the two of them recovering: wounded, yes, and more cautious—who wouldn't be, after what they had been through?—but still able to laugh, eventually. Still able to whisper to each other in the dark at night, still able to be *them*.

It dawned on him that he hadn't just pictured it. He had *expected* it. Taken it for granted. They had survived so much: of course they would survive this. And he'd forgotten that it wouldn't just happen. It took *work*.

He'd been waiting for her to save him.

He grabbed his phone, flipped it open—

I have to tell her this.

—ignored the voice saying it wouldn't matter, that it would sound just like everything else he had said to her—

1, SEND.

—determined to explain, to make her understand that he really did get it, that he really was still here.

"YOU HAVE REACHED. ALINUH. COL-MES. LEAVE YOUR MESSAGE AFTER THE TONE."

BEEP.

He hesitated, unsure whether to leave a message or try back later, and had the revelation that she may never answer a call from him again.

"Alina, it's me. I just . . ." He took a deep breath, trying to steady his voice, and it helped a little. "I just wanted to tell you that you're right. I *have* left you alone. I know. I've been . . . well, an insufferable jackass, for one thing, but . . . I haven't been *working* on it. On us. On me. I need to. I know I do. I've just . . ."

The backs of his eyes were burning. He clenched his teeth, forced his voice level.

"I've been sitting here, all night, thinking about it, and I'm so sorry for how I've treated you. You've been hurting as much as I have, and I've been acting like I'm the only one who . . ."

He waved it off. He didn't want to go down that road.

"I just wanted to tell you that I understand that. And I'm going to start working on it. Right now. I called Shauna, I'll still be going to the Wednesday sessions. I know you probably won't be there. But whether you are or not, I will, and I'm going to be asking her about seeing someone else, too, and doing whatever I need to in order—"

"YOU HAVE. TEN. SECONDS TO COMPLETE YOUR MESSAGE. BEGIN AT THE TONE."

Jesus *Christ*, he hated that thing. He stared at the wall,

off-balance, as the beep sounded. The seconds ticked past.

"I love you," he finally said. "And the man you love is still here, somewhere. Just . . ."

The tears resurged; his whole face pinched trying to hold them back.

"Don't give up on me yet."

86

The phone hung in his hands while he stared at the carpet and drew long, shuddering breaths. Alex asked what was wrong, and Ian shook his head.

"It's okay, Daddy," Alex said. "You can tell me."

Ian looked up at him. The boy's eyes had gone as dark as the ocean, heavy with concern. Ian was supposed to say, *Grandma's gone.*

"I just really miss your mom," he managed. "I wish she were here, is all."

"Where did she go?" Alex asked.

"You remember how I told you that some people take the people they love for granted, and they don't treat them very good? And that actually it should be the other way around—you should treat the people you love better than anyone else?"

"Where did she go?" Alex asked again.

"Well, Daddy didn't do that. I messed up, and I hurt your mom, and now she's left to stay with her dad."

"And she'll never come back?" The question bulged with dread.

"I don't know, kiddo. I hope so, but I just don't know."

The boy's eyes dropped to the floor, disbelieving, and Ian finished the conversation correctly.

"Give me a hug," he said. Alex came up to him at once.

On the day Alina's mom died, that embrace had flooded Ian with solace. Alex had given him one of those long, close hugs that had started to grow more and more rare. His smallness and his heat and his coiled energy and the sheer, pleasant weight of his *dependence* had soaked into Ian like a balm, and the two of them had gotten up together and gone to share their strength with Alina.

He knew that wouldn't happen now, and he closed his eyes, not wanting to see his son disappear again. He waited several seconds, remembering that hug from the year before, imagining that he could one day grant that same solace again to his wife.

Then he opened his eyes to the empty living room, and turned on the TV to escape its crushing silence.

87

Alina woke him with kisses.

One on the temple, three slow, gentle ones trailing across his forehead, another on the far temple, another on his ear. As his eyes opened she lifted her head to smile at him, her hair haloed in the sunlight streaming through the window, her dark eyes heavy and sensual.

"I love you," she said.

His every nerve blazed with need. He clutched at her hair, pulled her down, kissed her deeply. "I love you too," he breathed between tastes of her. "I love you too, oh, God, Alina."

She responded to him slowly, working her leg against his, lapping at his tongue and his lips and his neck. She was *there*, finally, she was *with him*. He wanted to bury himself in her hair, drown in her scent.

He grabbed a handful of her hair and yanked her onto her back. She gasped, but she loved it. He knew that, because he knew *her*, and he took one of her nipples into his mouth and nibbled at it, and she arched her back and gasped again, and Alex screamed.

Her fingers scraped across Ian's back. He took her other breast in his hand, massaged it while he kept working with his tongue, and she moaned his name like a plea.

Alex screamed again. He needed help. He was *calling*, just as his father had made him promise to do.

Ian pulled back. "He needs me," he begged. "Can't you hear him?"

Alina looked away, her face stony and betrayed.

"How can we ignore him? Can't you *hear* him?"

"Get the fuck away from me," she hissed.

88

He opened his eyes to a spray of cold morning light across the wall. From the living room, he heard Alex sobbing.

The sound drove him to the edge of the bed, where he sat up and endured it for just a second; buried his head in his hands and tried to figure out what was real. Then he heard Eston's voice, and his eyes opened like a pair of knives sliding from their sheaths.

"Fucking disgusting," the rapist said.

Ian threw his bathrobe on and stalked into the living room, hatred smoldering in his chest. Alex was on the floor there, curled in a ball, facing away from his attacker. Eston stood over him.

"I put a pot in this room, didn't I? And you fucking go and piss yourself?" He was pacing, shaking his head in disbelief. "You can't even hold your own piss? What the fuck is wrong with you?" He spun abruptly, leveled a sharp kick into the boy's back, and Alex screeched.

"I oughtta rub your face in it!" Eston shouted. "Like a fucking pig! Is that what you are? A fucking pig?"

He reached down, grabbed for Alex's hair, and Ian roared, "Hey, you fucker!"

Alex disappeared at once; again, Eston's head snapped up, this time toward the ceiling, casting about like he'd just heard a sound from upstairs.

Why can he look for me? What happens if he finds me? But the thoughts were swept out of Ian's mind on a river of rage.

"You're done with him! You understand me? You're *done* with him!" Eston whipped his head the other way, staring toward the front window. Ian darted toward him, screamed at the back of his head: "Hey dumbass! I'm *right fucking here*!"

The kidnapper fairly leapt in terror; he fell over, scrambled backwards toward the couch.

"He killed you! Don't you know that? You were killed by a fucking five-year-old! *Killed*!"

Eston was staring through Ian's chest, panic dancing in his eyes. It redoubled Ian's rage, made it burst from his throat like the explosion from a volcano. He clapped his hands and waved. "Jesus, you're stupid! I'm *right*! *Fucking*! *Here!*"

Eston's gaze snapped upward. For a single, eternal instant, he met Ian's eyes.

Then he was gone.

89

Ian grabbed the lamp and hurled it at the couch, where the kidnapper's head had been a second ago. The shade flew off; the bulb shattered. The cord popped out of the wall, snapping through the air like a leaping viper.

The lamp's body bounced to the carpet, somehow intact, so he grabbed it again and launched it into the wall, where it exploded. Ian flinched away, felt a hail of broken glass rain against the back of his neck, and snapped up the end table.

"You hear me now, you fucker?" he shrieked, and smashed it against the floor. It was metal, with a round base, but the top was glass and it flew out and crashed against the wall. "Come back here!" He straightened up and spun around, looking for Eston. "Come back here! You'll fuck little boys but you're scared to fuck with me? *Come back here!*"

He stood in the middle of the living room, robe gaping open, the table hanging from one hand like a club. His eyes darted savagely, finding nothing.

"*COWARD!*"

The scream tore his throat raw. The end table dropped dully to the carpet, and his fingertips twitched. God, he wanted to kill that man. His thoughts danced with violence.

But he's already dead. Listen to your own words.

He is already dead.

"Fuck," Ian whimpered.

He stumbled through the bits of shattered glass to sink heavily into a chair.

No. No, he was here, I saw him. He was tormenting Alex. Kicking him. But when he heard me, Alex escaped.

If he could spare Alex from reliving his torture at the hands of that man, he would intervene every time —no matter the time of day, no matter the consequence.

Maybe it would be cathartic, even if it wasn't real. Give him some sense that he was helping his son, when obviously he'd done nothing for the boy when he truly needed help.

Ian flinched from that idea. It stung. How pathetic, to try and make himself feel better that way. Everything he was seeing was already finished—he wasn't affecting it at all.

Unless Eston is here, torturing Alex again, right under my own roof.

His breath caught. He hadn't thought of that before. He'd assumed that Eston's appearance was just Alex trying to show Ian more of his final few weeks, but what if Alex wasn't controlling these new visions? What if Eston himself was somehow . . . ?

Ian shook his head and lurched back to his feet. He paced into the dining room while he thought, trying to avoid the ruin of his living room floor.

The cellar pantry. Alex's rape. Ian hadn't seen Eston, then; just Alex. It was the same the night he'd tried to convince his son to go into "the light." The boy had looked frightened, like he was running from someone, but Ian hadn't seen anyone.

It was different now.

Ian halted. His jaw clenched.

Good.

GOOD.

He *hoped* that fucker was actually here, somehow. Ian had been able to scare him. Eston didn't like being yelled at; he didn't like being seen. Anything Ian could do to bring him misery was good. The man deserved to burn in hell.

But his wild bravado leaked away as soon as it came on. If Eston was really in the house—like Alex was—

Alex is not *in the house, goddammit, you are* imagining *that!*

—Ian wouldn't be able to torment him forever. It was wonderful to have some power, to actually scare the bastard, but how long would it go on? Weeks? Months?

If I can get his attention again, maybe I can make him tell me who Kelly is.

Yes.

That felt right. *That* felt like a purpose.

Ian swung around, itching to see Eston again. But besides the shattered glass, the living room was empty.

90

He took a shower to clear his head. Before getting in, he had to dig a piece of glass out of his bare foot. He hadn't even noticed it until he started calming down.

The main floor shower was cave-like: there were no windows in the bathroom, and with the shower curtain drawn the light had to sneak in over the rod. He usually liked it that way. In the roar of the water and the enveloping murk, he felt like he was in a secret pocket of space outside the world, existing solely for him. Alina got annoyed by how much time he'd spend in there, but sometimes he felt like he had to gather his strength there just to face another day of work.

Today he couldn't get ahold of that rejuvenation. His thoughts were whirling too quickly to be paced by the torrent, and the dimness seemed to mask some secret treachery. He finished quickly and tore the curtain back, bracing himself to find Eston crouched like a predator in the steam, but the bathroom was empty.

After getting dressed, he grabbed a used plastic grocery bag from the kitchen and went to clean up. The sight of the living room drew him up short.

When he'd left it, the mess had resembled a battle-field: there had been a fight here, and of course, some collateral damage.

Now it looked more like the naked aftermath of a man who had lost control of himself.

He swallowed the insight and flipped on the TV, for some background noise while he worked. *Law & Order* wasn't on anywhere, amazingly, so he had to settle for some nature show. It was about fish, the weird ones that live way down deep.

As he finished collecting the biggest chunks of debris and got up to grab the vacuum, Silvia Kalen's face filled the screen. The reward was still $100,000.

Ian watched the whole thing. For once, it didn't make him angry, but he was still glad when it ended. He hated how happy she looked in that commercial. It was too keen a reminder of what he'd lost.

91

That night he tried again to dig up information on Kelly, but he focused instead on Leroy Eston, hunting for any reference to the woman in Eston's online presence.

Surprisingly, there weren't many Leroy Estons on Facebook. It felt like a long shot, thinking he could just comb through the man's friend list and come across a Kelly, but Ian went through each of the four hits anyway. Nothing.

He ran through many of the same searches he'd run on Kelly, and found little bits of the man's past. Eston had lived in Shakopee for a year or so before he died, but before that, he'd been all over the country. He had never been arrested before, or at least, he didn't show up as a registered sex offender. During Eston's year in Shakopee he'd held several different jobs as far as Ian could tell, either in town or close by—mostly at gas stations and little car repair shops. But there was no sign of a sister, or girlfriend, or wife.

After two hours Ian gave up. Behind him, Eston said, "That's what I like to see."

Fear slithered out of Ian's heart like a host of maggots. He was rooted to his chair, unable to move while that old, gibbering terror clawed at him.

Alex answered with a whimper. "Uh huh." It broke Ian's paralysis, and he slowly swiveled his chair around, nausea bubbling in his throat.

His son sat on the couch, his red turtleneck standing

out in the drab basement decor like a pool of blood. His hands and feet were loose. He wasn't gagged.

Eston had his arm around him.

"Pee in the pot. Like we talked about. You don't get that dirty piss on the ground, or in those . . . pretty pants. Put it in the pot, and Uncle Leroy will take care of it." He set his free hand on the boy's knee.

Ian gagged, a quick dry heave that left him trembling.

Alex looked away, and Eston frowned. "Hey, no," he said. "Don't look at her. Look at me."

The boy grimaced and clenched his eyes shut. He shook his head. Eston caressed his cheek.

"Get out of here, Alex," Ian breathed. "He can't hurt you anymore."

As Alex disappeared, Eston's eyebrows knitted in confusion. He started panning the room, eyes roving up and down the wall.

"Kelly," Ian said. "Who is she? Is she still alive? Were you working with her?"

Eston stopped his scan of the wall, cocked his head as Ian spoke.

"Answer me," Ian demanded. "What is she doing there? Where is she now?" *I'm going to find her and cut her fucking throat out.* "Do you care about her?" he pressed. "If she hurt my son, I'm going to kill her."

Eston's upper lip twitched; it made the whole side of his face spasm. Then he rose slowly to his feet, and resumed his careful inspection of the room.

For an instant Ian remembered the Ouija board, and wondered if he could force answers from the man that way.

Then Eston's meandering search finally met his eyes.

A wondering grin played at the corner of the killer's mouth.

"Well, well," he said.

From upstairs, Alex cried, "*Daddy!*"

92

The shout made Ian jump. Eston disappeared. For a second, Ian again found himself unable to move, every nerve struck senseless by too much impossible stimuli too quickly.

Then Alex called for him again, and his rubbery legs bore him up the stairs two at a time.

"Alex?" he shouted as he reached the kitchen. His hands were trembling. Eston's grin leered at him. "Alex!"

The boy was in his room, sitting up in bed, eyes wide.

"Alex," Ian breathed, relieved to have found him. "What is it? What's wrong?" He crossed the room and sat down on the bed next to his son. He started to reach an arm out, to hold him, but stopped himself before they touched.

"I want Mr. Tuskers," Alex whined.

Alex's stuffed elephant was his guardian against nightmares, monsters, and "bad animals." Ian or Alina would set it at the foot of his bed every night, where it would stand vigil until sunrise. He and Mowsalot, the kitty, were Alex's two favorite stuffed animals: one for standing guard, and one for snuggling.

Ian bit his lip. "God, I'm sorry, kiddo. Mr. Tuskers isn't here."

"Can we go find him?"

No, it's your bedtime. You wait here and I'll go get him.

"No, bud. I'm sorry." He longed to give Alex what he wanted. The request wasn't surprising, after the number of times Ian had seen Alex with his attacker in the last few days. It was a request for reassurance, a simple yearning to be safe again.

But the elephant had to be buried somewhere in the garage, if they even still had it at the house at all. More likely it was thrown out, with most of the other things they'd taken out of Alex's room.

"Daddy, *please*," Alex urged. "You have to find him."

"I can't, honey. I wish I could."

"What about Mau-zlot? Is he gone *too*?"

"Yeah," Ian said heavily. When Alex had lost the two animals while he was alive, bedtime could be held up for half an hour while his parents tore the house apart searching. "Yeah, Mowsalot is gone too."

Alex was stricken. He looked back at his pillow like it was a hornets' nest. In the darkness, Ian again envisioned Eston's grin.

"It'll be okay," Ian said. "I promise." It's what he'd said when his son was alive, too. He'd promised a hundred times that everything would be okay. Now, the words scraped from his throat. He'd never been so wrong about anything in his life.

"But what will I *do*?" Alex moaned. "What will I do without Mr. *Tuskers*?"

Ian forgot himself. He reached for his son to pull him into a hug, and found himself in an empty room, sitting on a stack of boxes.

93

The night passed in fits of dozing on the couch, as the TV droned. His dreams were of his son running and screaming toward a lake, of Eston grinning as one eye ran with blood, of Alina marrying Justin.

Sunday he went to Cub to pick up a few basics for the house. When he left the house, he found the air giddy with snow. The radio said it would continue through the night, and into the coming week.

Alex again asked him to stop wearing his black hat. He asked what would happen if he didn't. Alex said, "The eyes are scary on that black hat." Ian chewed this over as if just hearing it for the first time, but couldn't make any more sense of it than he had before.

Cub took about twenty minutes. It was good to be around people, even strangers; the respite from his constant sightings gave him room to breathe. As he walked across the parking lot back to the car, he realized he was in no hurry to get home. He wished, not for the first time, that he knew somewhere trendy to go.

A coffee shop, he mused. *Or a . . . I don't know, some place downtown. I have no idea.*

He frowned. That was the whole problem.

Even when he was at the U he'd never really been cool, though he'd had plenty of friends who were. He'd gone with them a couple times, to First Ave or the Lagoon, but a lot of the places they'd visited were closed now. The ones that were still open he couldn't even picture himself in anymore. He'd just look like a buffoon.

He and Alina used to commiserate about how uncool they both were. But they'd done it cuddled together on the couch, under a blanket, watching TV and secretly feeling like they were the lucky ones.

"Screw it," he muttered. He went to the library.

The woman behind the counter gave him a little smile as he came in. They knew him here, mainly from when Alex was still alive. Ian used to bring him in on Saturday mornings, to give Alina a little extra time to sleep in. Once, when he was almost three, Alex had somehow located a copy of *The Pimp's Bible* and run wild through the place, brandishing it like a prophet with a sacred text. Ian had been mortified and apologized profusely, but remembering it still made him smile, and the staff here still talked about it.

He wandered over to the little Fantasy/Sci-Fi section, relishing the ambience: hushed footfalls, murmured conversations, muted taps on a keyboard. It matched his mood. All the people he required, none of the noise.

"Daddy! Can I get this one?"

Ian jerked his head toward the voice, his heart hammering, and saw a little girl in a pink jumpsuit and pigtails. She had a SpongeBob picture book clutched in one hand. She wasn't talking to him.

When the library closed at five, the sky was already growing dim. The clock in his car read *6:04 PM*. He realized grimly that Daylight Savings Time had ended yesterday, and he hadn't set his clocks back. It was the first time in years he had missed that.

Fuck.

It was another one of those little signs, like staring into the sink for ten minutes, like the dirty pizza cutter. Signs that he couldn't hold it together.

I'll talk to Shauna on Wednesday, he told himself. *I'm gonna get help. I already decided. Let it go.*

But he couldn't.

94

He started toward home, but a heavy knot of dread settled into his gut at the thought of walking into his living room. He didn't want to see Eston there again, not after the way the man had grinned last night. *Well, well.* Those two simple words had bled Ian's courage dry.

So he flicked on the signal, not sure where he was going but sure he didn't want to go home. As he eased into the turn lane he imagined Eston at home, raping Alex while his father was away.

He jerked back out of the turn lane. The car that had started rolling forward to take his spot slammed on its horn, and Ian tossed it the bird.

What the hell had he been thinking, not going home? Alex had been in the car earlier, but what if he was there now, back in the cellar pantry, while Eston molested him unchecked? What if Alex was calling for his dad again, right now, while Ian was busy dicking around having a pathetic day on the town?

He eased into the gas, pushing it up to sixty-five even though the last sign had said forty.

God *damn* it.

The light ahead was red, but Ian kept his foot on the gas, watching the cross traffic blink past. There were no cars ahead of him, and the cross light was already yellow. His anger at himself wouldn't let him ease up.

His light turned green, like he knew it would, but that

didn't stop the giant Suburban hurtling into the intersection from the left.

Ian tore his foot from the gas and onto the brake, but his shoe, slick with slush, slipped off the pedal and slammed back into the gas. It was only for a split second. But it was enough.

The Suburban's horn shrieked. Ian jerked the wheel to the right, aiming for the curb, but the street spun too fast. A building flew by his vision, then the cross street, then the road he'd just come down. He jammed his foot onto the brake as everything went past.

Thud. The world tilted, then tilted back.

He didn't realize he was screaming until he stopped.

95

The Suburban rocketed out of sight to the left, still on the street, unfazed and untouched.

Ian's car was straddling the curb. It was still running. He hadn't hit anything. These insights dripped into his brain slowly, like percolating coffee.

I'm alive. I'm okay.

He peeled his trembling fingers off the steering wheel as his heart galloped up and down his throat.

The airbag didn't deploy, he realized. *It couldn't have been that bad, if the airbag didn't deploy.*

"J-Jesus," he muttered. He was shocked to hear himself stammer.

The door opened easily, and he took a walk around the car, as much to calm himself down as to look for damage.

"Hey!" a man called, climbing out of a blue Prius. He

was parked about twenty feet back, just this side of the intersection. Next to him, traffic crawled and gawked. "You okay?"

"Yeah," Ian called back. His voice was steady this time. "Yeah, just—you know, just shaken up."

Prius Guy slammed his door and walked up. He was short and heavy, white, wearing a pair of geeky glasses. "That was crazy! What a maniac! If you need a witness, I saw it. Freaking crazy!"

"Yeah," Ian answered. One of his tires looked sort of scuffed to him. Had it been like that before? Everything else looked all right.

Prius Guy caught him eying his car. "The car okay? God, I thought you were gonna flip for a second when you hit that curb. Isn't it nuts? It's barely even snowing!"

"Yeah," Ian said again. His whole brain was ready to beat the tar out of something, or run screaming. It had no capacity for any language more elegant than he'd managed thus far.

The other man approached the car, staying opposite Ian, and appraised it. "Doesn't look too bad." He sounded disappointed. "You got off lucky." As if it had only just occurred to him, he said, "Should I call the cops?"

Ian shook his head, still inspecting his tire. "I didn't get the plate." He looked up. "Did you?"

"Nah, I saw the driver though. She was texting, I'm pretty sure. Can you believe that shit? What the hell is wrong with people?"

Ian waved this off. "It's all right. At least I'm alive." His hands were still shaking. He couldn't calm down. Why couldn't he calm down?

"You okay to drive?" Prius Guy asked.

"Yeah," Ian said, though he wasn't honestly sure. His legs felt like water.

He remembered Eston kicking his son.

"Yeah," he repeated, with more conviction.

"You sure? You want me to follow you home or anything, just in case?"

Ian looked at the guy like he was losing his mind. "No. Thanks. I'll be fine."

"All right. You just look pretty shook up."

No shit, he wanted to say. He'd only been in a handful of accidents in his life, and none of them had even involved another driver. He felt like he should be angry —*Texting? Seriously?*—but he just couldn't muster the energy.

"I'm fine," he said, and got in the car.

He was facing oncoming traffic, so he had to wait for the light to change before he could pull out. When the chance came, Prius Guy pulled into the street, blocking traffic for him. Ian saw him beckon self-importantly from inside the cabin.

Ignoring Ian's earlier claim that he'd be fine, Prius Guy followed him for maybe half a mile. Then he waved again and turned off.

Ian's hands were still quivering when he got home ten minutes later. It was almost dark already. The wind chimes danced on the front porch, jangling madly.

The living room was empty when he came in.

He held his breath, listening. His own heart hammered in his ears. He didn't hear anything else.

96

That night he dreamed he was spinning. Spinning and screaming.

Getting out of bed was a relief, even if he was still exhausted. The clock said *6:17 AM* when he flipped off his alarm. It hadn't had a chance to ring.

In the shower he closed his eyes and pulled in the heat: faced it so it would lash him directly, bowed to it so it would trickle over his lips and down his limp arms, breathed it in and out like a monk seeking *om*. It helped, for a time. Then, he started feeling that *spin* when he closed his eyes, and he got out.

Long, quiet mornings to get ready had been the norm for him once, before Alex was born, but he rarely got them now. He could appreciate them, normally, but as he prepared his coffee and flipped on the TV to check the weather he was constantly listening for Eston, or Alex. There was no peace; only anticipation or dread.

Yesterday's delirious swirl of snow had matured into a steady, ponderous blanketing. The front walk was doused in it, the yard transformed to infinite white. The street had been plowed, thank God, but beyond that lay pure, deep winter, come like a thief in the night.

The heavy flakes drifted around him as he scraped off his car. The air was still. It was cold, but not yet bitter; the kind of whispering snowfall whose perfect, fragile beauty called like a siren.

Most Minnesotan kids loved snow, and Ian had been no exception. Then he'd grown up, and started driving, and winter's mystery and grandeur had sloughed slowly away—replaced with despite for the long commutes it brought and annoyance at having to clear off the car in the mornings. That old sense of wonder had crusted over a little more with every year, starved out by the practicalities of his adult life.

Then Alex was born, and winter had become beautiful again.

He stopped in mid-scrape, his eyes stinging. He could've looked down, to try and get himself together, but instead he looked up: into the broad, grey-and-white expanse of falling snow. Nothing else existed when you looked into a snowfall like that. It eclipsed the sky.

He remembered sitting in the front seat as a little boy and looking out the car window at night. The snowflakes were like stars, hurtling past a starfighter as it blasted through space. Infinite and unknowable. Sometimes, when Alex had been in the backseat staring out the window, Ian had wondered if he'd thought the same thing. A couple times, he had almost asked. But it was too private. He had contented himself knowing that his son was free to look, and wonder, because Dad was taking care of the driving.

The snow caressed him, and he closed his eyes. Drew in a deep breath. When he'd gotten control of himself, he finished his scraping and climbed into the car.

Alex was in the backseat, dressed in black slacks and a grey button-down shirt. He had Mr. Tuskers in his lap, and was staring quietly at the back of the driver seat.

God, it was hard seeing him. Every time Ian had a moment like he just had in the snow, a moment when he said goodbye, the boy returned. *Because I have no right to forget him. Because I have no right to move on.*

"Found him, huh?" Ian said, trying to ignore the guilt.

Mr. Tuskers was too important to risk on casual car trips: he'd only been allowed in the car when Alex was staying at Grandma and Grandpa's for the night. And on the day of Alina's mom's funeral.

Alex didn't answer; Ian didn't expect him to. That had been one of the few days when the boy had been quiet for an entire car trip: staring at the backs of the seats, trying to understand death.

"Well, good," Ian said. He flipped the rearview mirror up so he wouldn't have to see his son, and pulled carefully into the street.

97

Sheila was with Justin in his cube when Ian got to work, huddled and whispering. She had some kind of tight purple leggings on—they weren't *pants*, exactly—with the word *Princess* scrawled across the ass in sequins, and a garish, tight-fitting yellow top. The two of them turned to glare at him as he stepped out of the elevator.

If he didn't have both of them over a barrel, Ian would've been pissed. Livid, even. But he did, so instead he looked them in the eyes, waved, and smiled. "Morning!" he called.

Jorge was reading a book at his desk as Ian walked by. *Good. I could use a slow morning.* He fired up his computer, got logged in, and checked his office email while he waited for a call. One message caught his eye at once.

From: Kari Alefson
Subject: Candidacy for Senior Pos.

Mr. Colmes—
Thank you for your interest in the Senior
Technical Specialist position. Unfortu-
nately, we have determined you are ineli-
gible for this position due to your
current corrective action.

It went on to quote the relevant sections from the
employee handbook, but Ian didn't read all of it. He knew
what it boiled down to: Justin had written him up last
week, so he couldn't post out of his position.

Fuck. His left hand tightened into a fist. He was
madder than he would've expected.

*I should go back to Justin. Tell him to get that write-up out
of my file, or else.* The temptation was powerful. It was
intoxicating to feel like he had some power here, some
recourse.

But he didn't. Not really. He believed Justin when he
said that Barb already knew. He'd only met the woman a
handful of times, but her reputation preceded her: she
was a nosy, micro-managing bitch. Since she'd taken over
the call center, he'd lost one of his breaks and become
accountable for every second of his workday. He couldn't
take a piss that lasted longer than three minutes now
without having someone come track him down.

Even if Justin did as he asked and removed the write-
up, Barb would ask questions. That was a great way for
Ian to lose his job.

Besides, when push came to shove, Ian wouldn't have
the heart to deliver on his threats, and he knew it.

He growled a sigh and leaned back. *Goddammit.* He'd

been looking forward to the new job. Some part of him had already decided it was a done deal.

Stupid.

98

At lunch he grabbed a sandwich from the cafeteria and took it down to his car to eat. He wasn't in the mood to talk to anyone.

The snow was still coming, and the cold had a definite bite to it now. He turned the engine and cranked up the heat. As he did this, he gave a jaw-crunching yawn. Maybe a nap wouldn't be bad, either.

He drove to the far end of the parking lot—he hated napping in the car where people would see him—and nestled into his favorite corner, back against a growing pile of plowed snow. On public radio, some Republican was ranting about people being able to get health care. He would've preferred music, but it seemed like every other station just had commercials.

The sandwich was one of those pre-made things, probably a relic from yesterday's batch, but it wasn't too bad. He finished it off, set his cell phone alarm for thirty minutes, and leaned the seat back. The gentle rumble of the engine, the roar of the vents, and the drone of the day's news soothed him, and he let himself drift.

Untethered, his mind wandered to the job he'd been kicked out of the running for. Should he tell Alina? He'd told her he applied, so it seemed like he should. But if they were really over, why would he tell her anything? The job wasn't going to make a difference to her coming back one way or another.

He wondered if she'd heard his message now, or if she'd just deleted it. If she had heard it, had she believed him? He wasn't sure she would. And really, did it even matter? He had to go ahead with what he'd said he'd do, whether she believed him or not, because he didn't want to go through the rest of his life treating her this way, thinking of her this way. His betrayal of her in the aftermath of their son's death was staggering. He wanted to remedy it, as best he could, and that was all.

His thoughts blurred as he plunged deeper toward unconsciousness. He'd known he was tired, but some part of him marveled at how quickly sleep was taking him. A respite from his headache would be wonderful. Sometimes these little naps really helped with things like that. Alina couldn't take them. She always said they left her groggier than she'd started. If she had a headache, it invariably got worse; if she didn't, she got one. His head was hurting worse too, he realized. His naps could misfire too, sometimes. He hoped that didn't happen today.

Unbidden and without transition, an image of Eston leapt to his sleeping mind: sitting on the couch in the basement, staring at him. *Well, well.* Eyes keen and hard.

Ian wanted his bravado, he wanted his hate, but all he felt was a mewling, miserable terror. He pounded up the stairs, threw the door open, and was back in the basement. Eston was raping Alex on the couch.

Stay down here, Eston grunted to Ian over his shoulder. *Stay.*

Ian's guts twisted with nausea. *Get off him,* he tried to say, but the words wouldn't come. He didn't have enough breath to form them. His head was pounding.

He took a step toward the kidnapper and staggered to his knees.

Eston chuckled.

From upstairs, Alex called. His voice was a ray of sunlight trying to penetrate the ocean, muted by the water, quivering and broken.

Eston was sitting on the couch now, just looking at Ian and waiting. Ian wanted to challenge him, but he'd gotten too tired.

In the dream, he closed his eyes. It was black, still, and silent. He wasn't falling. He was nowhere. He tried to wonder what was happening, but was too tired.

Alex shrieked at him and the sound was barely audible, like it was echoing on the other side of several steel walls. It was a bare whisper, accompanied by the acrid tang of exhaust.

Ian ignored it, and it went away. He was growing cold. He was lonely. No one would miss him.

Then he heard Alex crying. It was the pure, simple wail of a child who needs help, and he responded to it without thought.

A bare slit of light accosted his eyes. It was all he could manage. They wouldn't open all the way. He saw fog in the cabin.

Alex was in the snow outside his window, still crying. He had fallen down. He was only two. The snow scared him. He didn't understand.

Why was there fog in the cabin?

Panic seized him, and he yanked at the door handle. It snapped back closed. The door was locked.

His head throbbed and grated; his eyes started to sink

closed again. He yelled incoherently, trying to make noise just to keep himself awake and moving.

He fumbled at the lock, trying to pop it open, but it kept slipping out of his grip. It was a tiny nub, nearly flush with the door frame, and his fingers were fat and clumsy.

He forced himself to slow down, to swallow his panic. Darkness nibbled at the edges of his vision. He settled the nub of the lock between his quivering thumb and forefinger as if he were trying to pick up a tick. Then he squeezed and pulled.

The lock popped up. He threw the door open and tumbled into the snow, gasping.

He climbed to his feet and leaned against the car. The world swirled gently around him. He closed his eyes for an instant, trying to ease the dizziness, and immediately opened them again to fight off a wave of drowsiness.

A fissure of pain split his head from front to back. He wanted to reach inside and turn the car off, but he'd need to hold his breath to do that, and it was all he could do to keep dragging at the air. It burned in his throat, cold and caustic. There wasn't enough in the world.

Suddenly he remembered Alex. He threw a look backwards, into the snow bank, but the boy was gone. Ian was alone.

What the fuck. The thought clattered down the chasm of pain in his head like bouncing scree. *How . . . ?*

He had slept in his car with the engine running a hundred times. This had never happened. It was supposed to be safe anyway, there were catalytic converters and all kinds of safety technology, he was out in the open air instead of an enclosed space, how did—?

Maybe he had parked too close to the snow bank. He inched his way toward the back of the car, his head spinning. There were at least a couple feet clear behind his back bumper.

But his tailpipe was bulging with snow.

He stared, shaking his head slowly, still panting. Someone had stuffed his tailpipe? Why would anyone—?

Justin, he thought at once. *Or Sheila.* They wouldn't really be pissed enough to *kill* him, though. Would they?

He craned his head around the side of the car, but the snow was unblemished. No one had come that way. He looked behind him, and saw nothing there either. The only tracks were his own.

99

The headache got worse as the day went on. He couldn't catch his breath. More than once he put himself into *ACW* to delay the next call, wondering whether he should leave for urgent care or an emergency room visit. Each time he decided against it. He didn't want to give Justin the satisfaction of seeing him leave, or risk another event that Barb might notice.

By four thirty he could barely think clearly. He went to his normal urgent care clinic in Maple Grove, but they wouldn't see him; they sent him over to the ER, where the staff drew some blood, put him in a mask, and had him lie down. The air was cold and startlingly pure. He stared at the ceiling and breathed.

"That helping?" the doctor asked as he came in. He was an older man, maybe early sixties, with thinning hair and a craggy smile.

Ian nodded. It was actually helping quite a bit.

"Good." The other man took Ian's chart from the nurse and sat down. "You're lucky, you know," he said, flipping through it. "Napping in the car like that, with the engine on? Risky stuff."

I've never had a problem before, Ian wanted to say. It felt like being at the dentist.

As if picking up on his frustration, the doctor came over. "I'm going to take this off so we can talk a bit. I may want to put you back in it for a bit, later." He reached around, loosened the straps, and pulled the mask from Ian's face. The normal air felt dingy in comparison.

"Thanks."

"I'm Doctor Synech." He pronounced it *cynic.* They shook hands.

"Thanks," Ian said again.

Synech nodded. He told him his labs looked good overall, CO a little high but not dangerous. He walked through Ian's symptoms—Was his headache improved? Could he catch his breath better?—and made some notes.

"I'd like you to stay overnight for observation," he said. "Your symptoms sound better, but I like to be careful in situations like this."

Ian imagined Alex in the basement, without his father to banish Eston.

"You know, I think I'm doing all right." Ian gestured at the mask. "This helped a lot."

"Are you sure? Sometimes people think they're doing better than they are. CO poisoning can be tricky business."

"No." *I can't afford it anyway,* Ian thought to add, but

skipped it. While it was true, it would lead down another avenue of argument he'd rather avoid. "I'm really doing better."

"All right." Synech gazed at him. "How old is that car you were napping in?"

"It's a '91," Ian admitted. The Check Engine light had been on for the last year or so, but he didn't mention that.

"Well, you need to get it checked. Even a '91 shouldn't be leaking that much CO."

"Yeah, I told the nurse—I backed up too far, hit the snowbank. The tailpipe got clogged with snow."

"Yeah," Synech said. "Listen, Ian. If you need someone to talk to, I know a guy—very approachable, very easy going, no pressure. I'm gonna give you his card here."

Ian scoffed. "I didn't do this on purpose, doctor."

"Well, I believe you. But I'm giving you the card anyway." He took Ian's hand, pressed the card into it. "Call if you need to, and if that headache comes back or you start getting lightheaded or short on breath, come back in."

"All right." Ian shook his hand.

100

The snow had dwindled to a whisper by the time he got home. He trudged up the front walk, buried under the day's snowfall. As he fished in his coat pocket for the house keys, he wondered with dread what awaited him inside.

He eased the door open a crack and fished inside for the light switch, flipping it on before stepping through. His brush with his own mortality had left him shaken. He didn't feel equal to encountering Eston in the dark of his living room tonight.

The couch was empty, the room silent. He stepped inside and stomped his boots on the entry rug, shaking off the snow, waiting for the call from Alex or the whispered greeting by Eston. Neither came, but that only left him expectant and unnerved.

"Alex?" he said. When there was no response, he picked up his boots and crossed into the kitchen. He glanced down the hallway to Alex's room as he passed by, but the room was dark and empty.

At the door to the backyard, he paused to put his boots back on. When he finished, he said again, "Alex? I need to talk to you."

His eyes darted around the room, but found only a sink full of stinking dishes, an old yogurt container on the counter, a small collection of empty, unrinsed milk cartons. The room grew more disgusting every day. To get away from it, he turned and went outside.

The snow shovels were in the little, one-car garage behind the house—along with the lawnmower, a mess of broken-down cardboard boxes, a stack of Alina's defunct painting projects, and a host of other miscellaneous crap. They'd filled the little garage so quickly after moving in that instead of fighting over who got to clean and park in it, they both opted to just park on the front street. Besides, the door opener was busted, and the only way to get in was through the little side door.

The lock gave him some trouble—it always stuck a bit in the winter—but he jiggered his way past it. As he swung the door open he caught his breath without thinking about it, bracing to find something horrible on the other side.

The sullen light from the streetlamps hung heavy in the windows, framing a single, long silhouette that comprised all the junk in the garage. He scanned it for just an instant. If Alex or Eston was here, he'd be able to see them in the dark. But they weren't.

He let out his breath—it plumed from his mouth in a long, curling cloud—and flipped on the light. It took five minutes of hunting to find the snow shovel.

He should've done the back walk, too—the one leading from the house to the garage—but wasn't in the mood. He'd be keeping the shovel in the house for the rest of the winter, anyway, and he wasn't likely to make a lot of trips to the garage for any other reason. So he just did the front.

Other than the drone of a distant snow blower and the *scrape-whuff* of his own work, the street was silent. The snow was plentiful, but not too wet. It took him about twenty minutes to get through it. He spent the time wondering how much a new catalytic converter would cost him, and whether it was time to buy a new car.

He cleared up to the front step and paused to stretch his back. He hated shoveling those two stairs. One of them had a crack, and he could never tell where it was under the snow. His shovel would always catch on it. It was maddening.

He rolled his neck, determined not to spend all night trying to deal with that stair crack, and caught a glimpse of Leroy Eston through the front curtains, pacing.

For a long moment Ian stood still on the step, waiting. When several minutes passed and he saw nothing more, he carefully and deliberately finished shoveling the porch. Then he went inside, his heart pounding.

Eston was sitting on the couch. He said, "Where the fuck have you been?"

Ian's mouth worked, but he had nothing to say. The sight of the man was like the scream of fingernails on a chalkboard. *Is he talking to me? Does he see me, or is he just—*

"Whatever," Eston answered. "Answer your fucking phone next time." He glowered at some response that Ian neither heard nor delivered. "I'll talk to you however I fucking please. Now get in here, and close the door."

Ian realized he still had the door open. He closed it, staring carefully at the kidnapper, who had stood up and was chewing his lip.

"I think you're right," Eston finally said. "I think we need to move to your place."

A heartbeat. Eston fixed his gaze on a point somewhere around Ian's jaw. "Yeah. Careful. Thank God you're here. I could never pull this shit off on my own." He snarled. "Why the fuck do you think I said anything in the first place? This isn't working, it's—there's too many people. That boy is so goddamn mouthy, if he starts screaming at the wrong time—"

His eyes widened, affronted. "You must think I'm an idiot. No, I haven't told him that. Why the fuck would I tell him that?" Eston cocked his head, just slightly. "No. No, no, no. If anyone's going to let anything slip, it's you. You've been nothing but a constant fuckup since day one. You're lucky I share him with you at all."

He snapped his head toward Ian, lip curling. "Listen, bitch, you are in this as deep as I am. Don't fucking start with me. Just start getting the shit together." He yanked a palm up, his eyes blazing. "*Don't*. It's a twenty-minute drive. I think even you can manage that. Just get the shit together. Now." He stalked into the kitchen.

101

Ian followed, but Eston was gone. So he stood staring into his empty kitchen while his thoughts smoldered.

Kelly had been Eston's accomplice. If that hadn't been obvious before, it was glaringly so now. He had to have been talking to her. *Had* to.

She had hurt Alex. Eston had *shared* him with her. She had worked with Eston to keep the boy under control. She had volunteered her place to keep him—

Was that where they had been going, when Alex had somehow gotten out by O'Dowd? *Kelly, I lost him, get down to the shore.*

And they hadn't caught her. The police didn't even *know* about her.

Ian's fist clenched. She was still *out there*.

"You son of a bitch," he muttered to his empty kitchen. "You fucked up tonight."

And suddenly, he knew. He was absolutely certain. *This* was why Alex had come back.

Because Kelly was still out there, someplace, and Alex couldn't rest until she was dead.

102

He thundered down the stairs, even leapt the last three. Stabbed at his computer's power button like he was murdering a bug.

When the desktop finally came up, he didn't go to the internet. He brought up an empty text document, and started typing.

- **Kelly. Girlfriend? of Eston.** He backed up, added: **(Coworker? Partner? Maybe he beat her)**

In the basement Saturday night, when Alex had looked away from Eston, Eston had said, *Don't look at her, look at me.*

Her. He typed: **Definitely a female, even though Kelly can be a guy's name.**

Then he entered down and wrote:

- **Black hat? Ski mask? Something to do with shoveling?** Pause. **Lives in Minnesota, maybe. Still needs to shovel snow.**

Enter.

- **They were moving. Going from Eston's place to hers. She must own a place. Or rent a place. Or HAD a place - this would've been in March or April. Maybe not any more.**

Enter.

- **Call the PD, see if they had any leads on her.** Pause. He added: **Or had even heard of her.** Then he highlighted the entire entry and deleted it.

- **She was out running an errand, or**

something. Eston was pissed she took so long to get home. Maybe she picked up the supplies for them? Maybe people saw her, at the grocery store or something?

Enter. His fingers shook.

- HE SAID HE SHARED HIM WITH HER.

ENTER. He knuckled it that time, as if he were pounding on a door.

What else. What else.

- They were at the lake. Eston sent her down to the shore. A terrible thought occurred to him. **She might have fallen in. She might be dead. Check obits or news for a body showing up in Shakopee?** But if they'd found a body in O'Dowd—a second one, after already finding Alex—he would've heard about it.

Enter.

As if he had just lunged headlong off a cliff, he realized he had nothing else on Kelly. His freefall lasted twenty seconds. Then he wrote:

- Donnie went off the road. Followed by: (?????????)

Enter.

- I don't like that black hat. Could be Kelly. Could be something else.

Enter. He rapped feverishly on the table four times.

- Delilah. New girl at daycare. Reference to Kelly? A "new girl." In retrospect it seemed obvious. If Alex could only repeat what he'd said in life, then he'd latch on to any kind of reference he could manage to a second person, or a female that Ian hadn't heard of before.

He froze. *Jesus.* He arrowed back up to **Donnie went off the road**, added: Another car went off the road.

That was always how the game went. It started with Donnie, then another one. Someone had to come help them both. *There were two cars.*

Of course there were. The van for Eston and Alex. And something else for Kelly.

Alex had been trying to tell him since *the first night*.

Enter. *What else?*

"Daddy?"

Ian's heart nearly punched out of his chest. He snapped his head toward his son, standing on the bottom step, and stifled a scream.

"Jesus, Alex," he managed. "You scared the shit out of me."

The boy's eyes were heavy with sorrow. He was in his favorite footy pajamas, festooned with cars and race-tracks. "I can't find Mr. Tuskers."

Ian took a shuddering breath. "He's not in your room?" He turned one eye back to the monitor, typed:

- **Mr Tuskers?** and
- **What's that noise????**

"I can't find him," Alex repeated. "May you look for him please?"

"Alex," Ian said. He felt a flush of annoyance, but swallowed it. "I'm trying to find Kelly. I'm trying to write down everything you've said, okay? And use it to find her. Because she got away, right? I think I finally figured out why you're here. Because of her, right? She hurt you, but she never got caught, and Daddy's gonna catch her." His vision blurred. His heart thundered. "Because I won't let anyone who hurt you live."

"Okay, but Daddy I can't find Mr. Tuskers."

Ian shook his head. "What?" He had expected *some*thing from Alex, some sign of relief, or happiness—

"I can't find Mr. Tuskers. *Please*, Daddy. Can you find him, please?"

The annoyance resurged, sharper than before. *God damn it.* "Alex, I'm doing this for *you*. This is what you wanted me to do. Remember?" He glanced back to the monitor, typed:

- **Raped in the basement.**

"But Mr. Tuskers—"

"Alex, I can't find him! Okay? He's gone! We got rid of him when you ..."

God damn *it*.

"When we lost you. I'm sorry, pal, but I just don't have him. Okay?"

Alex's face broke with tears. Devastated, he turned and ran back upstairs.

103

Ian stayed at it for another two hours, eventually branching back online, looking for some leads on his new avenues of inquiry. He still found nothing.

His newfound reservoir of energy ran dry.

He just didn't have enough to work with. Even with the clues Alex had given him—even with everything Eston had let slip—there were too many holes.

What was Kelly's last name? Was her house in Shakopee, like Eston's, or somewhere else? What kind of car was she driving?

He briefly considered driving to Shakopee, to the neighborhood around Eston's house, to see if anyone remembered seeing her. But he didn't even know what she looked like.

A night of work, and nothing to show for it. Alex could find a way back from the dead, but his dad couldn't find the boy's other kidnapper.

Ian slammed his fist into the table. It rattled through his bones like a thunderclap. He did it again, then again, then struck himself in the forehead. His ears rang. "*God damn it!*" he shrieked. "*You fucking idiot!*" The accusation echoed in the basement twice and faded away.

His headache sprang back as if summoned. His wrist hurt; the soreness in his elbow from his tantrum with the Ouija board suddenly started throbbing again. He drew one deep breath, trying to calm down, then another, then he was weeping. His fist flailed weakly at the table.

"What the fuck am I doing?" he whimpered. For just an instant, like the clouds parting for a ray of sun, he realized how mad his little text document—now up to three pages—would look to his wife. He resolved, again, to seek help. Then he wondered: if he told Shauna what he was seeing, would she even let him leave the building? Could she have him committed the same night?

His hands still trembled, but his tears dried. He saved his document, shut off his computer, and went to bed.

104

The next morning he stood in the dimness of his shower and realized he just needed to wait.

Eventually, Eston would give Kelly's last name, or a clue to where she lived. Or Alex would say something else, something more useful, now that he knew Ian was on the right track. *Some*thing. He had come too far now. Something would break. He just had to wait it out.

He bowed his head and let the water run over him, cascading from his hair like a waterfall. He'd slept terribly. That was nothing new, no, but still—it was wearing him down. Alex might not be screaming all night any more, but Ian still woke up several times every night. He couldn't remember the last time he'd gotten a full night's sleep.

The water ran until it grew lukewarm. Ian blinked and opened his eyes. He had washed his hair, but couldn't remember if he'd scrubbed all over. He got his pits and his crotch again, just to be safe. The water grew cooler. He turned the knob as far into the hot as it would go.

Had he washed his feet? God, this was pathetic. Screw it. It was almost time to leave for work. If his feet stunk he'd just be sure to take his shoes off by Sheila's desk.

He gave a weak chuckle and shut off the water. As he stepped out, something *pushed* him.

The floor slipped away, and the corner of the sink lunged suddenly for his temple. He threw out an arm, bounced off the vanity, and felt a singing pain in his neck. The toilet dug hard into his gut before he thudded into the floor, wet and heaving.

In the sudden, indifferent silence that followed, he stared at the ceiling and wondered if his neck was broken.

"Ah," he groaned. He lacked even the strength to curse. "Ah."

He turned his head toward the wall. His neck let him

move it, but God, it hurt. His shoulder groaned too, and the side of his stomach felt like it had been kicked.

Wincing, but fairly sure his neck was in one piece, he tried to sit up. His hand slipped on the glistening bathroom floor as he leaned on it, but he grabbed the rim of the sink and managed to keep his balance. As he sat up, the room spun lazily.

The shower curtain rod had gone askew when he fell; the curtain twisted from it like a cripple's wasted limb. He stared, panting, daring himself to pull it aside and see what was there. *Eston. Don't be an idiot, you know it's Eston.*

He pushed himself shakily to his feet, then sat down hard on the toilet. His neck had the world's worst kink, like it had jagged rocks jammed between the vertebrae. His mind was racing. He didn't know what to think.

Finally, he pivoted his shoulders toward the shower— it hurt less than trying to turn his head—and yanked the curtain aside. The shower was empty.

What the fuck. He pushed an arm in, waved it around as if he could catch Eston crouching in the murk. *Jesus.*

You fell. You slipped in the shower. Jesus Christ, it's not like you're the only one who's ever done it. You're just lucky you didn't knock yourself out.

He tried to place his head in his hands, then recoiled from the sudden wrenching pain in his neck.

"Ah, fuck!" He grimaced and faced straight ahead, whimpering and cursing.

He hadn't fell. Something had *pushed* him.

Eston tried to kill me.

He waited for the reflexive scoff, the litany of reasons why this couldn't be the case.

Instead, he remembered Eston telling Alex, *I will come to your house, and I will kill your mom and dad.*

The phone rang. The bathroom's silence shattered like glass.

105

Ian whipped his head toward the sound, then pulled it back with an agonized groan. He made his way out of the bathroom slowly, feeling along his surroundings like a blind man.

"Hello?" He braced himself for Eston's voice.

"Ian?" A woman's voice. Kelly?

Ian's hand shook, though with fear or fury he couldn't tell. Maybe both. He clenched the phone like a knife, growled: "*Who is this.*"

"It's your mother." Like ice. Affronted ice.

"Oh." He relaxed his hand, slightly. He suddenly felt very stupid.

"Yeah. Who did you think it was?"

"I don't . . . . I don't know."

"Is everything okay? You sound—"

"Yeah, everything's fine. I was just getting out of the shower." Inspiration struck. "I've been getting crank calls every morning."

"Oh, those are the *worst.*"

He gave a shaky sigh. Crisis averted. "Yeah."

"Well I'm sorry to call so early, I just wanted to catch you before you left for work."

Ian stole a sidelong glance at the bathroom. The light was still on, steam curling into the hallway. "Okay?"

"It's been a long time since you've been over. I thought maybe you could come over for dinner tonight."

He tensed immediately—he always did at the thought of going to see his mom—but the thought of getting out of the house was intensely appealing. "That sounds nice," he said. The words surprised him. "What time?"

"Oh, just after you get off work." She sounded pleasantly surprised herself. "I can make tater tot hot dish. Your old favorite."

Ian grunted acknowledgement. "Okay. I'll be there."

"All right!" He could hear her smiling, and tried to ignore the vague sense that he was wandering into one of her traps. *Maybe it'll be different this time. Maybe she's just worried about me.* "I'll let you finish getting ready for work then."

106

There was nothing sinister about the bathroom once he got off the phone. His earlier certainty that he had simply fell reasserted itself, and he got dressed as quickly as he could.

The commute was like trundling through a minefield, as little explosions of neck pain detonated all around him. He winced when he checked his side mirror, hissed every time he had to brake too suddenly. When he reached the office building, the handicapped spots right by the front door beckoned. He weighed the idea of using them, imagined his car getting towed, and drove past.

The tender space just above his right hip ached as he climbed out of the car, and he wondered how badly bruised it was. He had some ibuprofen in the glove box, but his neck hurt too much to lean over to it, so he walked around to the passenger side door, opened it, and knelt. As he reached for the compartment latch, Eston hissed, "God damn it."

Ian's heart lurched; he reeled backwards as if he'd touched a live wire. Eston was in the driver's seat, his eyes flicking back and forth from the front window to the rear view mirror. "Right now?" he demanded.

From the back seat, Alex whimpered, "I really gotta."

"We'll be at Kelly's place in fifteen minutes," Eston seethed. "Why do you have to piss right now? What the fuck is wrong with you?"

"I'm gonna pee on the *floor*!"

"No!" Eston barked. Something resembling panic flickered in his eyes. "Don't! Fuck!" He glanced over his shoulder, yanked the wheel to the right. "Come on," he snapped. "There's a lake here."

"Morning, Ian!" someone called from across the parking lot, and Ian jerked again, sending a shock of pain through his neck. Eston was gone.

107

He stalked across the parking lot, neck stiff and eyes riveted to the distant door. When he finally got to his desk, he leaned his whole body over to look in his personal pharmacy drawer. He was just throwing four tablets in his mouth when he heard Billi's voice say, "Morning, Ian. This is Kelly."

Ian turned around, the pills scraping jaggedly down his throat. A thin, mousy woman smiled timidly and extended a hand. Ian stared at it.

"She's starting in the new training class today," Billi explained. "She'll be on our team when she gets out."

"'Kelly?'" Ian repeated back. Her smile widened as she nodded. Ian shook her hand once, and dropped it like a used wad of toilet paper.

A flicker—*Dismay? Concern?*—crossed Billi's face, but she didn't say anything. "And this is Sheila Swanson," she went on, ushering the small woman onward.

Ian stared at Kelly's back until Sheila turned around, beaming with fake welcome, and he was forced to turn away.

108

Between calls, he investigated.

He looked her up in their email system, but she hadn't been added to the group yet. He checked the team roster on the intranet site, but that was worse—it didn't even show Jorge yet, and he'd joined the team nearly a year ago. Finally, he found a little faux-news story on the corporate intranet site, announcing the new trainees.

```
Kelly Dennon


Kelly comes to us from Star Pointe Credit
Union, where she helped to maintain the
Maple Grove branch's computer network and
troubleshoot issues as they arose. Kelly
has extensive experience in Windows
networking. She will be joining Justin
```

Keplin's team in the First Contact
Support area.

The piece included a little picture of her, wearing the same timid smile he had just seen.

Star Pointe. The name sounded familiar, so he Googled and found that it had gone out of business during the big banking crisis, while the likes of AIG and Citigroup were raking in federal bailout money. He must've heard the story on MPR or something.

If that had really been her last job, she'd been unemployed since early 2009. She'd been out of a job when Alex went missing.

That doesn't mean anything. But he dug further anyway, trying to find out where she lived, and found a Dennon, Kelly; Employer: Star Pointe CU; Location: Zimmerman, MN.

Zimmerman was north of the Twin Cities, over an hour's drive from Shakopee. Eston had said, *It's a twenty-minute drive.*

He stared at this data, his head twitching slightly in denial, ice racing in his veins.

It's not her. You have no reason to believe it's her.

But what if it is her, and this is what he's been trying to tell me, and I just ignore *it—*

It's not her. All you have to go on is the name. It's not enough. There are a million Kellys out there.

But this is the one that came right to my desk, this is the one that I've been presented with—maybe he was warning me about her, I can't just ignore—

Then what are you gonna do? some incredulous part of his mind demanded. *Kill her?*

His earpiece beep-beeped. He moved his mouse to the X, and hovered.

"Hello?" someone on the line said. Ian closed the window with Kelly Dennon's home address and asked the caller how he could help him.

109

He thought about Kelly Dennon through lunch. He thought about her the rest of the day. As he drove to his mom's after work, he pondered ways to make her confess.

There was one *Law & Order* spinoff where the detective always made the perps admit to their crimes. It happened every show, without fail, and all the guy had to do was tilt his head in an unsettling manner. Ian doubted that would work for him.

On *Dexter* the main character often made his victims confess before he killed them. But that required stripping them naked and tying them down with plastic wrap; essentially, scaring the living shit out of them.

Ian pondered this. There were other ways to frighten people.

He thought of sending anonymous emails (*"I know what you did"*) and immediately rejected the notion as asinine; he considered cornering her in an alley or something and beating her until she admitted what she'd done, but in addition to the moral conundrum of possibly assaulting an innocent woman, there was the simple reality that dark alleys were hard to find in the suburbs.

This problem made him chuckle once—a sound more closely resembling a grating bark than a laugh.

He could follow her home. Make sure she really lived in Zimmerman. Or look up the address and see when the property was purchased.

He glanced in the rearview mirror, about to make a lane change, and saw Alex in his seat. He was still in his funeral clothes, staring at the back of Ian's seat with heavy eyes as he clutched Mr. Tuskers. Something about the sight made Ian feel intensely guilty, which in turn, as always, made him mad.

"I met a woman today named Kelly," he said. "She came right up to my desk. Is that who you were trying to warn me about? Did she hurt you?"

Alex was wearing his heavy winter coat now. The stuffed elephant disappeared. "Daddy, please!" he shouted. "May we listen to something *else*?" It was phrased politely, but it was more of a demand. There was some music Ian used to play that his son had absolutely hated.

Ian drew a breath, tried to focus on his son's meaning rather than his words. "You don't like this music?"

"No." Alex curled his lips in disgust. "No, it's all wrong. I want to listen to Sesame Street Musical."

Ian's heart suddenly started twanging like a taut guitar string; his hands shuddered. *It's all wrong.* He was grasping at straws, desperate, and all day he'd actually been thinking about how to corner Kelly Dennon and—

"All right," he said, as much to stop his self-recrimination as to answer Alex. "All right. Forget it."

In the backseat, Alex nodded. He stared out the window in silence while Ian imagined headlines.

*HOPKINS FATHER OF KIDNAPPED BOY IMPRIS-
ONED FOR ASSAULT*

MURDERED BOY'S FATHER COMMITTED TO STATE MENTAL HEALTH FACILITY

IAN COLMES, 34, FOUND DEAD IN HOME

He had imagined this last one as a suicide scenario, but as soon as he pictured it, he realized it could easily have happened this morning in the shower. Or:

IAN COLMES, 34, KILLED IN COLLISION

Or:

IAN COLMES, 34, FOUND DEAD OF CO POISONING IN SMARTLINK PARKING LOT

He'd had a lot of close calls lately. They disturbed him —they would've disturbed anyone—but it was more than that.

He chewed on it as he made the last turn toward his mom's house, rolled up the quiet street, and crunched into the snow of her unplowed driveway. As he knocked on her door, he finally figured it out.

On Sunday morning, Leroy Eston had looked at him and said, *Well, well.*

That day and every day since, Ian had nearly been killed.

110

It was amazing how quickly the old superstitions tried to come back.

He sat at his mother's table, while the gentle but condemning eyes of Jesus Christ gazed out at him from a portrait on the far wall, and mercilessly smothered the urge to tell her he was under spiritual attack.

She would believe him, at once. That's exactly why the idea was so enticing. She had never doubted the existence of demons and angels, never for an instant believed that anything they said at the local Assembly of God might only be metaphor.

But he wouldn't be willing to accept her solutions. And his refusals would only pile tinder on the fire of her convictions, sparking a new battle in the War For Ian's Eternal Soul that he simply didn't have the energy to wage.

The last round of combat had ended in an uneasy truce; she had sworn to pray for him every day, and to be there for him if he needed her, but she conceded that Jesus would need time to "work on his heart." Exhausted from a grueling year of fending off her constant church invitations and fervent letters, Ian had gladly agreed to this logic. If the truce were still valid, he sure as hell didn't want to be the one to break it.

She said grace. Ian closed his eyes and clasped his hands, feeling like a hypocrite.

"It's been years since I made this," she said afterward, nodding at the pan brimming triumphantly with tater tots.

"It's been years since I had it."

She scooped out a serving for him. "How is the counseling going with you and Alina?"

He bit his lip, then carefully chewed through a bite of food to give himself time to think about how to answer. "Not great," he finally admitted. "We had a fight last week. I don't even know if she'll be at the session tomorrow night."

She looked genuinely concerned. "Oh, honey, I'm so sorry."

"Me too. The stupid thing is that it was all me, being

stupid. She's been wonderful with me. Very patient. I need to meet her halfway." He was surprised to hear himself telling her so much.

"I thought you said before she was rushing you?"

She had good reason. She's pregnant, he almost said. But he didn't want to tell his mom that much. It would result in too many questions Ian wouldn't have the answers to. "I think she had good reasons. And it doesn't matter. I don't like the way I've been treating her, so it's going to stop."

She had a quizzical look on her face, but she let it go. Behind her, Jesus gazed on.

"Well, I've been praying for both of you. I know this has been really hard."

They ate in silence. Ian wanted to say thank you, because he knew praying was her way of expressing support, but he didn't want to encourage her, either. So he said nothing.

"I miss him, too, you know. Every day," she said finally.

Ian was surprised by this. He hadn't let Alex near the woman, except on holidays and family events. The prospect of the boy coming home, spewing some nonsense about how he or his family would be going to hell if they didn't start speaking in tongues, repulsed him. And he'd known that trying to bring up his reservations with her was a lost cause.

"I'm sorry you didn't get to see him more often," he said. That was safe, wasn't it? Even if it wasn't completely true.

She gave him a sad smile. "He had your father's eyes, you know. That's where he got that blue."

Ian returned it. "I know." She'd told him this theory before.

The whole time growing up, Ian hadn't cared that his father had left them. It was irrelevant. The man hadn't been integral to their lives, obviously. Ian had never met him. He hadn't harbored a secret grudge, or a fuming inner heart of rage, or an unfulfilled longing to meet him, or any of the other clichés. He simply hadn't cared.

One night when he'd crept in to check on Alex, he'd promised the sleeping boy he would see him in the morning. Suddenly, he'd realized what his own father had truly done. It was like driving headlong off a cliff. *How could you do that?* he had wondered. He'd gazed at his son, small and vulnerable in the dark, and his heart frothed with outrage. *What kind of asshole would you need to be?*

"They still ask about you at church."

He realized he'd been staring at the Jesus picture, and focused again on his mother.

"You remember Jim Bentley? You used to play with him all the time. He still asks about you."

Ian had been friends with Jim Bentley when they were six years old.

"Mom . . ."

"I know, I know." She raised her hands in mock surrender. "It's just so hard to see you like this, Ian. It's like you're adrift at sea. You need a rudder."

Regurgitated bullshit. He drew a deep breath. Let it out. Not a sigh; a calm step away from a precipice.

"I've been praying for you every day since—"

He'd needed that one moment of space, that instant to center and calm down. Her invasion of it kicked him off balance. He snapped. "Mom, I really don't want to do this. It's not why I came over here."

"Anyone can see you're in pain, Ian. I just want—"

"Of course I'm in pain, mom! My son is dead and my wife left me! Is Jesus gonna bring Alex back to life? Because if not, I'm really not interested!"

"He can help you with Alina. And He can help you with the pain."

Ian put a trembling hand to his forehead. He felt like an idiot. What had he expected? If he wanted good company and quiet reflection, he should've called Derek.

"Mom, I don't want to do this," he repeated, fighting to stay calm. "Please. I don't want to fight about this. I'm thirty-four, for—" He'd been about to say, *For Christ's sake.* "I've made up my mind. All right? And we can't spend the rest of our lives with you hounding me all the time. You need to figure out how to respect the fact that I'm an atheist."

The word stabbed into the air like a knife. Growing up, it might as well have been *satanist*, or *serial killer*. He had never admitted it so baldly to her.

"I don't harass you constantly about being a Christian," he went on, trying to rush past the sudden pain in her eyes. "I can respect your beliefs, even if I don't share them, and I understand that it was hard for you after my dad left, and the church was there for you. See? I don't believe it, any more, but I can respect it. I just . . . can you do the same? Can we talk, without . . ."

Without all this bullshit?

"Oh, Ian," she mourned. "How did you get so lost?"

He felt a tight knot of rage clench in the back of his throat. He clamped his lips closed around it.

Lost? *How the fuck did you get so* stupid? *You're a smart woman, why do you just devour every ounce of bullshit they send your way?*

How did I get lost? *How about when Alex was kidnapped less than three blocks away, and raped, and shot in the face? How about when Alex had to kill the kidnapper himself, since no one was there to fucking help him?*

He wouldn't say that, he *wouldn't*, because it would turn him into the classic Wounded Sinner, and she would see hope for him. She would think she just needed to explain that we can't understand, that God always has reasons, that it doesn't mean God doesn't love us.

He wanted to break things; his hands twitched with the need to do it. He wanted to rail and scream.

He refused. He was done with that. He was *done*.

Instead, he said, "Well, let me put it in terms you can understand.

"God told Abraham to kill his own son. He threatened him, to make him do it. Abraham took his boy to the top of the mountain and he would've done it. He would've *killed his own son*, but God finally said, 'Just kidding,' and let him off the hook."

She was shaking her head. "That's not how—"

He kept his voice level, but he raised it to be heard over her. "I will not serve that God, I will not pray to that God, and I will not acknowledge that God. I would rather burn in hell."

Silence. Finally.

"Thank you for dinner," he said, and grabbed his coat.

111

Stupid, stupid, stupid. He didn't blame her; he blamed himself. But he was still furious.

His speed inched upward: sixty, then sixty-five, then seventy. The limit was forty-five. Suddenly he remembered his accident, and practically slammed on the brakes until he was at a legal speed.

The drive home took about forty minutes. By the time he walked in the front door, he'd realized that despite storming out on his mother, he'd held his temper pretty well. No tantrum, no screaming, no smashing anything.

He snorted as he flipped on the light. *Almost like a grown man.*

Of course, he hadn't left on good terms, but what the hell. Just because he was trying to be more level-headed didn't mean he had to sit there and listen to her bullshit. He could respect her beliefs; she had to respect his. It was that simple. He loved his mom, but he wasn't going back to her church.

It was about quarter after seven. He paused in the dining room, remembering how he'd been planning earlier to do a little more checking up on Kelly. But Alex had said, *It's all wrong.* So he went back to the living room instead, and tried to find something to watch.

Alex came in around eight, in worn jeans and a backwards t-shirt. "Daddy," he said, "I think I'm getting so tired."

He'd only ever said that once. Ian remembered it immediately, because he and Alina had looked at each other as if their son had just announced he'd acquired his driver's license.

"Tired?" Ian asked. "Do you feel okay?"

"Yeah. I feel okay. But I'm only getting so tired. Is it time for bed yet?"

They'd checked his head then, and found him burning up. He'd gotten Tylenol, several kisses, and an early bedtime. But Ian couldn't check his head now.

Despite that, he felt certain he knew what Alex was trying to say.

He wetted his lips, trying to imagine a response that might allow Alex to clarify. "You can go to bed whenever you need to, pal."

"I need to go to bed soon. Okay, Dad?"

Whatever Alex wanted Ian to do, time was running out.

112

When Alex left, Ian went downstairs, and stayed up re-reviewing his notes until he started nodding off at the keyboard.

In bed that night, his thoughts swirled as he waited for sleep: *Donnie went off the road, I don't like that black hat, Where is Mr. Tuskers?*

When he fell asleep, his brain assembled dreams to try and fit the pieces together. Alex asked about Mr. Tuskers over and over, each request growing more urgent, and Ian realized that the toy was critical, though he couldn't imagine why. Why should he brush off the only concrete request his son had made, the only one Ian could actually comprehend how to fulfill? There was no harm in finding Tuskers, certainly, and it might be more important than he could understand. His dreaming self resolved to find the stuffed toy as soon as he woke, if he could.

Later, Alex screamed in the car. *"What's that noise?"* The sharpness of his shriek made Ian want to scream back, but he realized he had no point of reference for that event. He could place everything else Alex had ever said, could remember the exact moment the boy had spoken while he was alive, but not that. What *was* that noise? It tickled at the back of his mind, but he couldn't grasp it.

Alex had to go to bed. He would be leaving soon. He'd come to his father, asking him for help, and would have to leave without getting what he'd come for. His father had failed him in life; now, he would fail him in death.

He woke feeling unsettled and tired, the revelations from his dreams fading quickly. He started toward the bathroom, intending to take a shower, but the sight of the twisted curtain drew him up short. He decided to skip it.

As he brushed his teeth, some deep part of him began to wonder how Eston would try to kill him today.

113

He got to work alive. He saw Kelly Dennon as she headed toward her training room, and thought to give her a smile to make up for yesterday. *See? I'm not so crazy after all.* But he couldn't.

Sheila left him alone for once, and with no one to look up on the internet, the morning dragged past. At lunch he left the building, just to get out. The sandwich shop was only about three blocks away, but the traffic lights wouldn't cooperate. He was stuck at the third one, staring at a power line across the street, when he noticed the tornado siren mounted on top of it.

What's that noise?

It had been a tornado siren. A scheduled drill had gone off while they were driving, and Alex had hated it.

Just cover your ears, Ian had urged him. *It'll be over pretty soon.* They'd been right below the siren when it went off, just like Ian was now.

He itched to write this revelation down in his journal. When he got back to the office, he sent an email to himself at home: *"What's that noise" - tornado siren.*

114

"Ian!" Shauna exclaimed. "It's great to see you."

"Yeah." Ian glanced around at the metal chairs. The seat Alina had been taking for the last three weeks was empty.

"She . . . called me," Shauna said, as if he'd asked where his wife was. "She won't be able to attend any more sessions."

"I know," he said. "I talked to her."

"I'm really glad you decided to come back."

Ian managed a brittle smile that he didn't feel. "Well, thanks. I've been thinking, though . . . this is a couples' session . . ."

"Oh, *no!*" She threw her arm out in an exaggerated dismissal. "It's fine! You're more than welcome to stay!"

"I know. You mentioned that on your voicemail. But I don't think I'd be comfortable being here alone."

Shauna's face fell; her boisterous appeal died.

"You mentioned that you could maybe refer me someplace, though? I still want to . . . talk about this. I just think a more personal setting might work better for me."

To his relief, she nodded. "I could see that working better for you." She took out a card, circled one of the names on it. "I've worked with Dr. Bellweather for years. I'll let him know you'll be calling."

Ian nodded and took the card. As he turned to leave, he saw the Bensons coming in. "Hi," he said, and smiled. George gave him a nod.

Hey, I just wanted to apologize for freaking out like that last week. Ian wanted to say it, but he froze. He couldn't. They walked past. Ian took a step toward the door, then turned.

"Good luck," he said. "I hope they find Evan."

115

When he got home, he went downstairs and updated his document. Then he went online and tried to find the locations of the tornado sirens in Hopkins and Shakopee. He'd been hoping for a map or something, with all the sirens marked, but an hour of searching turned up nothing.

Another dead end. How could Alex have told him so much, but given him so little to work with?

But that wasn't fair. The boy was only five, after all. He had tried his best; so had Ian.

"Daddy," Alex said. "I think I'm getting so tired."

Ian turned toward him. He *looked* tired. "I know, bud."

"I think I'm getting so tired."

Alex deserved to rest. If his son stopped speaking to him tomorrow, Ian would be relieved and anguished at the same time. He didn't know what he wanted anymore. "Alex," he ventured, "what will happen if I can't figure out what you want? What if you have to go to bed before I finish?"

The shirt changed to stripes and a collar. He must've been in the middle of getting dressed; he was naked from the crotch down. "Daddy!" he protested. "You *promised*!"

Ian nodded, chastised. He had promised. But what was left to do? Other than driving down to Shakopee and talking to everyone Eston had ever worked for, he had no idea what to do next.

"Okay," he said. "Okay. But is there anything else you can tell me? Anything?"

Alex rolled his eyes and scampered upstairs, his bottom half still nude.

Ian sighed and turned back to his computer, but nothing new was occurring to him. He *did* have the list of Eston's old employers that he'd put together, but he couldn't just drive down and start talking to them. What would he say? *Do you remember Leroy Eston? Did you ever meet his girlfriend, someone named Kelly?*

He waited for the backlash against this idea. It didn't come. Instead, other ideas began to occur to him: questions he could ask, cover stories he could use. What if one of them *had* seen her? What if he could find out where she lived?

This last thought froze him solid. What if, indeed? What then? Go and talk to her? Go and *kill* her?

He went upstairs to use the bathroom, shaking his head. It was crazy, like all his other ideas. He didn't even know her last name, for God's sake.

But it didn't require telling anyone what he was

seeing. And if he questioned everyone Eston had worked for, and found nothing, then he could at least say he'd tried. He'd done everything he could.

He flushed the toilet and washed his hands at the sink. As he turned to use the hand towel, he caught a glimpse of Leroy Eston in the mirror, staring.

Then his heart seized.

116

He staggered, clutching at his chest with one hand. His legs started folding. He tried to take a breath and couldn't make his lungs work. It felt like they had collapsed.

He shot out a hand, grabbed hold of the doorknob trying to keep his feet, but the door swung on its hinges and he toppled forward, face-first into the carpet.

I'm having a heart attack.

I can't be having a heart attack. I'm only thirty-four.

Sharp, silvery pain shot from his chest and into his shoulders and neck. He dragged for breath, the carpet fibers tickling at his lips.

Where was the phone? Where the fuck was the phone?

Alex, he tried to say, but all he heard was a thin wheeze. Alex couldn't bring him the phone anyway. Alex was dead.

I will kill your mom and dad.

I will come to your house, and I will kill your mom and dad.

Eston.

"Daddy!" Alex screamed. He was in his room, visible in

the darkness. *"You have to find Mr. Tuskers! You have to find him right now!"*

Ian tried to get to his feet, but could only struggle to his hands and knees. At the sides of his vision, the walls were turning black.

"Daddy, he's here! In this box! This one!"

He clawed his way forward, dragging himself through the carpet as the strength bled from his arms. Every breath was a struggle. His heart was in a ratcheting vise.

Alex stood by one of the boxes in his room, pointing and shouting. Ian could no longer hear what he was saying. The words were like blasts of light. They rocketed from his mouth and streaked into space, leaving a shining trail.

He reached the box and somehow rose to his knees. The box wasn't taped, but the flaps were folded in. He fumbled at them like a child.

Alex helped. He was blazing now, too brilliant to be looked at directly. Sparks from his body leapt into the darkening air around Ian, gleaming like the jagged edge of a migraine.

Then the box was open. The stuffed elephant was at the top of the pile, its trunk somewhat flattened from months of being pressed against the cardboard, its glass eyes narrowed and hungry for violence.

Mr. Tuskers is here to protect you, Alex. He and I have talked. I told him: "I won't be in here, but it's very important that Alex be safe. So you need to guard him just like I would." And he promised to do that. He can see in the dark, and he's going to stay awake all night, and beat up anything that tries to hurt you. So you're safe. Okay?

Ian grabbed the toy, and the vise released his heart.

He fell to his side, gulping air, his eyes squeezed shut against Alex's brilliance.

117

Luminance boiled in front of him, bright as sunlight. He threw his hands over his eyes, and could still see the shining red wall of his eyelids.

There was a roar, and thunder like a stampede. The floor shuddered beneath him. He heard trumpeting.

Eston shrieked, and the temperature in the room plummeted. Ian's arms crawled with the sudden cold.

Then a blast of heat rolled over him. Eston's cry ended in a gurgle.

The light faded.

When he opened his eyes, Ian found himself alone in Alex's dark room, holding Mr. Tuskers like a drowning victim clutching a life jacket.

118

```
Alina -
```

He paused, staring at the blinking cursor. Mr. Tuskers sat on the floor to his right, glaring at the stairs.

```
I know this will sound crazy. Leroy
Eston, the man who murdered our son, is
trying to kill us. Alex tried to warn me,
and I realized, nearly too late, what he
```

```
was trying to say. Somehow Mr. Tuskers
can keep us safe. I can't explain it. I'm
begging you to believe me. Please just
keep Mr. Tuskers close by. I don't know
how it works, but
```

He stopped mid-sentence, reread the paragraph, and grimaced. Then he deleted it and started over.

```
Alina -
I've been having dreams about Leroy
Eston. He keeps telling Alex that he is
going to kill his parents. Then Alex
tells me that only Mr. Tuskers can keep
us safe. I know it sounds stupid, but I
don't want you to be hurt. I unpacked Mr.
Tuskers and would like you to keep
him close.
```

His nostrils were flaring as he finished the sentence. *Stupid. Pure fucking stupid.* He deleted this paragraph too.

The old Crazy voice tried to tell him there was no point in even doing this. He had had an anxiety attack, nothing more or less, and digging out his son's old animal had helped to calm him down. There had been more hallucinations too, of course. But there was no need to get the toy to Alina. There was no need to try to keep her safe, because all of this was in his head.

But Haunting said something else. Haunting said that Eston had promised to kill *both* Alex's parents—and if Alex's protection was keeping Ian safe, then it left Alina vulnerable.

He stared at the screen, paralyzed. The instants dripped past like sand grains in an hourglass. Alina could be getting attacked right now. Eston could be choking her, like he'd choked Ian. Maybe her father was calling 911, if he was even home, or maybe she was lying on the floor, face slowly draining—

Ian couldn't take that chance. But she wouldn't just accept the toy. She would think it was just another sign of his craziness.

"Dammit," he hissed. His fingertips quivered above the keyboard. The situation was impossible. If he hadn't been such an ass to her, if she still trusted him—or had a willingness to humor him—like she used to . . . .

But she didn't. He had ruined it.

God damn it. They should have been going through this *together*.

His heart twisted, and he started writing.

```
Alina -

I'm so sorry I hurt you. I didn't mean
to. I wish I could have been stronger
about this. You needed me as badly as I
needed you, and while I leaned on you so
hard you nearly broke, I gave you nothing
back. I see that now, and I want to
change it.

I said terrible things that must have
killed you to hear. They weren't true.
They weren't fair. I would take them back
if I could, and I wish to God I could.
```

I'm not asking you to come back. I know I can't. I just wanted you to know that I understand, now. If you do ever want to call, and talk about Alex, I think I can do that now. We don't have to dance around it anymore. You've dealt with it much better than I did, to your credit, but I know you are still hurting, at least as bad as I am. I don't want you to have to go through it alone anymore.

I've done some things to try to come to terms. I've been dreaming about Alex, a lot. Good times, and bad times both. Some dreams about how he might have been hurt. But also dreams about reading books at night, or about playing hide and seek, or sitting on the couch watching Law And Order :) They've helped. Yeah, they make me miss him even harder. But they also make me think that just maybe he doesn't hate me, wherever he is. If he can forgive me maybe I can forgive myself. I'm trying.

I've also set up some appointments with a doctor that Shauna recommended. I'm going to be seeing him once a week. And today I finally went through Alex's things.

I know we went through them together, but
I wasn't ready then. I was ready today.
It really hurt, but I went through all
the boxes in his room. I'm ready to get
rid of most of it, but I saved two
things: Mr. Tuskers and Mowsalot. I was
hoping you could take one, and I'd keep
the other. If by some miracle you are
ever able to forgive me, maybe our next
child could get them both. If not, we
will each have something to remember our
family by.

I'm sorry to drop it off in the middle of
the night like this. I know it's weird. I
just felt like it was important to finish
this task, and I don't want to leave it
until the morning. I've been putting it
off too long.

I love you.

- Ian

119

He printed the letter, folded it up, and wrote her name on
it. He'd told a lot of lies in it. But somehow, at the same
time, it was the most honest of the tries he'd made.

Outside, the night sky was one of those endless
winter slates: grey and featureless in the haze of the

streetlamps. His breath curled from his lips in short, fierce bursts. Halfway down the sidewalk, he stopped.

It had sounded like Eston was killed in Alex's room, but his threats against Alina had been too pointed to ignore. That was why Ian was bringing the toy to her father's house now. But if he left Tuskers with Alina, what would keep Eston from coming after Ian again?

"Fuck," he muttered, chewing it over, trying to figure out a way to make it work. Nothing came to him.

I could keep Tuskers, just until Alex is gone, he thought. But what if Eston went after Alina before that? Or—

Oh God.

If Eston could make Ian have a heart attack, how easy would it be to kill their baby?

The thought left him pale and shaking. No. If it meant letting Eston kill him, so be it. But he would rather that than risk any harm to his wife or his second child. He would kill *himself* if he had to before he would allow Eston to hurt another of his children.

He finished his walk to the car. As he grabbed at the door handle he thought of the other toy Alex had always slept with. Mowsalot. Not the guardian against monsters and bad animals—that had been Tuskers. But still a powerful symbol, at least. A well-loved companion. Ian had used to give it a voice, in the dark when Alex couldn't see his mouth moving. *Good night, Alex! I love you!* And, *Oh, Alex, I missed you today! Will you give me a hug?*

He glanced down at Mr. Tuskers, whose beady eyes glinted righteousness in the lamplight. The cat wouldn't be as good.

But shit, it was worth a shot.

120

He pulled out twenty minutes later, Mowsalot and Tuskers perched importantly in the passenger seat. He drove carefully, watching the limit and the road, on guard for a sudden jerk of the wheel, or a slip of his foot, or an abrupt traffic light change that would put him in the path of an onrushing semi. It didn't happen.

Ham Lake was nearly an hour's drive from Hopkins, especially driving cautiously as he was, but his vigilance and fear for his wife kept him awake. He hadn't been to Alina's parents' place since her mother had died last year, so he had to backtrack several times trying to find it. Eventually he wound up rolling slowly through what he thought was the right area, brights on, peering through the window looking for landmarks. When he finally found it, though, he knew he had the right place. Alina's mother had been a lawn gnome lover, and the lawn was still festooned with them, shoveling, planting, waving, and of course, Alex's personal favorite: mooning.

He killed the lights and rolled up onto the shoulder. The houselights were dark. Feeling like a thief or a peeping tom, he grabbed the two stuffed animals and stole up the long driveway toward the house. A pair of brilliant garage lights flared to life, and he froze in place, thinking he must have been seen—but it was nearly midnight now, and after a second he remembered the lights were simply motion-activated.

Still, they made him feel exposed. He trotted across the driveway and up on to the porch, expecting at any moment to see the front door open, and dropped Mr. Tuskers—letter taped to forehead—behind the screen door. For a long, agonizing moment, he considered ringing the bell. But the fact that he was here in the middle of the night was already weird enough—and besides, if he actually spoke to Alina he might say something desperate, something that would prompt her to reject his gift. He had to hope that Tusker's position on the stoop would be close enough to keep her safe until morning. He heard a dog bark inside, and fled.

On the way home his caution doubled. He heard a train whistling, and even though the signals hadn't dropped yet, he stopped and waited it out. As the train screamed past, he reached out to Mowsalot. Its fur was nearly brittle with cold, despite the heat blasting from the vents, and the reflected crimson from the train signal lights burned deep in its eyes.

121

He tried to sleep, but there was a coiled spring of live wire in his mind, sparking and flexing when he closed his eyes. He wanted to pace, to talk out loud, to check the mirror and make sure Eston wasn't behind him. He wanted to open his document, to find all the tornado sirens in the state. Alex was leaving soon. He'd said as much. Ian couldn't waste time sleeping.

The transition from thinking about these things to doing them was frighteningly smooth. He didn't even remember making the choice to get up. Part of him wondered if he was dreaming it.

He went over everything again—what he knew about Kelly, what he knew about Eston. Every clue Alex had given him, whether Ian had deciphered it or not. He hunted for tornado sirens and black hats, daycares or preschools with girls named Delilah; he read through *More More More, Said the Baby*. Alex slept on the couch behind him, curled like a kitten against a pillow, and Ian remembered covering him with a blanket on the nights he had fallen asleep watching his dad play computer.

He'd had the idea before of checking out Eston's employers, so he paid special attention to that—gathering as many details of the man's work history as he could.

A sea of empty pop cans grew on the desk as the hours passed, threatening to spill over the edge. The sugar and caffeine helped him keep working, but forced him to the bathroom several times. He went upstairs for these trips instead of using the basement toilet, because the upstairs bathroom was cleaner, the movement kept his legs awake, and he wanted to make sure Eston still wasn't there.

He brought Mowsalot with him. The toy felt normal again, not like it had been sitting in the freezer as it had briefly in the car.

As he emerged from the bathroom on one of these trips, he saw the first dreamy glimmer of dawn leaking from the living room curtains. His enthusiasm—running unbridled for hours—burned out. It was the same old story. A whole night spent investigating, and he was no closer to figuring anything out than he had been.

The clock said *6:41*. He had an hour and twenty minutes to get to work.

Suddenly, he longed to go to sleep.

"Fuck," he whimpered. "God damn it." Last night, he had been attacked by his dead son's dead murderer. The event should have changed his life, illuminated every-thing, made him certain what to do next. Instead, it had left him feeling even more powerless.

He could go to Shakopee on Saturday maybe, try to see if anyone had seen Kelly. But that was a thin thread at best, and he still wasn't sure he even wanted to do it. It seemed like a great way to end up getting committed.

He turned toward the shower, fighting back a yawn, and started getting ready for work.

122

Mowsalot sat on the sink; Ian sat in the shower. The water pummeled him like hot rain. He wanted to disap-pear in it.

Every few minutes he peered around the curtain, to make sure the stuffed cat was still there. One time, steam curled from its fur like a hot coal thrust into a puddle.

He could have stayed in the shower all day, but he forced himself out and went through the motions. He didn't hear Alex playing in his room. He didn't see Alex at all until he threw on his coat at the front door.

"Goodbye, Daddy."

Ian looked at him, yearning to reach out, desperate to understand. "This weekend, Alex. We'll drive down there, okay? I don't know what else to try. If there's anything else you can tell me—"

"I love you."

Usually, Ian said it first. He nodded, tightly, several times. "I love you, too." Then, because it was so important, he said it again.

"I love you, too."

123

It had snowed again, lightly, during the night. He scraped off his car as the engine warmed, the voices from the radio mumbling behind the windows like bodies moving beneath a blanket.

Inside, he stripped off his gloves and rubbed his hands in front of the vent, relishing the heat. From the passenger seat, Mowsalot stared out the front window, its mouth caught in a familiar and perpetual grin.

He pulled away slowly, double-checking for someone slipping out of control on the ice behind him, and rolled around the corner, angling gradually toward 494. The street was quiet. The taut vigilance he had struggled to maintain since the trip to Alina's father's house last night began to relax, dulled by fatigue. He blinked, long and slow, then slammed on his brakes, his eyes riveted to his rearview mirror and his heart screaming in his chest.

Leroy Eston's van was parked at the curb behind him.

The van's rusting sides were the molding white of an old basement wall. Its lights were off, and the cabin was dark. It crouched at the street's edge like a gorged, pale maggot, waiting.

Ian slipped the car into reverse and rolled carefully backward, watching the van's cabin. There was someone inside, but he couldn't make out a face.

Then Alex was on the sidewalk, his red turtleneck brilliant as a blood spot against the empty snow.

Ian heard his thoughts gibbering. He had seen too many horrible things happen to his son, but this . . . .

This!

The boy was singing, or talking to himself; Ian could

see his lips moving. He trailed his backpack along the ground behind him by one long, broken strap. He stopped just as he passed the van's front bumper and looked up, as if someone had greeted him.

Ian's heart wrenched. *Run, Alex!* he screamed in silence. *Run!*

And he did. He *did* run. Just like Dad had told him to. He pounded up the sidewalk, his song forgotten, his backpack capering after him, and then his arms were yanked back. He opened his mouth to scream, and his eyes widened. Ian couldn't see his attacker—it was like the night he'd seen him being raped in the cellar pantry —but Alex was fighting for breath, kicking, and then his eyes rolled into his head and he sagged downward. He hung like that for a few seconds, limp in his kidnapper's invisible grip. Then he was lifted into the air, carried like a baby behind the nauseating grub-like wall of the van and out of sight. The backpack went with.

Alex hadn't been tricked. He was too smart for that. He had run. He had tried to cry for help. They hadn't fooled him.

Ian was screaming.

The van's back door swung into sight as it gaped open to swallow his son. Just as quickly, it slammed back shut and the passenger door spasmed. It opened, then closed, and the van sidled casually forward, the maggot bloated and slow from its meal.

As it rolled past, Ian saw Leroy Eston in the driver's seat.

124

He shuddered and whimpered, at the mercy of his visions. He had always been powerless while watching Alex replay his life, but to be powerless *then*, at the one instant when his involvement could have changed everything, broke him. He heard a guttural wail gurgling from his own throat. His stomach, his heart, were ash.

Maybe Alex would re-live these moments again and again, forever. Maybe Ian's failure to figure out what the boy needed was damning him.

I should have been there.

His shoulders shook as if some giant beast had grabbed him in its jaws and was toying with him. Heaving sobs wracked his chest. His arm bumped the car horn, which protested absurdly on the silent street.

He fumbled for something to cling to. His wife loathed him. His son had died. But he craved their touch, was desperate with longing to hold them. His fingers closed on Mowsalot, and he pulled it to him with a ragged wail, clutching it like his son must have clutched it in the blackness of his room. There was a place in his mind that was ashamed to cling to a stuffed animal like a child, but he was far beyond it. For him there was nothing but raw, blistering pain, and the screaming need for comfort.

But the cat felt as if it had just been pulled from the fridge. It wasn't caustically frigid, as it had nearly been last night; but it could have been, recently. When the van had still been near, maybe. Something analytical began to speak in Ian's mind, wondering if the toy's sudden turns of cold were a sign that Eston was near, or that it was holding him at bay.

Slowly, the thought dragged him back to himself. As he fought to correct his breathing, wipe his face, find a tissue, he realized he had seen Eston driving.

If Eston had been driving—

Kelly had snatched Alex from the sidewalk. Kelly had smothered him. Kelly had lifted him into her arms, bore him into the van while he was helpless. *Kelly* had.

Right then, at that very instant, she was out there, somewhere, alive.

His hands tightened until his nails dug into the meat of his palm. Slowly, carefully, he put the car into gear and turned toward home.

PART III

125

He printed his document, in case he needed to check his notes, and while it rattled out of his old bubblejet he pulled up and saved a map of each of the places on his list where Eston had probably worked. Once he had them all he printed those too, and threw them in a folder.

Then he went into the bedroom and carefully loaded a clip before pulling the .22 from its shelf in the closet. He flicked the safety, refamiliarizing himself with how it worked. Off, then on; off, then on. How quickly could he do it? Could he remember? Could he do it *too* quickly, or might this miniscule obstacle prevent him from doing something stupid, like shooting the wrong person?

It was only a .22, but it weighed as much as a corpse.

His hands shivered with cold sweat. He shook his head once, tightly, and set the gun back on the shelf. He stalked out of the room. He was passing under the threshold when he remembered Alex's eyes rolling back, his body drooping in the invisible grip of his attacker before he was scooped into her arms and carried like a baby.

Ian had carried him that way: swaddled him to make him feel secure, anchored him against the crook of his arm, and paced with him in a circuit from the kitchen, through the dining room, into the living room, and back again—over, and over, and over. He had gazed into his fathomless eyes, waiting for them to close, wondering what they were seeing, falling in love with them. When the boy had grown older, too old to be carried that way, Ian had sometimes done it anyway. *I used to carry you this way when you were a baby,* he'd say, and Alex would close his eyes with a silly but deeply contented grin, and play along, and Ian's heart would sing.

He halted in the doorway, fingers curling and uncurling, lips and eyes twitching.

Then he went back and grabbed the gun.

126

It went in the glove box. The folder, he tossed on the passenger seat. Mowsalot followed suit, grinning vacantly at the front window. Ian glanced into the backseat, expecting to find Alex there, but it was empty.

The first place on the list was Todd's Gas, just off 169. He stared at the words, at the address, imagining that Kelly was working there right now.

If you find her, what then?

It was an old question, and it didn't matter. He pulled out.

It was 9:27. The morning traffic on 169 had cleared, and the highway flew past. He missed his exit, unsure of where the place was, but turned off at the next one and angled back. The path took him to Main Street, a quaint through-way that reminded him of growing up in Monticello: little, single-owner shops and restaurants with names like Corner Cafe and Peterston Antiques.

The street was quiet and uncrowded. He crept along at half the thirty mile-per-hour limit, combing the buildings for a sign of his destination and watching the street names roll past.

At the next corner he saw it. It was a little place, like the other shops around here, and even still had a full-service lane. The garage was just big enough for three cars at once. A sign in the front promised *$19.95 Oil Changes—30 minutes or less.*

He parked across the street and double-checked his notes. When he finished, he saw that Mowsalot had tumbled to the floor in front of the passenger seat.

"Shit," he muttered. He hadn't thought about what to do with the toy. Eston might attack him if he left it in the car. But there was no way anyone would talk to him if he brought it with.

He picked it up, set it back on the seat, and swore again. *Screw it.* He couldn't risk another of Eston's attacks, so he snatched the cat up and opened the door. But as he set his foot on the blacktop, he felt like an absolute idiot. He turned back and froze, paralyzed with indecision.

His cell phone trilled. The screen on the front read: *Smartlnk Rscrs.*

He only hesitated for a second, then flipped it open. "This is Ian," he said.

ADAM J NICOLAI

"Ian." The voice was cool and feminine. "This is Barb Shantic at Smartlink."

Justin's boss. Son of a bitch.

"I need you to come in immediately so we can speak in person. When will you be here?"

Her directness put him off balance. "I . . . can't, I won't be in today."

"I need you to come in immediately," she repeated.

"Well, that won't be possible," he rejoined, incensed at her tone. "If I'm fired, just tell me."

"I've spoken with Justin Keplin about your recent performance. There are some matters we need to discuss in person."

"I won't be in today," he said again, but his voice held a slight tremor. Why wasn't she just firing him? What he'd done to Justin could be considered blackmail. Did she know?

"You are scheduled to work today, and you have no personal time remaining. What time will you be in?"

"I told you, I *won't*," he snapped. "I have a family emergency that needs to be taken care of right now."

"Then your employment is terminated, effective immediately." She sounded as smug as Sheila.

"Fuck you," he said, and snapped the phone closed.

He left the cat in the car.

127

A bell over the door jingled as Ian walked in. A skinny kid in jeans and a simple striped shirt glanced up at him from behind the counter. "What's goin' on?" he said.

230

"Hey," Ian answered. "I'm looking for Ben. Is he around?"

"Oh, he's in the garage," the kid said. "You can head in there." He jerked a thumb toward the door, and Ian did as he suggested.

The sides of the garage bristled with tools and toolboxes, cardboard boxes filled with bottles of engine oil and dirty rags. Two of the stalls were empty; a rusted blue '94 Civic was hoisted atop the last one. Ian heard the distinctive whining of a power screwdriver.

"Is Ben here?" he called, trying to be heard over the din.

An older man in a jumpsuit glanced back from a computer, nestled on a counter between two hubcaps. He had a thin line of a mouth, crow's feet, and black hair shot through with grey. "Yeah!" he shouted. "Can I help you?"

Ian stepped toward him and offered his hand. "I'm Ian Jones, with the Shakopee Sentinel."

Ben shook his hand. "With the Sentinel, huh? Don't see that everyday."

"Right." Ian tried a smile, not sure how to respond, but it faltered. "Well, I'm doing a story on Leroy Eston, the man who killed that Colmes boy earlier this year, and I'd heard he worked here for awhile." He was amazed at how easily the lies rolled off his tongue. "Is that right?"

Ben's gaze darkened. "Yeah, that's right," he said. "Maybe four years ago. What do you need to know?"

Ian fought to keep his cool. *Did he have a girlfriend?* he wanted to ask. *Do you know anyone named Kelly?* But the questions were too pointed, too incongruous. He forced himself to wait.

"How well did you know him?"

Ben snorted. "Not well enough, apparently. He was quiet. Had a hell of a temper. I never would've thought he'd do something like that, though." He shook his head. "Fucking crazy. Pardon my French."

"A temper?" Ian asked. "Why do you say that?"

"Oh, you know." Ben waved the question off, then continued, "He'd throw tools if he got pissed about anything. Scream and curse and carry on. I had to ban him from talking to customers because if they had any questions he'd get real nasty with 'em. One day he and I had a little conversation about his paycheck and he ended up breaking the window on a customer's car." He paused expectantly.

"Wow," Ian said, a bit late. "So how long was he here?"

"Workin' here?"

"Yeah."

"Oh, God—six weeks? Not even? I fired him after that thing with the window. Knew he was no good." He shook his head. "But still, you never expect . . ."

Ian nodded. "Did he ever talk about his home life, or his friends, or—"

"No, no, nothin' like that. Not that I heard, anyway. He always seemed like the kind to get his shift done and get the hell out of here."

Ian couldn't help himself. "He never mentioned a girlfriend, or a sister? Maybe someone named Kelly?"

Ben paused, sneered in concentration for a second, and finally shook his head. "No. Sorry. Not that I remember. That someone he knew?"

Ian shrugged. "I don't know—just a name that showed up in my notes. Probably nothing.

"Thanks for your time."

128

It was the same at the next place, and the third was just a gas station: the garage had closed down the year before, and the clerk behind the counter had only been working there a few months. Ian scratched them off his list, which eliminated all his leads in Shakopee, so he got on 13 and headed in to Prior Lake.

Shop and Shop was by far the most upscale place Eston had worked; attached to the fading remnants of an old strip mall, it boasted that its patrons could shop while they waited for their car to get done. The sign proclaiming this opportunity appeared to have been propped in the front window for at least ten years, the white lettering nearly absorbed into the fading green around it. But inside, at least, it looked relatively fresh and well-kept: clean floors, a leather waiting couch (but who would want to sit on it, when they could go shopping?), and a flat-screen TV mounted on the wall opposite a broad, floor-to-ceiling window.

A young woman who couldn't have been much older than Sheila was on the phone behind the counter, wearing a name tag that said *Wendy*. She gave Ian a smile and a hand signal—*One second, almost done here.*

As Wendy negotiated an appointment time with the person on the phone, Ian noticed the clock on the wall behind her. It was almost noon. He'd pissed away another day at work, incurred some kind of penalty that sounded as if it would not only cost him his livelihood, but maybe a day in court as well, and he'd found nothing. The pendulum between fierce, driving mania and utter despondence began to swing away again, stealing his anger from that morning and his certainty that he was doing what Alex wanted. He wondered if he would ever be able to explain this to anyone. He wondered if he would ever see Alex again. He wondered if his wife was okay.

His mind snagged on this last thought, and he considered calling her. But the receptionist finished her call just then, smiled brightly at him, and asked what he needed.

"I need to find Kelly," he said. He hadn't meant to be so blunt, but when he reached inside for the story he'd been telling up until this point, he found nothing but surrender. "I heard she worked here."

"Kelly Baker?" Wendy asked.

"I—" Ian started, thrown off balance. "Yes, right, Kelly Baker."

"Sure, she's in the garage—are you a friend, or . . . ?"

"I—no, I just—my name is Ian Smith, I was just hoping to speak with her for a few minutes." Was Smith the right pseudonym? His heart was pounding. *She's here. Jesus Christ, she's here.* His gun was in the car.

"Oh, okay." Wendy's smile faltered. "Do you know her . . . ?"

"No, I—" Ian rolled his eyes, managed a nervous smile. "I'm sorry. I've just had a lot of interviews this morning and I get a little flaky when I skip breakfast. I'm from the Shakopee Sentinel. I just wanted to speak with her for a few minutes about—" He couldn't say Eston, not now. What if it tipped her off? "We're doing a piece on the Shop and Shop."

"Oh!" Wendy seemed pleased to hear this. "You want to talk to Doug, then. He's the owner."

"Oh, no. No. Ah—Kelly contacted us. She requested the piece. If you don't mind I'd just like to talk to her first."

"Oh," Wendy said again. She looked confused.

"It'll only take a few minutes," Ian pressed, and walked past the counter to the shop door. He tried a smile, to put her at ease, but couldn't make it stick. It didn't matter. He wasn't going to wait, no matter what she said. "Thanks," he said, and pushed through the door.

There were eight stalls in this garage, and a line of computer stations set up against one wall. At the nearest station, a nondescript, twiggy woman with limp, dark hair was hunched over a printout, reviewing it with a customer. She tapped and circled, her lips moving but inaudible over the clamor. Her nametag said *Kelly*.

Ian's heart clawed into his throat; a roar or scream danced on his tongue. His gun was in the car, but he could go back and get it. Several stalls had open garage doors—he could get the gun, walk right through one of those, march up to her and make the six o'clock news.

She grabbed him. He stared at her arms, at her mouth forming silent words, at her height and her dull, flaccid hair. *She carried him like a baby. She shared him with Eston.*

He imagined stalking up to the counter. *This is for Alex, you bitch.* The gun would take her by surprise. He would have it to her forehead before she could react.

You might've dodged the cops, but I'm his dad. Do you fucking understand me? I am his fucking dad.

He saw three gunshots. The first caught her in the forehead and yanked her head back, the second blasted through her open, screaming mouth and out her cheek, splattering the wall behind her with blood and flesh, and the third caught her in the neck, turning her scream into an impotent gurgle. She fell back against the wall, her hands scrabbling toward her face, as the first customer began to scream. One of the mechanics lunged into him, knocked the gun from his hand and smashed his head against the concrete, but it didn't matter. He had fucked her up. She hadn't gotten away. As the guy twisted his arms back, shouting for someone to help, grab his legs, call the police, Ian would only laugh. Or sob.

Kelly finished with the customer, and her phone rang. She picked it up, her lips still churning enigmas.

Go! Get to the car! Now!

And that night Alina would see his face on the news, on the internet; the next day the Star Tribune would have him on the front page, and he would look insane. He'd never see his wife again, never meet his second child.

Get the fucking gun!

Kelly's eyes locked on him, the phone still cradled to her ear. She nodded. Her mouth formed the word *Okay*.

"Mr. Smith?" she shouted, loudly enough to be heard, and beckoned Ian her way.

Fuck all that! Get the gun! Do what you fucking came here for! SHE KIDNAPPED YOUR SON!

"Mr. Smith?" she repeated when he didn't move. She stepped toward him, holding out her hand; when he refused it, her brow tightened. "Wendy told me you were looking for me. I'm Kelly Baker?"

He lunged forward, grabbed her around the neck and bore her to the ground. Choked until her face turned blue, then black. Roared and screamed, smashed her face with his forehead.

Except he didn't.

"Did you . . . ?" Ian started, but he had no idea how to finish that sentence. "Did you . . . was there a Leroy Eston that worked here?"

Her face soured immediately. She inched backward, as if the very mention of the man's name made Ian repulsive.

"There *was*," she said. "I thought this was about some kind of publicity piece?"

"Did you . . ." he started again. He couldn't keep those two words off his tongue. "Were you two friends?"

She narrowed her eyes. "What does that—? *God*, no. The man was disgusting."

She's lying. You're going to let her lie her way out of this?

But she didn't seem to be lying. Her tight shoulders, her pinched eyes—every muscle in her body conveyed loathing.

He got a sudden image of a late night at the garage. Eston tried to force himself on her, and she screamed, and kicked him, and got away. He had no idea if it was real or not, but it *felt* right.

He couldn't meet her eyes. He looked past them, to the station behind her, and saw a picture taped to the side of the monitor. Kelly was pushing a little girl in a swing, both of them grinning hugely.

She has a daughter.

No one with a daughter could have done it. No one.

"Mr. Smith?" she asked. "If you have questions about Leroy, you should probably talk to Doug. He's—"

"No," Ian said. "No, that's okay." His knees quivered. As he turned away they nearly spilled him to the floor. "Thanks," he said over his shoulder, and fled.

129

He drove two blocks and pulled over, his hands shaking and his stomach in revolt.

She has a daughter!

Jesus Christ, she has a daughter! You could have made an orphan!

What the fuck are you doing out here?

On the passenger seat, Mowsalot crouched, grinning.

Ian glanced at the rearview mirror, panting and sweating, on the verge of hyperventilation. He expected to see the police, but there was nothing.

You could have killed an innocent woman! You were ready to do it! Jesus Christ, *Ian!*

He started to reach for the gun, thinking to throw it into the street, but his hands were quivering too hard to get a grip on the glove compartment latch.

What the fuck are you doing? he demanded of himself again, but there was no answer. Nothing made any sense.

He was driving around Prior Lake, a city he had never visited before in his life, with a gun in the glove box, looking for someone to kill. That's what he was doing.

"Alex!" he called, and craned his head to look in the rear seats. "Alex! Where are you?" There were Burger King bags and old pop cans on the floor, discarded junk mail scattered across the seats. No car seat. No smiling little boy, no blue eyes.

"*Alex!*" The demand scraped from Ian's throat in a choking wheeze. "Answer me! Where the hell are you?"

His eyes darted to the passenger seat, and again to the rear. Nothing.

"Dammit, Alex, *please*! I am here because of you!

You sent me here! It was hard enough losing you, but you are the one who came back, made me go through all this . . . *shit*! Now you fucking tell me! Enough fucking around! Tell me what I'm doing here!"

He waited for maybe half a second.

"Goddammit, Alex, I almost killed a woman! *I almost killed a little girl's mom!*"

A man had stepped out of a little cafe. He peered towards Ian's car, brows knitted, and Ian slapped his mouth shut.

Shut up. Shut up. He's not coming. People can see you.

Go home. Just go home.

He put the car in gear and peeled away, shooting up to fifty miles per hour on the little, urban street. He hardly slowed down for the next turn. His tires squealed as he angled around, heading back toward 13. The speed helped to calm him, to give him something else to focus on.

Get home. It's over. He's gone. Go home.

13 north was just ahead, and he could take it back to Hopkins. The last place Eston had worked was in New Prague, though, and that was south.

Ian turned south.

130

This time, he skipped the front desk and walked straight in through the garage. He saw a pair of guys talking in the corner and said, "Hey, is Curtis here?"

One of them, a greying, reed-thin man who was easily in his early sixties, pointed a greasy finger toward the back corner. Ian followed his gesture and saw a large, balding man behind a desk. "Thanks."

Ian's heart began thrumming nervously as he walked to the back of the room, memories of his encounter with Kelly Baker flashing in his mind. He tried to get around them by focusing on the man sitting at the desk: middle-aged, fat, with a flushed red face and fingers like sausages. *How do you get that fat working in a garage?* he wondered. Curtis must have been a manager, sitting in a chair, for a long time.

"Curtis?" Ian asked, and the larger man blew out a breath.

"Yeah."

"Hi, my name is Ian Jones." Ian held out a hand; Curtis took it. "I'm with the Shakopee Sentinel. Could I talk to you for just a few minutes?"

Curtis sighed again, his eyes squinting toward the monitor on his desk. "I'm really kind of busy here, Mr. Jones. Could you—?"

"Five minutes. I swear. I would come back another time, but my schedule has me out of town for the next two weeks."

Curtis gave him a look that said, *What does that have to do with me?*

"I'm doing a story on Leroy Eston, the man who kidnapped Alex Colmes earlier this year. They found him up in Shakopee, by O'Dowd?"

The other man's face changed from mild affront to caution. "Shit," he said. "That was five years ago Leroy worked here. I didn't know anything about him."

"But you remember him, then?"

Curtis scoffed. "Barely. He was an asshole, that's about

all I remember. Always late. Always getting into fights with the other guys. I wasn't surprised at all to hear about what happened. That guy was a real piece of shit. Ten miles of bad road."

"Yeah," Ian said. "Listen, I'm actually trying to find out if there was a woman he would hang around with—a girlfriend, or a sister, maybe? Someone named Kelly?"

"Kelly?" Curtis barked, as if the name were preposterous. "No, I don't remember anything like that."

This was the last place on Ian's list. Curtis' denial hit him like a punch to the gut. He bit his lip, trying not to scream or cry. "Are you sure?" he asked, feeling like a beggar.

"Yeah, I—Ed! Hey, Ed!" He threw out an imperious arm, beckoned for the older man Ian had seen earlier.

Ed walked over; he had remarkable posture and speed for a man of his age. "Yeah, boss," he said flatly.

"You remember Leroy Eston?"

Ed's eyes smoldered. "'Course I remember Leroy Eston."

"You remember if he had a girlfriend, or anything?"

"Or a sister?" Ian put in.

Ed barked a humorless laugh. "A girlfriend? That guy?"

Curtis shook his head. "That's what I said, too." He looked back to Ian. "Sorry. If you don't mind, I really have to get back to—"

"Someone named Kelly," Ian pressed. "Anything, a picture, or someone he might have just mentioned once—"

"Look," Curtis said, at the same time Ed answered, "*Kelly*. You talking about that Kelton guy?"

"Oh!" Curtis said. "*Kelton*. What was his first name? That jaggoff friend of his, he tried to get him a job here. What was it?"

Ian felt dizzy. He put a hand on the desk to keep himself steady. "Kelton?" he repeated, trying to keep up.

"Yeah," Ed said. "Can't remember his first name. He'd drop by here like he owned the place. Skinny guy. He and Leroy would go around back and toke up on his lunch break, like they didn't think anyone knew. Didn't Leroy call him Kelly sometimes?"

"That's—" Ian put a hand to his temple, trying to calm his breathing, his spinning head. "That's got to be it. Do you know his first name, or how I might get ahold of him?"

"That had to be six years ago, now," Ed grunted. "I doubt he even knew the guy anymore, Leroy didn't seem like the kinda guy to keep friends around."

"He tried to get him a job here," Curtis said again, nodding. "Shit, I bet you . . ." He pivoted his chair toward an ancient metal file cabinet, ran his fingers down the drawers. Ian watched, tense, quiet, as Curtis backed up to the second drawer, labeled *Apps*, and thumbed through the files.

"There!" Curtis announced, tearing out a thin folder. Inside was a single sheet of paper. "'Tim Kelton'. April 2004. I knew he'd tried to get a job from me." He scoffed. "What a joke! I was about ready to fire Leroy, and he tries to get his loser friend in here." He was grinning.

"'Tim Kelton,'" Ian repeated, disbelieving. "Did he leave you an address, or a phone number, or anything?"

"Well, I can't give you that, you know."

"Right." Ian's heart thundered in his ears.

"And it was—what'd you say, Ed? Six years ago? Guy's probably not even there any more, anyway."

"Maybe." Ian licked his lips. "A hundred bucks," he said.

Curtis' grin froze on his face. "What?" he said, incredulous.

"A hundred bucks," Ian repeated. "Come on, what do you care? You said yourself the guy was a jackoff."

The grin melted away. "What, does he owe you money or something?" Curtis tossed the folder on the desk and crossed his arms over his bulging gut. "Get out of here, pal."

Ian's fingers twitched. He looked Curtis in the eyes and saw Justin: smug, defiant, challenging.

Fuck that.

Ian snatched the folder. Curtis saw him going for it—his eyes widened and he started to reach out—but Ian was too quick. He broke for the open door.

"Hey!" Curtis screeched. "*Hey!*"

Ian tore across the parking lot, hurled himself into his car, and turned the engine.

"Get back here!"

Ian peeled into the street, his blood screaming in his veins.

131

He drove without a plan, eyes glued to the rearview mirror, just trying to put as much distance behind him as possible. He kept expecting to see Curtis coming after him in some beat-up old F-150, or the lights of police cars cresting the hill. Neither happened, and finally, he slowed his racing mind enough to think it through.

Curtis wasn't chasing him. As far as Curtis was concerned, Ian was just some nutty old friend or enemy of Kelly's, trying to find the guy. He wouldn't call the cops —and even if he did, they wouldn't give a damn. A six-year-old, most likely out-of-date job application had been stolen. So what? It didn't matter; wasn't that exactly why Ian had been so pissed at Curtis lording it up in the first place?

A sign ahead said *Southside Park*. He pulled into the lot, his breathing finally calming, and took out the application. It was an old generic thing, dark blue with white printing and light blue fields, pocked with grease smears.

Timothy S. Kelton. Date of birth: August 17th, 1967. A phone number in the 952 area code. An address in Lonsdale. A signature smudged beyond recognition. No cell phone number, no e-mail address, no picture.

Compared to what Ian had had to go on before, it was an absolute treasure trove.

He thumbed the phone number into his cell, then imagined Kelly seeing *Ian Colmes* pop up on his caller I.D. Part of him wanted that. He *wanted* Kelly to see his name, to know that Ian was coming for him. He wanted him nervous, even panicked. The thought of Kelly's blood running cold when the name popped up made Ian feel like a predator. Or an angel of justice.

But he didn't want Kelly running. So he went into town instead, hunted for nearly half an hour to find a payphone, and called from there.

"Hello?"

A little girl's voice. Ian felt his heart sink.

"Hi, I'm looking for Tim Kelton. Is he there?"

"*Hello*?" the girl repeated. She couldn't have been older than four.

"Who is it, sweetheart?" a woman said in the background. "Give it here."

"He's looking for his kitchen," the girl said. Ian heard the scuffle of a phone being reclaimed.

"Hello?" the woman said.

"Hi, hello, I'm looking for a Tim Kelton?" Ian said. "Does he live there by any chance?"

"You have the wrong number."

"Ah—my information is a few years old, sorry about that—can you at least tell me, did he maybe used to live there?" Pause. "Is this number in Lonsdale?"

"This number is a cell phone. I've had it for two years, and no, I've never heard of him. You have the wrong number."

Shit. "All right," Ian said. "Thanks anyw—" he started, and she hung up.

132

He considered going home. It was already after two in the afternoon, he hadn't had anything to eat all day, and he could use the time to sit down at his computer and plan his next move: look up the address, run Tim Kelton through the old amateur internet research routine. But he felt *close*, for the first time, and he wouldn't be able to get home and back to Lonsdale before dark. So he went into the gas station, got directions ("You can take 19 right in"), and hit the road.

The drive was about twenty minutes. When he got

into town he stopped and bought a map book, but it still took him another twenty minutes of driving around before he found the place.

He parked across the street and took a minute to look at it. The house was a 50's cream-colored rambler. In the front yard, a big willow sagged and a plethora of weeds broke the snow cover. A sidewalk ran past in the front. The other houses had been shoveled out; this one hadn't, and the driveway was likewise unshoveled, though a pair of beaten tracks indicated that at least someone was still using it. All the shades were drawn.

"Is this it?" Ian said. He glanced around the empty car, but Alex wasn't there, and the cat wasn't talking.

Ian's hand started shaking again as he reached for the glove box latch, but he got the compartment open and pulled out the .22. The safety was on. He shoved it in his waistband and covered the bulge with his coat. Then he crunched through the snow to the front door, his rapid breath rolling in front of him. The bell was busted, so he knocked.

Thunderous barking greeted this intrusion. The door shuddered; Ian heard claws scratching at the other side. He imagined a massive pit bull, with a head like a battering ram, and fought the urge to rest his hand on the gun.

A muffled, "All right, all right," came from within the house. "Jesus Christ, it's just the door." A lock clicked, deadbolts rolled back, and the door opened to reveal a grizzled, mangy man in a bathrobe and ratty slippers, with one hand on the knob and the other clutching the collar of a straining black lab. "Yeah?" he grunted.

The breeze died; the world held its breath. *That's him.*

Ian's hand twitched toward the gun, stopped. *He grabbed Alex.* "Timothy?" Ian said as his head buzzed.

"Who wants to know?"

Don't fuck with me, Kelly. But he spat out something he'd heard on MPR. "Census. Are you Timothy Kelton?"

"He ain't lived here for years." The dog strained against the man's fist, wheezing, its face contorted with a snarl.

"Where is he?"

"Fuck if I know. He used to rent here, but his mom died and he got her place. Still owes me almost two grand."

"Do you know where his mom lived?"

"No idea." The man peered at him. "Ain't the census over with?"

Ian let out a shuddering breath, at once relieved and despairing, every nerve in his body jangling. "Thanks," he said, and went back to his car.

133

The drive home took nearly an hour, the sun sagging low on his left. He went through a Burger King and got some food—his first meal of the day—but barely tasted it. He kept looking in the back seat, hoping to see his son.

He hadn't found Kelton today, but he had learned the man existed. It was a huge victory, a revelation, and yet he felt completely empty. He hadn't seen Alex since witnessing the boy's kidnapping on the way to work, and he was growing certain that the cryptic farewell they had shared that morning had been final.

As he opened the front door he caught himself

holding his breath, hoping to hear the boy cry his name or come bounding around the corner, grinning hugely, but the living room was silent. He went into Alex's room, but it, too, was empty.

For the millionth time, he tried to flip the switch, but the light connected to it was dead as ever. It suddenly occurred to him that there had never been a more succinct analogy for what had become of his life: standing in an empty room, impotently flipping a light switch, knowing that he was trying to interact with a thing that was dead but doing it anyway, over and over again, always mildly surprised when it didn't react.

Even if he found Kelton now, his son was gone. Alex would never know the peace he had come seeking.

He sank to his knees in his son's darkening room, and wept.

IIe wept because he didn't understand Alex's request sooner. He wept because he had locked the boy in his room, because he had screamed at him and berated him, because he hadn't spent enough time just *listening* to him while he had been back.

He wept because he missed him. God, he missed him.

That's all any of this has ever been about, of course: how badly you miss him. And everything that's happened has been in your head. You know that. There is no afterlife; there are no spirits. You saw what you needed to see, because it gave you a chance to tell him how sorry you were, and an opportunity to believe there was still something you could do.

Tim Kelton had been an old friend of Eston's. Eston might have even called him "Kelly" in front of other people, just like Ian had seen in his hallucination.

But Ed hadn't been sure of that, and the two hadn't

been seen together for six years or more. No one else Eston had worked with had ever seen him with a friend of any kind.

It was something for you to pursue, to feel like you could make a difference. That's all. And it's done now.

He remembered the kidnapping: how Kelly had scooped Alex up from the street after knocking him out with some kind of chloroform.

That was in your head, *Ian. That didn't really happen.*

He remembered Alex staring past Eston in the basement, and Eston saying, *Don't look at her. Look at me.*

Her. *You see? Your hallucinations don't even match up with reality. You were looking for a* woman *when you set out this morning, remember?*

He winced, put his hands to his face and pinched his eyes shut. "Alex," he whispered. "Tell me what to do." But the boy didn't answer. He was gone.

You aren't going to kill a man based on your hallucinations. All you know about him is that he used to hang out with the man who killed your son. That's not enough. Is it?

A cold, firm clarity settled into Ian's mind at this thought.

Maybe it was.

When Alex had been kidnapped, Ian had stayed at home despite the urge to hunt for his son, waiting for a ransom call that had never come. When the investigation's resources had been diverted to searching for Jarrid Kalen's daughter, he'd listened to his wife and his mother and everyone else who assured him that the police were still searching just as hard as they were before, instead of trusting his instinct and taking matters—somehow—into his own hands.

In the last month he had guaranteed that his wife would leave him, he had blackmailed his boss, and this morning, he had lost his job—all for this belief that somehow, he was doing what Alex wanted. Now even the boy had disappeared.

What was left?

Maybe the question wasn't, *Is there really a good reason to kill Tim Kelton?*

Maybe it was, *Is there really a good reason* not *to?*

134

He went downstairs and turned on his computer. For the first time since that morning, his hands had stopped shaking. Despite not having slept in nearly thirty-six hours, his mind felt clear.

Compared to the hours of painstaking research he had done on "Kelly," finding Tim Kelton was laughably easy.

His mother, Martha Kelton, had died on November 26th, 2004. Her home had been located at 1541 W. Hill Road in Shakopee, MN. On the Shakopee city website, he was able to confirm the current owner as Kelton, Timothy S.

He stared at this information for maybe two minutes —waiting for the phone to ring, or Alex to appear, or a mysterious window to pop up that said, *Don't do it.*

Then he printed out directions, grabbed his gun and his stuffed cat, and got back in the car.

135

The clock in the dashboard read *4:17 PM*. It wasn't dark yet, but it was drawing close; by 5:40 it would probably be pitch black outside. He could wait an hour, head to Kelton's house under cover of darkness, but he didn't want to. He wanted it to still be light out. He wanted Kelton to see his face.

A gentle snowfall began as he eased on to 169. He drove in silence for nearly ten minutes, then turned on the radio. It was set to the Current, and they were playing Dessa again: some haunting, *a cappella* piece he had heard before but didn't know the name of. It matched his mood perfectly, so he listened to it until it ended, and then he was almost there.

West Hill Road was at the southwest edge of town, past the main drag and the more newly developed areas, surrounded by broad fields and slowly freezing creeks, and not far, he noted distantly, from O'Dowd lake. The street sign hung from its pole at an angle, faded with age, at the base of an aptly-noted hill dotted with snow-shrouded trees. He flipped on his signal and angled up the street toward the hill's crest. There were no driveways on the incline, but ahead he saw a battered minivan turning out of a cross street and heading down the hill.

As it passed him, he caught a glimpse of the driver. He was short and gaunt. His black baseball cap blended into the gathering murk of the vehicle's cabin, and Ian wouldn't have even noticed it if it hadn't sported a stitching of a pair of glaring, bloodshot eyes just above the brim. For a split second, the driver met his gaze; then he was gone, disappearing into the distance of Ian's rearview mirror.

Daddy, I don't like that black hat.

His calm evaporated, boiling away like dew from morning grass.

The eyes are scary on that black hat.

"Jesus Christ."

He slammed on the brakes, his feet moving faster than his brain, and cranked the emergency brake into place before jumping out of the car, craning his head down the hill.

At the bottom, he saw the rear bumper of the minivan turning out of sight. It was going right, into town.

Every instinct screamed to follow him: to jump back in the car and tear down the hill, maybe ram him off the road. But the guy might see Ian coming, he might have a weapon—or even worse, someone else might see the vehicles collide and try to get involved, maybe even keep Ian off him.

No. He couldn't chase him. But he knew where the man had come from. He'd probably come back.

Ian got back in the car, groping for some sliver of his previous calm, but the sight of the man's hat had completely undone him. He released the emergency brake and rolled up the hill, his eyes locked on the outlet the van had come out from. The mailbox came in to view, shrouded by the surrounding trees, but his lights caught the number. 1541.

Tim Kelton's house.

He started to turn into the driveway, but stopped and backed out. He wanted to catch Kelton by surprise. If the man came home and saw a strange car in his driveway, that wouldn't happen. So he rolled past maybe a quarter mile, and parked in a shallow shoulder, brimming with dead leaves. He still hadn't seen another driveway.

He stuffed the .22 in his waistband again, and hesitated for only a bare instant before grabbing Mowsalot. It was like clutching a chunk of dry ice.

"Fuck!" He snatched his fingers back and shook them, stunned, then hunted for some gloves. He found an old, unmated one in the trunk, put it on, and used it to stuff the toy under his arm. Then he hiked back up the road to the house, his heart hammering in his ears.

1541 West Hill Road had a long, dirt driveway, winding through a wooded lot; it ended in a wide loop in front of an old rambler. All the windows were shaded and dark. A rusted metal swing set sat decaying in the front yard, like the bleached skeleton of some old dinosaur.

It made Ian's stomach turn, but it wasn't the last thing to catch his eye. A utility pole stood just before the tree line, and near the top of it jutted a tornado siren.

The black hat. The tornado siren. Ian's stomach did lazy pirouettes.

Alex must have been here. He must have heard the siren. His references to it had been attempts to explain where he had been—where Kelton still was. They had to have been.

He darted to the front porch, tried the front door. He

wanted to wait in ambush for Kelton from within the house, but the door was locked.

He stole around to the side and found a window, but it was barred. The next was the same. But in the rear corner of the home was a third window. On the other side, within the house, it was covered by some kind of wooden plank; Ian couldn't see through it to the interior. He broke the glass anyway, then reached through and tried to pry the plank aside.

It wasn't a plank nailed across the window. It was something like a bookcase. It started rocking as he jostled it, until finally it tipped, spilling into the house with a crash.

He froze, Mowsalot burning with cold beneath his arm, his breath whistling in his lungs as he listened for a shout of surprise from inside. After thirty seconds he heard nothing but the dull whine of an engine on the road beyond the trees, its headlights flickering between the boughs as it passed. The ghostly light was a reminder. *He'll be coming back. Hurry.*

Ian used his gloved hand to brush the broken glass from the threshold, then climbed inside, being careful not to drop Mowsalot. He wished he had brought a flashlight. He didn't want to turn the lights on, to alert Kelton to his presence should he happen to return. But even with all the windows covered, there was still enough light to make out the little dining area he was standing in; enough to see the galley kitchen stretching ahead of him, exiting back to the living room on his right, forming a circle; enough to make out the rolled-back rug, and the trapdoor set into the floor of the dining room.

"Jesus," Ian breathed. He remembered Alex in the

basement at home, whimpering and sobbing inside the cellar pantry. "God."

I should put the bookcase back, try to make it look normal, hide in the kitchen and jump him when he comes in. There's no time to check the door. I don't want to be down there when he comes back. And that was true, all of it, of course it was, but he was heading into the kitchen anyway, hunting for something that would let him get the padlock off that trapdoor since he didn't have the key. He was sure that Alex had been here, now, and he had to see it—he couldn't come so close to the place where Alex had felt such pain and not do what he could to share that burden. He had to see it.

In the kitchen he found two boxes of breakfast cereal —the sugary kind with the cartoon characters on the front—and a carton of fruit snacks. Each of these turned his stomach, made him want to scream or vomit, but he kept rummaging through until he found what he needed: a claw hammer, hanging from two hooks beneath the sink, and a flashlight.

He snatched them up, set Mowsalot down, and went to work against the trapdoor's padlock. But he was a nerd who worked in a tech support phone bank, for Christ's sake, and he didn't have the strength to break the lock.

"Dammit," he hissed. He resettled himself on the floor, threw his shoulder into it—and his hands slipped, cracking into the floor and bouncing the hammer out of the lock with a clatter. "Fuck!"

The lock was marred, though. Starting to bend. So he grabbed the hammer again, jammed it into place, and stood up to lean into it with his foot, with all his weight. He imagined his foot slipping just like his hands had, the hammer leaping upward and smashing into his face, and stole a glance at Mowsalot to reassure himself. *Don't worry,* the cat's brazen grin seemed to say. *Eston's here, but I won't let him try anything.*

In the end, the whole plate came off the trapdoor, tearing loose with a squeal. He kicked it aside, the padlock still hanging off it, and yanked the door open. Inside was a cement staircase—so steep it was nearly a ladder—plunging into blackness.

Again, he noted that going down those stairs would be a terrible idea while Kelton was still gone. The basement wasn't going anywhere; he could check it out later, after his business with Kelton was finished.

But this warning was never more than a passing curiosity. He felt closer to Alex than he had since the boy died, and it suddenly occurred to him that maybe *this* was what the boy wanted, what he had been trying to show him for weeks. He had died alone. Maybe he just wanted someone to share what he had gone through. If that would buy him peace, then it was important—more important than anything else.

"I'm coming, Alex," he muttered, and began to lower himself down the steps. He was swallowed by darkness immediately, alone with it save for the erratic beam from his bouncing flashlight. The steps were cold cement, old and uneven. He counted sixteen of them as the walls seemed to close in around him and the silence grew total. At the bottom he saw a hanging pull chain, and when he clicked it, a naked bulb flared.

He was standing at the end of a long, narrow passage made of bare cement. A heavy door stood in the wall on the right, this one locked with a deadbolt. He approached it slowly, his enthusiasm dying now that he was so close, curdling into dread. The bolt didn't fit well, and took several attempts to crank open, but finally it gave way.

When he opened the door the stench of stale shit and piss assailed him. A nearly unrecognizable stock pot sat in one corner of a squalid little room, overflowing with human waste. The walls were festooned with posters of SpongeBob and Mickey Mouse. A smattering of naked or headless Barbie dolls lay scattered across the cement floor, and there was a bare mattress crammed against one wall.

Sitting on the mattress, her gaunt face stained with resigned horror, was Silvia Kalen.

137

She scrabbled backwards, her eyes wide, shaking her head. She ducked over the far edge of the filthy bed, and disappeared.

"Oh, my God," Ian said. "Silvia? Silvia, is that you?"

The room was silent. Ian took a tentative step into it, and his foot kicked something on the floor. It skittered a few feet across the cement, then came to a stop. Ian stared at it, his mind churning for several seconds before he finally recognized Alex's backpack.

He couldn't process this. He looked up. "Silvia?"

There was no answer. The room might have been empty. A horrible thought flitted through his mind: that she wasn't real, that he was imagining her.

"Are you Silvia Kalen?"

She didn't answer, but he heard her: breathing, whimpering.

ADAM J NICOLAI

She thinks I'm here to rape her.

He clenched his eyes shut, put his hand to his temple. "No. Honey. Sweetheart. I'm gonna get you out of here. Okay?" He walked carefully around the bed, his palms up as if trying to calm a wild animal. "I'm not gonna hurt you. Okay? I swear. I swear to God."

He saw her then, and the sight tore the air from his lungs.

She was hugging her knees, her back to the cement wall, rocking back and forth in a tight ball. Her dress was filthy, torn; her face was criss-crossed with bruises, caked with grime.

She couldn't have been more than five years old.

"Oh, kiddo," he breathed. "Oh, I'm so sorry."

She flinched from his words, turned her face away; seemed, impossibly, to draw further against the wall.

"Silvia," he said, "I'm going to get you out of here. Okay? We're going to leave. Your dad is looking for you, and I'm gonna bring you to him. I won't hurt you, and I won't let anyone else hurt you." These last words sparked on his tongue, ignited something in his chest that caught and blazed, roaring, and he said them again. "*I won't let anyone hurt you.*"

She wouldn't look at him, still. He imagined what she might be thinking; how many times she had heard these promises or something like them before. *Eston told Alex he'd bring him home too.*

He stole a glance toward the door. The flickering light from the bulb in the hallway danced around its edges. There was no one there. Yet.

"Just take my hand, and we can go. All right?" He held out his hand and she recoiled from him, trembling with raw panic. His voice went up an octave. "Oh, hey, no, no, no . . . it's okay, I swear I won't hurt you. I *swear*, okay? Please, sweetheart, we need to get out of here. Don't stay here. I'm here to get you out. I'm gonna take you to your daddy, okay? We're gonna—"

But at the mention of her father she started shaking her head, furiously, disbelieving. *She's heard that before. She's heard it too many times.* She pushed herself to the floor, to worm underneath the bed.

"Silvia, please," he begged. "I'm Alex's daddy."

She froze. Even her breathing stopped.

"Yes. Okay? He told me where you were, and I came." As he said it, he knew it had to be true.

I'll just call for you.

His sight went blurry, brimming with tears. *Oh, Alex.*

"I'm sorry I didn't get here sooner. I didn't understand. I *wanted* to, but I just didn't. I just didn't. I'm so sorry. But I figured it out now. Okay? He sent me here to help you, and I'm here." He blinked hard, pushed the tears from his eyes. The feeling in his chest had grown to an inferno.

And finally, she looked at him. Her voice, when it came, was fragile as glass.

"He said you would come."

138

She stood, and he took her hand. It was fragile, and little, and warm—it made memories of his son burst in his thoughts like suns—and for an instant, it struck him dumb. He clenched his eyes closed, fighting with himself.

Get her out.

Get her safe.

"Okay," he said as they started toward the door, "Okay, good. Stay close to me, all right? Even when we get outside. You stay close, and we'll get you somewhere safe. We'll get you—" He started to say, *To your daddy,* but bit it off. "We'll get you safe."

He reached the door and peered around the corner; held his breath, and listened. Nothing. They hurried up the hellish corridor to the narrow steps, and he pressed her ahead of him. "You go first," he said. "Can you do it?"

She looked at the steps, nodded fervently.

"Go ahead. Be careful."

But she stopped, staring at him, eyes wide.

"I'll be right here. I promise. No one's gonna hurt you. He's not home. Okay? Go now. Quick!"

When she still hesitated, her lip trembling, he took her hand and set it on the second step. "Climb it like a ladder. Can you do that?"

After a heartbeat, she nodded again. Then she started up. He watched tensely, ready to catch her if she fell. She was wearing a dress. He saw that she had no underwear, and had to swallow a surge of bile.

As she reached the top and began to climb out, he followed. The shadows in the dining room had grown longer; the light outside was a strip of red, burning beyond the western tree line. In the dimness she was just a silhouette. "Okay," he said. He tried to smile at her, but there was nothing inside him capable of it. "You did great. I'm gonna carry you for this part now, okay?"

He held out his arms, and she came to him. He scooped her up, careful to keep her dress smoothed so his hand wouldn't touch her bare bottom. As he straightened up he waited for the familiar, dependent weight of her legs latching on to his belly and hip, but she wouldn't do it. Her legs jutted stiffly from her body, and he would not ask her to do otherwise.

"Okay," he breathed. "I'm going to lean you back to carry you." He set the crook of his arm against the back of her neck, his other arm behind her knees, and rested her backward, carrying her like a baby. Like he had carried Alex, even when the boy was older and giving him that silly, contented grin. "Okay." For a mad instant he tried to figure out how he would get through the window with her; then he realized he could just go out the front door. "Okay," he breathed again, and turned to cut through the kitchen.

As he rounded the corner he saw Tim Kelton in the front door, a plain, brown grocery bag on the floor at his feet. He had a handgun aimed at Ian's chest. "Drop her," he said.

Silvia's head whipped around at the sound of Kelton's voice; her entire body stiffened.

"I said drop her," Kelton repeated.

"Fuck you," Ian rasped, and Kelton shot him.

139

The muzzle flared, coughing sparks. A concussive blast thundered in Ian's ears, as if he'd just been smacked in the side of the head with a cinder block. He wanted to turn, to grab his gun, to dodge or run, but in the instant these notions flashed through his mind, his leg gave out.

Silvia spilled from his arms. He toppled sideways, clutched at the door jamb, and smashed face first to the kitchen floor. The stink of gunpowder was everywhere. The world filled with a long, scraping buzz.

His ears throbbed with pain; they had to be bleeding.

Kelton was behind him, shouting, but the words were a thousand miles away. He couldn't make them out. Ian scrabbled at the gun in his waistband, yanked it free, turned painfully on to his back. When Kelton rounded the corner he hoisted it and pulled the trigger, but nothing happened. He'd forgotten the safety.

Kelton flinched out of sight when he saw the weapon anyway. *Fuck,* Ian thought. *Oh, fuck.* He fumbled at the safety switch, got it off. The floor was slick with blood. It was coming from his leg.

Silvia, Ian said. He couldn't hear his own words. He craned his head back to find her, trying to keep one eye on the corner in case Kelton came around again. She had run into the dining room, curled herself into the corner. *Come here,* he said. It felt like he was talking into a gag; he could feel his words pushing against his jaw, but not hear them. *Come to me.*

Kelton darted back around the kitchen corner and fired twice, the sound like twin sledgehammers to Ian's eardrums. The fridge handle blew loose, ricocheted to the floor; a chunk of wooden counter exploded. Ian screamed, twisted back, and squeezed off three shots of his own, but Kelton was already gone.

Compared to Kelton's weapon, the .22 was lobbing firecrackers.

Goddammit, Ian whined or thought, the words swallowed in the onslaught of rushing wind in his ears. He kept his eyes glued to the corner where Kelton was taking cover, but the corner led to the living room, which joined around to the dining room behind him. Kelton could appear at either side of the kitchen any time.

Ian felt curses dribbling from his lips. He clenched his teeth, snorting, and pushed his back to the cabinets, trying to gain his feet while keeping watch. As he maneuvered, he felt a weird tugging sensation within his thigh. As he put pressure on the leg, the tugging bloomed into a fiery pain.

Silvia screamed from the dining room, loud enough to be heard through the mountain of cotton jammed in his ears. Ian twisted to look that way, but the sudden motion cost him his balance. He slammed into the floor, his teeth biting hard into his tongue.

Kelton shoved the dining room table over, forming a makeshift barricade so Ian couldn't shoot him. Then he darted behind it, grabbed Silvia, and pelted for the front door as she shrieked.

No! He felt the word tear from his throat, but it was impotent, silent. Again he forced himself to his feet as his leg threatened to buckle beneath him. He staggered around the corner, saw the screen door banging closed behind Kelton as he hauled the girl toward his van. Ian heaved his .22 up and fired at the fleeing man's back, missing twice.

Fuck!

Ian limped to the front door, pushing through a dizzying sea of whining static. He reached it just as Kelton pushed Silvia into the back seat of the minivan. The vehicle was parked facing down the long driveway, giving Kelton cover. As he slammed the rear door closed, Silvia hurled herself against the back window, banging and screaming.

Ian shoved through the screen door, dragged himself to the porch rail, and emptied his clip at the van. One window erupted in spiderwebs; the rear right tire blew and sagged to nothing. Then it was driving.

Get the plate, something in Ian urged. *Call the cops.*

But it was drowned out by the deafening horror of Silvia in the back window, her mouth moving silently, her fists pounding at the window. She had believed him. She'd thought she was safe. He couldn't save Alex, and he couldn't save her; the incredible weight of his failure struck him dumb.

The van lurched forward, kicking plumes of snow and dirt behind it, and hurtled off the driveway and into the ditch. Silvia jerked and fell out of sight.

Curses, silent nonsense, flicked from Ian's tongue. He started for the porch steps, but his leg screamed a protest. He stumbled, then fell, toppling to the frozen ground. He wanted to stay there, to cry and moan and beg for help. Instead he levered himself upward through a heavy fog of pain, and dragged his wounded leg to the van.

Silvia! he felt himself screaming. *Silvia!*

Kelton leapt from the van, hurled the rear door open. Before she could scream again, he smashed his fist into her nose. *"Shut up!"* he roared, so loudly Ian could actually make it out. She tried to pull away, and he grabbed her by the back of the dress, yanked her forward, and hit her again. *"Shut up! I fucking told you!"*

Silvia! Ian bellowed, the sound echoing from the bottom of a well, and Kelton snapped his head toward him. *Let her go! The cops are coming! Let her go!*

Kelton snarled and yanked his gun out.

Ian was in the middle of the driveway, wide open, still

thirty feet or more from the van. On instinct, he dove to the ground, covering his head. Bullets whined past him like mosquitoes. Pockets of snow erupted everywhere.

Something punched into his ribs, something that weighed a thousand pounds. His mouth gave a long, squeaking gasp. Blinding pain shot through his body.

At the van, Kelton's pistol went empty. He cursed and grabbed another clip from his pocket. As he loaded it, Silvia jumped from the van and ran for the tree line.

He snapped something inaudible, stole a glance back at Ian, stuffed the gun in his waistband, and ran after her.

Ian couldn't get up. He was done. It was over.

He got up anyway.

He dragged himself toward the ditch, wincing and hissing. He clutched one hand to his side, but it did nothing. Every inch of movement evoked shrieks of pain from his body. It felt like a shattered rib bone was grinding into his lung.

Just beyond the tree line, Kelton tripped Silvia, sent her sprawling to the snow, and fell on her like a mountain. She twisted, snarled.

Bite him, Ian tried to cry. His laboring lungs could barely muster a whimper. *Get his . . . his eyes.*

She couldn't have heard him, but she still fought like a devil: a storm of flailing limbs, of gnashing teeth. She must have struck him in the nose with her skull—he recoiled, grabbing at his face, but when she scrambled to her feet he dove forward and tripped her. Her face smacked into a rock as she fell.

Ian was at the ditch. He dropped on to his butt and scooted painfully down. His vision was swimming, his ears clamoring with phantoms.

She tried to crawl away, but Kelton had her foot. He dragged her back to him as she clawed at the ground, his fists climbing her leg while she screamed. As he grabbed her waist, Ian finally reached him, and gouged his fingers into Kelton's eyes from behind.

Kelton shrieked, flailed—he pulled his gun and squeezed off a shot over his shoulder, another blast of thunder that made Ian's vision swim and his tortured ears sob. The shot went wide. The kickback bounced the weapon out of Kelton's awkward grip and into the snow.

Ian bore him to the ground, one arm locked around his neck. He squeezed. Kelton kicked impotently, locked his hands onto Ian's arm, and started prying him loose. Then he hurled his weight to the side, and Ian landed on his wounded leg. His grip on Kelton's neck evaporated in a scream. He toppled sideways and crashed to the ground, a rock digging into the small of his back.

Coughing, Kelton climbed to his feet. Behind him, Ian saw Silvia. The side of her face was covered with blood, pouring from her nose and the wound on her forehead. *Run,* he tried to say, but his tongue betrayed him. It had no strength left. *Please run.*

Kelton cast about for his gun, but settled for a broken tree branch at least two feet long and almost as thick as his arm. He rasped a taunt, his bloody face mouthing the words behind a veil of silence, and crashed the stick into Ian's wounded ribs.

Ian knew he was screaming, but he couldn't hear it. He tried to roll away, and the rock in his back jammed into his spine. Kelton hit him again, and then again. Brilliant flowers of pain detonated in his ribs.

Kelton cried something over his shoulder to Silvia,

grinning. *"Remember what I said about anyone who tries to help you?"* his lips said. *"About what would happen if you tried to run?"*

Ian reached behind him, trying to dislodge the rock so he could roll away, but it wasn't a rock. It was Kelton's gun.

"Get over here!" Kelton demanded of her. *"You gonna watch this! Open your fucking eyes, you gonna watch this!"*

Ian brought the gun up, and shot him in the stomach.

An explosion of blood burst from Kelton's back. He took a step backward, trying to keep his balance as the front of his shirt slowly darkened, then crumpled into the snow.

Ian crawled over to him.

Kelton's mouth was moving; he looked bewildered, plaintive.

Ian grabbed the stick, braced it against Kelton's neck, and pushed.

He felt the blood from the man's stomach gushing against his own belly; felt his feeble kicks as Kelton tried again to fight loose. But as weak as Ian was, Kelton was weaker.

Kelton scrabbled at the stick, at Ian's face, at Ian's hands. His legs kicked impotently, silently, into the snow. His face turned red, then purple.

When he stopped moving, Ian grabbed the gun and blew his skull open.

140

Silvia was huddled against a tree, her eyes clenched shut, her face a pale mask.

Silvia, Ian managed. He felt light-headed. He wondered how much blood he'd lost. He wondered if he'd die. The thought didn't frighten him. Maybe he'd see Alex, and if he did, he'd tell him, *Don't worry. I saved her.*

Her eyes were still closed. She put her face in her hands.

Sweetheart, he tried to say, but it came out as a choked croak, and he coughed. The gun fell out of his hands and he sank to his knees in the snow. Suddenly, he realized how cold he was. Every muscle shook.

He tried to clear his throat. *Sweetheart,* he said. *It's okay. He's gone. The police—*

Someone might have heard the gunshots and the screaming; they might be on their way. But he pulled his phone from his pocket, bending every bit of his will toward holding on to it, not fumbling it into the snow. He punched in the numbers as if wrestling a bear. *9. 1. 1.*

On the other end of the line, someone mumbled an incomprehensible greeting.

Yes, he said. *I found her. We're at fifteen . . .*

The sun was setting. The trees' shadows loomed suddenly, darkening everything. He was so *cold.*

Fifteen forty-one. West Hill. Please hurry. We're in the trees.

The voice murmured something in response; it wanted to know more. But the phone had fallen from Ian's hands, spinning slowly away into the snow. He watched it go, wondering how it had happened.

Then he lay down, and didn't wonder anything.

141

Voices, and shouting. Exclamations. Brilliant, strobing lights. He was lifted, carried.

From the other end of a very long tunnel, someone said, "Can you hear me?" and he answered, "Yes."

Sirens. Jostling. He remembered something important, and opened his eyes. There was a woman crouched next to him, bouncing with the bumps in the road. She was wearing green, peering at some kind of electronic device mounted against the vehicle wall. He asked her his question, but she didn't hear. She was talking, muttering something to someone he couldn't see.

He groped for her arm; when he took hold of it, she snapped her eyes to his, and he repeated himself.

She hesitated. He was afraid she wouldn't answer, for fear of upsetting him. Then something flickered inside her eyes and she said, "Yes, Mr. Colmes. She's going to be okay."

The world drifted away, and the pain went with it.

142

Eventually he felt the play of light across his eyelids, and opened his eyes to an empty hospital room. The shades were open, letting in a shimmer of bleary sunlight; on the far wall, a silent TV flickered with *The Price Is Right*. He stared at this for awhile, assessing the dull throb in his left side and right leg.

The door opened, and a nurse came in: a small, plump woman in her late forties. "Ian?" she said, smiling gently.

"Yeah," he croaked, and her smile broadened.

"I brought you some water here," she said, and as he downed it, she busied herself checking his monitor and his wounds, answering some of the questions he didn't yet realize he had.

Her name was Shelly, and he was at St. Francis Regional Medical Center. His wounds would be painful, but probably not serious (he was very lucky!) and the doctor would be in later to take a look at them and answer any questions he might have. In the meantime, if he needed anything he could just push the call button.

"Thank you," he said. His voice sounded distant, and he wondered if he was on some kind of pain medication. "Is Silvia okay?"

"Yes," Shelly answered. "She's over in Pediatric."

"Don't let anyone hurt her," he said.

Shelly gave him a long look. "I won't," she said.

When she left, the room fell silent again. He turned the volume up on the TV, watched an extremely over-weight white man try to guess the price of a bottle of shampoo. He thought he should be worried about what might come next—he was jobless, he had killed a man, he had been shot twice—but he wasn't.

For once, he just wasn't.

143

He got a lot of visitors at the hospital.

The cops wanted to know how he'd found Silvia. He said he'd heard her screaming in the house, while driving past. They didn't buy this—it was plain in their eyes—but he stuck to it anyway.

They asked him other questions, too. *Did you know Tim Kelton had been involved in Alex's kidnapping?* No, Ian answered, not until I saw Alex's backpack in his dungeon. *What were you doing in the Shakopee area?* Driving by the lake where Alex was found. I do it once a month or so.

They asked him: *You really expect us to believe you found Silvia Kalen by chance?* He didn't know what to say to this, so he started nodding off, and the nurse asked the police to leave.

Any one of the people he had questioned about Kelly could've ruined him—any of them could've called and reported his weird behavior earlier that day. But despite the media circus, despite his picture all over the news, none of them did.

Jarrid Kalen was composed when he entered. He was a hard man, wiry, but shorter in person than Ian had expected. He gave Ian a strong handshake and said, "I can't thank you enough." Then he proceeded to try.

He tripled the reward to 300,000 ("An extra hundred for each gun shot wound," he explained), promised Ian he would have his medical bills handled, and swore to defend him in court.

"You'll have the best legal representation possible. There is no way you're going to jail," he said. "Silvia says she screamed all the time. You were in his house because you heard her, and she's safe because of you.

"You brought her back from the dead," he said, and then his composure cracked a little, and Ian caught a glimpse of the wreck that had been festering beneath for months.

He nearly told Jarrid about Alex, then, but held his tongue. Instead he said, "Take care of her," and Jarrid swore he would.

Derek came, and Ian's mother. Billi, from work, visited too. But none of the visits—not the ones from the cops, not the one from Jarrid Kalen—mattered as much as Alina's.

144

She paused at the door when she entered, swallowed by her bulky winter coat, her head straddled by a pair of snowy earmuffs. They looked at each other for a long time. He read the pensiveness in her eyes and thought, *She's not sure she wants to be here.*

"I didn't know if you'd come," he said. He could've said, *Hello,* or, *How are you,* but the moment felt too fraught with consequence to risk empty pleasantries. They both knew who they were and where they stood.

"I didn't know either."

Why did you? he wanted to ask, but this felt too confrontational, so instead he said, "I'm glad you did."

She gave him a tight smile that didn't touch her eyes, and crossed to the chair at his bedside. When she sat, she carefully pulled the gloves from her hands, peering into her lap. "Are you okay?"

"The doctors say I was lucky. There should be no permanent damage. The worst thing was the blood loss. They just want to keep an eye on me for a couple days, otherwise I'd be home already. Or in jail, one or the other."

She looked up. "So you really killed him?"

"Yes." He held her eyes as he said it. Words clamored at his tongue—*I had to. He was hurting a little girl. He had hurt our son.*—but he kept them back. After a moment, she nodded.

"Good. Are they going to send you to jail for that?"

He let out a breath. "I don't know. Jarrid Kalen says there's no way he'll let that happen."

"You've talked to him?"

"He came to visit."

"How is Silvia?"

"They say she's all right. I'm sure she's a wreck, but at least she's home." *At least she's alive.*

"I heard they were together for awhile. Silvia and Alex. They said on the news that they were both at Eston's house for a week or two." Her tongue handled the word *Eston* like it was a wood splinter. "They were moving them to this other guy's house—Kelton?—when Alex got loose somehow."

"Yeah. I heard that, too. I think . . ." He hesitated, wanting to tell her but not wanting to scare her off. "I think Alex really cared about Silvia, even though he didn't know her long. I think he'd be glad to know she's safe."

Alina nodded, tightly, and looked at the wall. Ian reached for her hand, and she took it.

Through the window behind her, he saw snow falling.

Silence settled over them, but it wasn't one of those pits that he was always stumbling into. It was tense and heavy, but it was also expectant. And for those few minutes, he was too happy to be holding her hand to care.

"I got your letter," she finally said.

His heart jumped. He'd known this was coming, but didn't know what to say, so he waited. When she didn't say anything more, he asked, "What did you think?"

"Did you really go through Alex's boxes?"

"I went through enough to know that I'm okay with getting rid of them. I think we *need* to get rid of them."

She nodded. She still wasn't looking at him. "It was hard to read."

"Why?"

"Because it sounded very familiar, Ian. Because we've done all this before."

"We haven't done this. It may feel the same to you, but it's not. I'm different. I'm looking at things differently."

She did turn to him then. "How can I know that?"

"You can't, really, not without being around me. But if you give me a chance—just one more chance—you'll see."

She gave a pained sigh and turned away again, but not before he saw her eyes glimmering. "I'm sorry," she said. "I shouldn't be here talking to you about this while you're . . ."

"No, it's okay."

"You're in the *hospital*, for God's sake."

"It's okay. I don't care about that. I just want us to be okay again."

"You make that sound so easy."

"I know it won't be, not after how much I hurt you. I'm *sorry*, Alina. You were strong for me, and I wasn't strong for you. I want to be there for you, if it's not too late. I know I really hurt you. It won't happen any more."

"But you still think it was my fault, Ian. You still think I—"

"I *don't*," he urged her. "I swear, I don't. I was mad, I was scared, I wasn't thinking straight, but I'm thinking straight now. I was grieving and I said some really stupid things, and you put up with them for far too long. There are only two people to be blamed for what happened, and now they're both dead."

Silence again. She wasn't looking at him. But she still had his hand.

"If this isn't going to work, we have to decide that now. We can't wait until the baby is born. If we divorce, I'll agree to equal custody. You're a good father, Ian, and she should know her father."

A warm wind boiled in his chest: joy, humility, awe. *She.*

"But I can't pretend with her. And I can't stay with you just for this child. I *need you*, Ian. I can't pretend everything's okay when it's not."

"You won't have to." He realized he was smiling. "You won't have to, I promise. I don't want that either. Did you say *she*?"

Alina looked down at him again, naked vulnerability scrawled across her face. She looked as if she thought he wasn't listening. But when she saw his face, she gave a small smile of her own. "Yeah. It's a girl."

"That is wonderful."

"Yeah." She squeezed his hand. "I want to name her after my mother."

"Teres?" He tasted the name, found it beautiful. "Perfect."

Her face pinched; she looked away again. "I want to believe you, Ian. I really do. But people just don't change this fast."

"Maybe I'm not changing," he said. "Maybe I'm changing back."

145

They went back to the house together.

The first day, Alina changed the bulb in Alex's room. Ian called Derek and asked if he could help bring the boxes out to the car for a trip to Goodwill. Derek agreed, and as he and Alina worked, Ian helped by holding the door, which was all he could manage while still recovering. By sunset, Alex's room was empty except for a glowering stuffed elephant.

That night they lay in bed and talked. By midnight they were fighting. By two they were crying. Their discussion roamed from the bedroom to the dining room to the living room, but finally, they fell asleep together on the couch.

146

The marker read:

ALEX ISAIAH COLMES

2005—2010

WE LOVE YOU

As Ian knelt by his son's gravestone, the brittle grass crunched beneath his knees. He took off his gloves and rested one hand on the stone. A frigid shock stole into his fingers, but he didn't flinch from it. The sensation was welcome. He owed it to Alex.

"I brought you something," Ian said. "I was gonna keep it for your sister, but I don't think she'll need it anymore." He set Mr. Tuskers on the grass, where the animal surveyed the surrounding cemetery with protective menace. "I thought you'd like him here. I would've brought Mowsalot, too, but I lost him. I'm sorry about that."

He clasped his hands in his lap. An observer might have thought he was praying.

"Mowsalot kept me just as safe as Tuskers, did you know that? He might seem like just a snugglepot, but he doesn't screw around. He keeps your back. He did a good job.

"It's okay now, though. I'm pretty sure the bad man is gone. Tuskers hasn't gone cold on me ever since mommy brought him back to the house."

He smiled, a little bit. "And she is back. I don't know if she told you that." Alina had asked for a few minutes alone at the grave as well, before returning to the car where she was waiting now. "I won't say everything is perfect. But we're both trying, and she's staying at the house. What happened wasn't her fault. She was just worried about your sister. And she was right to be worried. I just . . ." He gripped the stone again, breathed a shuddering plume of steam into the winter air. "I just missed you so bad, Alex. I always will. I won't forget you, you know that? Neither will your mom. And if there's any way I can see you again, one day—if you are someplace that I can come—I will. You'll be playing, or whatever, and look up, and suddenly . . ." His jaw clenched, fighting for the words. "Suddenly, you'll see your daddy."

He let himself dwell on this idea. There was a time when he would've given everything to make it come true, to hold his son again at that moment. For the first time in months, though, he felt torn. If finding Alex again meant losing Alina . . .

"Maybe one day," he said. "Maybe. I told you, no one knows for sure, right? But your mom needs me right now, and I need her—and your sister will be here soon." He smiled again, just a hair, at the taste of the word. *Sister.* "*Teres Alexandra.* Don't you think it's pretty?"

He closed his eyes, gripped the marker with both hands, and kissed it. The sensation of cold, coarse stone lingered on his lips as he pulled away. "I love you, Alex," he whispered. "I always will."

Then he rose slowly to his feet, and returned to his wife.

147

When she was pregnant with Alex, Alina had done most of the work to prepare the baby's room by herself. For Teres, Ian made sure they worked together. They went with a pony theme—something girly, but not overwhelmingly so—with a lot of yellows and greens. The task wasn't strenuous, but for Ian's healing leg and ribs, it was challenging.

As they worked, they talked about what she would be like. Would she have inexplicable blue eyes, like her brother did? Would she be as picky about her formula, or share any allergies? Most concerning of all, Alina asked: What if she didn't like ponies?

If she didn't like ponies, Ian assured her grimly as he rested his throbbing leg, she would be shit out of luck.

They finished the final touches just before the sun fell behind the trees. As they stood back to take it in, Alina grabbed his hand. "She likes it," she said, and it was true: within her belly, Ian could feel his daughter's joyful kicks. He smiled broadly at his wife, and she kissed him. For a single, glorious instant, all was well.

Then they turned out the light, and that brilliant hope slowly faded as night came on. They went to bed early, exhausted, and Ian lay awake as his wife drifted off, his thoughts spinning with memories of those first nights with Alex, of the ways he had changed their lives.

Facing away from him, Alina began to whimper in her sleep. "No, Ian," she muttered. "I can't."

A chasm of despair opened in Ian's chest. *Just like before.* Even now, even months after they had gotten back together, her dreams were ruined—not by the horrors that had happened to their son, but by the memory of him abandoning her. He watched her tremble as he had watched Alex suffer: paralyzed and powerless.

Then he pulled her close. He didn't know what she was dreaming, didn't know his full place in it, but suddenly, he refused to let it matter. "I love you," he whispered. He lifted a hand to soothe her hair; kissed her forehead. "It's okay. Everything's okay now." As he shushed her, her breathing evened. With a deep sigh, she turned in her sleep and burrowed into him. When she calmed, he finally fell asleep.

In his dreams, Alex was smiling.

A NOTE FROM THE AUTHOR

I'm working on a collection of short stories called *These Morbid Gifts*. I generally write one a month. If you go to **subscribe.AdamJNicolai.com** and join my mailing list I'll send them to you for free, as I finish them, as a thank you for signing up. I'll even dedicate them to you. And, you'll be the first to get news from me on my new novels and sales on existing books.

If you'd like the notifications without any of the free fiction or other bonuses, you can also find me on Amazon and then press "Follow."

Thank you for reading. If you liked the book and would like to see what else I've done, just turn the page.

ALSO BY ADAM J NICOLAI

Young Sarah is a woman haunted – not by ghosts, but by crippling exhaustion, post-partum depression, and the unending cries of her newborn daughter, Rebecca. In fevered snatches of sleep she imagines a Messenger from God inciting her to unspeakable acts, and in her weakest moments his exhortations sound like sanity.

Estranged from her own mother and suffering from a deadly disconnection with her own identity, Sarah doesn't know how to love her daughter any more than she knows how to love herself. Alone with her baby in a tiny, sweltering apartment, she will suffer. She will weep.

But she will also endure.

Unforgettable and truly unique, *Rebecca* takes hold of you on the first page and drags you headlong into the hellscape of a tortured young mother's mind - a journey that will end with unspeakable horror, or the triumph of a mother's love over darkness.

Read *Rebecca* now.

ALSO BY ADAM J NICOLAI

TODD

You've read enough cookie-cutter horror. Now read *Todd*.

Without warning on a sunny June afternoon, all life on Earth vanishes. Reeling and alone in the aftermath, Alan and his son Todd scrounge through the ruins of civilization to survive.

Finding food and water is easy. Electric power is harder. But Alan has his own search, one he tries to hide from his son: after a lifelong struggle with depression, his scarcest resource now is a reason to keep living.

Through wildfires and tornadoes, as the deadly cold of a Minnesota winter draws closer, the two ask questions that may never be answered. Why did this happen? Why were they spared? They don't realize that behind the empty sky, the entity that did this still watches—or that its plans have only begun.

Fast-paced and brutal, *Todd* drags you forward from its first moment to its inevitable conclusion—an ending that will leave you in breathless disbelief.

It's time for a thriller that digs deeper.

It's time to read *Todd*.

ALSO BY ADAM J NICOLAI

CHILDREN OF A BROKEN SKY

A sin buried at the dawn of time. A world made to endure the consequences. For untold ages, darkness has built upon darkness. Now, at last, the hope of redemption glimmers.

Lyseira grew up in a little village beneath a mountain's shadow, where she and her friends discovered a secret long lost—a secret that would shake the world to its bones.

Now, as she comes of age, her friend Helix is accused of murder and sentenced to death. Forced to choose between watching him die and the staggering risk of rescuing him, she launches her friends on an unforgettable journey—one that will change them all forever, and set the world itself down the path of history.

Bestselling Kindle author Adam J Nicolai invites you to a world beneath a broken sky, where sorceries clash with miracles and nothing is what it seems.

Read now.

ACKNOWLEDGMENTS

Thank you to my mom, Senja, for knowing I was a writer before I did.

Thank you to my wife, Joy, for listening to the countless hours of second-guessing, elation, strategizing, and despairing.

Thank you to Brad Olson and Sue Hein, for teaching a class that made me discover how much I could do.

Thank you to my children, Isaac and Rydia, for helping me realize what really matters in life.

Thank you to Jason Godfrey for the modeling session with Mr. Tuskers.

Thank you to The Seven for all the encouragement (I still can't believe none of you thought Tuskers was over the top).

And thank you to you, for taking a chance. If you enjoyed *Alex*, please consider posting a review at your retailer's website (an author can never have too many good reviews!) or recommending the book to others.

Every positive review, no matter how brief, helps me more than you might think.

ABOUT THE AUTHOR

Adam J Nicolai is a father who constantly imagines the worst. He lives near St. Paul, Minnesota with his wife, Joy, and their two children, Isaac and Rydia. He has written several novels, all of which can be found on Amazon. He is a life-long nerd, game lover, author, Star Wars fan, Dungeon Master, and amateur game designer.

While he has never lost a child, his heart breaks for those who have.

His first novel, *Alex*, was extremely well-received on Amazon, breaking on to several bestseller lists. It remains one of the highest-rated novels by customer review in Horror, Thriller, and Suspense, and peaked at #3 top-rated in overall Kindle Fiction.

Adam loves connecting with his fans. He writes about politics and deep thoughts on Facebook and Twitter (@AdamJNicolai). You can also drop him a line at ajn@loneroad.co (not .com!). For more information on Adam's other books, see his website: http://www.adamjnicolai.com.

If you would like to receive free fiction from him every month, you can also join his mailing list at http://subscribe.adamjnicolai.com. He would love to hear from you.

41251644R00164

Made in the USA
Lexington, KY
05 June 2019